NOV -- 2020

D0962142

**ESTES VALLEY
LIBRARY**

THE
LAND

ALSO BY THE AUTHOR

The Night Birds
Little Wolves

THE LAND

THOMAS MALTMAN

SOHO

The characters and events in this book are fictitious.
Any similarity to real persons, living or dead, is coincidental
and not intended by the author.

Copyright © 2020 by Thomas Maltman
All rights reserved.

Published by
Soho Press, Inc.
227 W 17th Street
New York, NY 10011

Library of Congress Cataloging-in-Publication Data
Maltman, Thomas James, 1971– author.
The land / Thomas Maltman.

I. Title.

ISBN 978-1-64129-220-7
eISBN 978-1-64129-221-4

PS3613.A524 L36 2020   813'.6 — dc23   2020015486

Interior design by Janine Agro, Soho Press, Inc.

Printed in the United States of America

10 9 8 7 6 5 4 3 2 1

For my family, who first took me to The Land

In the midst of winter, I found there was,
within me, an invincible summer.
— Albert Camus

THE
LAND

A Dead Man
Casts His Shadow

Above all, Mr. Kroll told me, take care of the dog. We were standing together in the foyer, next to the last suitcases Mr. Kroll needed to lug to his Audi, and he lingered here as if he had something else important to tell me. Mrs. Kroll already had the Audi running in the driveway, where it huffed clouds of exhaust in the icy November air as she sat rigid, her arms crossed and her body tilted forward in the seatbelt of the passenger side, the posture of a snowbird who might grow wings and fly to South Padre Island for the winter by herself if he didn't hurry. When she gave a toot on the horn, Mr. Kroll grimaced. "Just between you and me, Lucien, I don't put much stock in this Y2K business," he said, "but if the world really does go to hell, I don't want to be stuck someplace cold."

I didn't say anything, but I couldn't have disagreed

more. If the world ended at the turn of the millennium, the last place I wanted to be was surrounded by busloads of old folks greased up in Coppertone and singing along to Jimmy Buffett. I couldn't wait to be alone, longed for what I hoped would be a winter of solitude.

Mr. Kroll handed me a schedule with his tight, military printing listing watering days for the ferns and spider plants, the exact temperature to set the thermostat (62 degrees), and a food and exercise program for a geriatric German shepherd named Kaiser.

"No parties," he said, taking hold of my other hand.

"I don't drink."

"You will clear the driveway of snow, just in case."

He didn't explain what he meant. His palm felt scaly and lizard-like. He tugged me closer to him as though he were about to confide a secret. "Harry said you were good. He said he was sorry he had to let you go."

If it wasn't for Harry Larkin, I'd be homeless as well as jobless. The Krolls were longtime customers at Bay City Mutual where I had worked before the accident. The place they were leaving behind was called "The Gingerbread House" by locals—a stone house set back in the pines with a red-tiled roof that curved like an elf's shoe, twin turrets on either side, and topiary bearding the lower windows—like some vision from the Brothers Grimm. The property sprawled over eighty acres of boreal forest above a deep canyon carved by the Wind

River, which ran swift and silver far below, spilling down to Cauldron Falls before pouring into Aurora Bay, miles and miles away, where I attended Northern Minnesota State University. The Krolls needed someone to maintain the property and I needed a place to stay. *Get some rest*, Harry Larkin had advised me before explaining the arrangement, *then get your shit together.*

I told friends and family that I planned to use the time to finish coding an open-ended computer game called *The Land*, a post-apocalyptic fantasy world I'd been programming since my freshman year with the little free time I had between work and school. I planned to release the game as shareware and dreamed of it becoming a cult classic. Already on academic probation, I was about to be thrown out of college, so I hoped the game might get me in the door at some place like BioWare up in Canada, where I could work on the next *Baldur's Gate*.

Mr. Kroll had a thin crop of oily hair, nicotine-stained teeth, his breath smelling of ashes and Listerine. "Do you know your way around guns?" He asked this in the same tone as someone might say, *Do you know the Lord?*

"Guns?" I was the only child of two overly protective parents who hadn't even let me own a toy gun as a boy.

"I keep a .30-06 fully loaded in the gun cabinet. You have the keys. We've discussed the things that are not yours to touch, but the rifle you may use when the situation calls for it. If wolves come around—and they will—let them have it."

"You want me to give them the gun, sir?"

Mr. Kroll had finally let go of my hand. "Lucien," he said, his mouth crimping at the corners, as though speaking my name aloud a second time pained him. I regretted my attempt at humor, just a little, knowing how much these old-timers hated a wiseass. When Mr. Kroll had visited the bank on business he preferred to be waited on by the pretty, young female tellers, especially Maura. Maura had been everyone's favorite. "Harry said you were smart before your time in the hospital, so I think you know what I mean." How much had Harry told him? And surely he knew that wolves were on the endangered species list. Mr. Kroll lowered his voice, though it was just the two of us in the foyer. "Wolves are vermin and you are on private property. Won't anyone know what you do out here. Got it? Also, it's okay if some of my wife's plants die, but not the dog."

AFTER THEY LEFT, I spent hours wandering the maze of rooms, at first careful of the old couple's privacy. My bare feet sank into lush, Berber carpets the color of burgundy, and the floors seemed to slope downhill, as if this entire house was drifting toward the volcanic ridge above the river, a quarter mile away. A spiral staircase led to a walkout on the lower level. Here a bearskin rug splayed before a towering stone fireplace. Bay windows looked out over a grove of birches already filling up with snow. In November of 1999, a wolfish cold had settled early over the woods, shaggy with snow. It was so quiet I swore I could hear the hush of each flake touching the ground. I could hear the thump of my heart in my ears, strong and insistent and traitorous. I only wanted to be alone, but I could feel something padding toward me in the snow, and I knew I would have to go out to meet it. I didn't know enough to be afraid yet.

MY MOTHER HAD CAMPAIGNED for me to come home to Chicago and enroll in Oakton Community College for the spring semester instead of housesitting this place over the winter. "You'll be so far from everything," she said over the phone.

"That's the whole point."

"But how will you keep up with your classes?"

"It's not a bad commute. Now that I'm not working thirty hours a week, I can focus better." I paused, mentally counting how many lies I'd packed in those sentences. My focus had been shattered. I missed two weeks of classes in the hospital and I should have withdrawn rather than take Fs, but I let the deadline pass without doing anything. Yet, I still attended. Some days I went to classes I hadn't even enrolled in, choosing random lectures on meteorology, the philosophy of Eastern religions, or astronomy, and sitting in the back taking notes. Once the registrar's office caught up with me, my time at Northern was done, but I couldn't wrap my head around why any of it was supposed to matter anymore.

"You *are* coming home for Thanksgiving."

Home? I wasn't sure where that was anymore since my parents had divorced. "We'll see, Mom."

I heard her swallow on the other end of the phone line. I hated talking on the phone, the way disembodied voices floated out of the ether. She knew I wasn't coming home. I couldn't. Not yet. There was something I had to do first. I was afraid she was going to start crying again. "I gotta go, Mom."

THE FIRST DAY OF the storm I took Kaiser out for a walk, trussing my hiking boots in antique snowshoes I'd found hanging beside the French doors in the lower level and grabbing a set of poles from an umbrella stand. I didn't bother with a leash, knowing the old dog would stay close. In the sandy, acidic soil of the property, the white pines grew immense, their trunks gnarled and gigantic, the upper reaches soughing in the wind. Grandfather trees with white frock coats and mossy, dripping beards.

Kaiser ambled along beside me. Released from his side yard pen, the dog appeared ready to bound through the snow, if only his body would allow it. He wheezed and struggled in the deeper drifts, his back legs stiff and arthritic. Balanced on my balsa wood poles, I commiserated. Under my skin I could sense the alien piece of ceramic prosthetic the surgeon had grafted to my hip bone.

Kaiser and I discovered a pond at the edge of the birch grove. Beneath the glazed surface of the ice, koi swam in sluggish circles, mottled blurs of flame. I cracked the ice with the hard plastic end of my pole and the koi squirmed away. Kaiser snorted beside me, a questioning bark, before using his paws to break more ice so he could slurp the cold water. Soon the small pond would freeze solid around those fish, leaving them trapped and breathless. Already a new skin of ice was forming around the holes we had made. The Krolls hadn't left any instructions about tending the koi and I felt certain they were going to die but didn't know how to save them. We were gazing down into their icy tomb, our shadows blocking out their light. Yet, it didn't seem like a bad way to go, all things considered. "The parable of this world is like your shadow," I told Kaiser, one of my notes from the religion class that got stuck in my head, though I couldn't recall who said it. Kaiser sat on his haunches, slobbery icicles dangling from his muzzle. "If you stop, your shadow stands still. If you chase it, it distances itself from you."

Tomorrow was Sunday. I had a shadow to chase.

MOST OF WHAT I knew about Rose of Sharon, a church just outside Ursine Lake, was that Maura's husband was a pastor there. The church sat in a valley between two round recently logged hills now humped with snow, the building a converted ranch house with a cross pinioned to the chimney. People parked on a flat plain just outside, no more than a dozen cars. A gated cemetery nestled in the crook of one hill.

After maneuvering my Lincoln Continental into a tight space, I almost turned around. And I would have, except this ridiculous boat of a car made such simple tasks trouble. My dad had insisted I buy the Continental with the insurance money after he viewed the crushed remains of my Civic. What did I think I was doing here? Perhaps there was time to pull out, before anyone recognized me. Would Maura's husband know who I was? I knew from Maura that her husband was named Elijah Winters and that he was a pastor who was mixed up in a movement similar to the apocalyptic, white supremacist stuff that got some members of Randy Weaver's family killed halfway across the country in Idaho. I knew that Maura had been afraid of him.

A tall man with a cadaverous face watched me from the front steps of the church, his hands on his hips. It was too late to turn around now. I had been spotted. I shut my engine down, got out of the car, and walked toward him.

The bulletin board beside the man identified the church as Apostolic/Christian Identity. I had little idea what that meant. Holy Rollers, my dad would call them.

My family was Easter-and-Christmas Presbyterians who attended a neighborhood church on holidays but otherwise didn't think much about religion.

I tried to disguise my limp under that man's gaze, but my hip had stiffened during the long car ride, so crossing the icy gravel lot seemed to take an eternity, the man watching with that smile frozen on his face. "Welcome," he said when I got close, extending one large, bony hand. "I'm Roland, one of the deacons here."

"Meshach," I said, taking his hand. The false name just slipped out. I winced as he pumped my grip, in part because his hand felt strong enough to break every bone in my body, and also because if Maura ever had a son, she had vowed to name him Meshach, who had stood in the fire for his faith and was not harmed. Maura knew her Bible, though she had not been devout. A seeker like me. I couldn't forget how lovely her singing voice had been. Those old-time hymns. She'd sung one for me once, late at night after the bank closed, her voice pitched with all the loneliness and longing in this broken world. There had been nothing between us then, but I was already in love with her. Surely her husband would know what she hoped to name a boy, if they were blessed with a second child. Already with the first words out of my mouth I had given myself away. Maybe that was okay. Maybe that was why I had come here. I had questions that needed answering.

A muscle twitched in Roland's long jaw. He had sun-burnt, weathered features, his skin still deeply tanned in winter, permanently marked from a life spent work-ing outdoors, even his hair burnt white as if scorched by frost and sunlight. "What brings you to our service this morning?" he asked, squinting at me.

"I was out for a Sunday drive, saw people going inside. Thought maybe I should check it out."

That caught his curiosity at least. Let him think I was led here by the Spirit. It surprised me how easily I took to lying. "Well, it's good to have you with us, Meshach," he said, setting a hand on my shoulder and guiding me within.

Organ music swelled and filled the small sanctuary where a congregation of around thirty or so people rose from metal folding chairs, and began to sing and sway. Roland insisted I sit next to him near the back, his tweed blazer falling open as he guided me to the row, revealing a holster and a big nickel-plated pistol strapped to his side. Roland passed me a red hymnal, showed me the right page for "As the Deer Pants for the Water." He had a big enough voice for the two of us, which was good, because I only mumbled along, my throat strangely thick, my armpits and hands clammy with sweat, my hip aching.

People think of the Deep South or someplace like Idaho when they think of the crazies. They forget that

Randy Weaver was born and raised and radicalized in Iowa. They forget about the Posse Comitatus in North Dakota or the Aryan Republican Army robbing banks across the Midwest or rumors of Timothy McVeigh cooling his heels in Elohim City before committing his act of terrorism. What kind of man carried a holstered gun into worship? I thought that Roland had likely been chosen to receive visitors like me, make sure I wasn't an ATF agent or spying on behalf of some other federal agency. Did I look like an agent? I had lost so much weight this last month, dropping to a hundred and fifteen pounds the last time I climbed on a scale, that I felt like my skeleton and brain were composed of tumbleweeds. Nonetheless, I was investigating a mystery. The mystery of Maura. Roland and his big horse pistol were here to remind me that I was an outsider and therefore under suspicion. I hoped this church at least served good coffee.

After the hymn finished and we sat again, the preacher prowled the front. He was an athletic, lantern-jawed man dressed in blue jeans and plaid, his tan sports coat with leather patches on the elbows, a Bible hefted in one fist like a football he might heave to a lumbering tight end. This was my first glimpse of Maura's husband. Black-haired, with a trim mustache and sideburns, and small gray eyes, the Reverend Elijah Winters looked more like a professor than a white supremacist who had done time in Stillwater. His gaze kept finding me, the lone stranger in the back.

So far as I could tell there was no official order to the service, no usual rigmarole of a few hymns, announcements, and readings. They didn't even print a bulletin, instead feeling the service out. Pastor Eli had a surprisingly deep voice for a thin man, a voice with a soothing timbre, rising and falling as the moment called for it. He opened by talking about a corpse, the body of a Buddhist that some "hippy" claimed hadn't rotted for a week after death, the congregation muttering and shaking their heads when he asked, "Is that some kind of wonder? One week before the devil's own stench settles in? Does it even compare to what our God can do?"

Then he read to us from the Book of Matthew about a little girl everyone writes off as dead before Jesus happens along and says, "She is not dead, only sleeping," and the child revives and her parents rejoice. He paused after reading the passage. "What do you think I said to that hippy?" There was laughter now, along with scattered amens. "Do you think he had the eyes to see, the ears to hear? What do we tell the world with our own lives about what our God can do? What do we say to them?"

He rocked on the balls of his feet to some music he heard inside himself. He had them now, leaning toward him, his voice lowering and softening. Hell, I was drawn in like the rest of them, even if I kept thinking of Maura. Here now, I could see why she had fallen for him. He was charismatic, handsome, hardened by the world in ways I couldn't understand yet, his voice promising currents of wisdom. "Have you wondered what it feels like to be dead? To be laid out on the cold metal table of the undertaker? Each of us here knows that feeling. To be dead. To feel like inside you will never know warmth again."

Are you dead, Maura? Is your body somewhere at the bottom of Ursine Lake, naked and lashed to stones to keep you under the ice? Are you buried in an unmarked grave in this barren cemetery? Or have you only gone away?

His gaze found me once more as he stalked among the rows, moving down the aisle, the Bible now tucked under one arm like a running back holding a pigskin so it would not be fumbled. Be calm, I reminded myself, he's never met you before. He never visited the bank, never attended the office Christmas party. He doesn't know what you've done. Yet, I couldn't hold his gaze. "We know what it feels like to be dead inside. Empty. And all the world can give you is a week before the rot sets in. Like that's something to crow about. That's all the world has to offer. A week before you stink like a dead fish. Is that all you want?"

He was looking right at me as if I was the only one in the room and we were having a conversation. No, I thought. My aim was to go out with as much stink as possible. "No," I said, in a raspy voice, and my face flushed with heat, for the question had been rhetorical.

"No," he repeated gently before lifting his voice again. "Jesus has so much more to offer. So much more. We were dead in our sin. Every one of us. Dead and cold in the grave. In the devil's own grip. But there is not a thing we have said or done that Jesus doesn't know. He knows everything. Our darkest sin. Our deepest shame. And still he comes to us. He comes and finds us in the grave we have dug for ourselves, and he says, 'You are not dead, only sleeping.'" He turned, releasing me from the heat of his gaze, and strode back up to the front, pausing to touch some of the elderly members on the top of their heads or their shoulders as he moved among them. Like he could heal them, wake them with a touch. I couldn't help noticing that for a white supremacist he seemed to have borrowed many of his speaking patterns from African-American preachers.

He paused last at the front, laying hands on a dark-haired girl. The girl lifted her chin, her look adoring. A girl so small I could see her legs swinging under the chair. Sarah. Maura's daughter. His daughter. I knew her immediately, even though the girl sat beside a blond woman who wore a bold, blood-colored shawl that made the rest of her pale features look bleached out. The woman had her left arm around the back of Sarah's chair, and she tilted her chin up with the same look of adoration. Pastor Eli ignored the woman as he continued up to the front. I tried to figure out how Maura could abandon her daughter. I still couldn't believe she would leave her behind.

Where are you, Maura?

"We have to die to this world, leave behind the stench of our sins. We are called out of the darkness of our own grave. And we wake and we rise and there is such a singing in heaven when we walk again."

I tugged at my collar, pinpricks of heat needling up my spine, like I had been touched by a fever. I wanted to mock him, but in truth I was moved by his words. Deep down, I was the very dead man he had just described. I should be dead. I hated myself for not dying. I vaguely remember rising once more to sing another hymn along with Roland and then the pastor was talking again, but I completely lost the thread of whatever he was saying. He kept calling the devil "The Enemy" and growling warnings about a force of evil besieging us all. It sounded like some scary stuff, but I couldn't follow any of it. If you crack a front windshield with your forehead it does things to your concentration, even a month after the stitches have been removed and your hair has grown in over the scars. If I stood too suddenly the dizziness overcame me, a glittering wave of nausea that could knock me from my feet.

I had not expected this. I had expected crazy talk about the "agents of ZOG" and how the UN was the "One World Government" trying to put the "Mark of the Beast" on our bodies. Blood moons and blood seas. I had plenty of time during my convalescence to read up on white supremacists and skinheads, though I had to read it in snatches because of concussion protocol. But except for Clint Eastwood here sitting next to me with his holstered Saturday night special, these people seemed kind of normal.

On our last day working together Maura had been remote for most of her shift, maybe sick with some kind of premonition. Alone in the break room, when I tried asking her what was wrong, she shook her head. She hadn't been eating or sleeping well, couldn't keep her food down. She was so frightened her husband had figured it out. "It's going to be okay," I tried reassuring her.

"No," she said. "It won't. It won't ever again." Her eyes, so round and shining most days, looked pink and bloodshot under the fluorescent lights, the skin pouched and bruised beneath the sockets. She looked lost, her face ashen. Later that night after closing the bank and locking the doors, she excused herself to the bathroom and when she came back out, she said, "You're going to have to drive me to the hospital, Lucien," her breathing shivery as she described fainting in the bathroom after a dizzy spell and hitting her head on the sink.

Had I been driving so fast because I was angry with her? Dangerous driving like that in the rain. "Slow down," she said, but I had acted as if I hadn't heard. If the car hydroplaned, if I had to brake suddenly. No way to know what might loom out of the storm ahead of us. But nothing happened on the way to the hospital. I got her there safe. I just didn't know I wouldn't ever see her again when I dropped her off at the emergency room entrance. I just didn't know there was five thousand dollars missing from the vault back at the bank.

My adrenaline up, aching with feelings I couldn't yet name, I still had my foot pressed firmly to the accelerator on the way home after dropping her off, and I ended up skidding right through a stop sign and into a speeding pickup that made mincemeat of my Civic. The guy in the pickup was hurtled through his windshield and across the road, his body blazing a thirty-foot meteor-like channel through somebody's front lawn. This turned out to be a good thing because after smashing into my Civic, the fuel line in his pickup caught fire. I woke to heat, gasoline burning in my nostrils, the frantic screel of metal-on-metal as paramedics tried to cut me from the pinned wreckage with the Jaws of Life before I passed out again. My own foretaste of hell. I know some of this because the pickup driver later came to visit me in the hospital, a lanky kid wearing a Twins baseball cap, his arm in a cast since they'd had to replace lost skin there with skin from the back of his legs. He was otherwise miraculously unhurt. "You got a raw deal here, dude," he'd said. "This is why I don't wear a seatbelt."

The cops searched my crushed car for the money and didn't find it. Harry Larkin cleared me of suspicion; the burden falling on Maura, who disappeared that night. She never checked into the hospital where I would spend the next ten days.

The more I thought about it, the more I wondered. If Maura had stolen the money, she could have lied about other things.

Where did you go, Maura, and why? Were you really pregnant and unsure about the father and what to do next? Did you really miscarry? Did you feel even a shadow of what I felt for you?

"Do you want to be saved?" the Reverend Elijah was asking from the front. "Is there anyone here who wants to get up and leave behind the darkness of the grave and walk into the light?"

Every head bowed while mine was still lifted. My throat parched and dry. Right there in the church I smelled burning gasoline. Reverend Elijah watched me. Even Roland had raised his head. I stood and stumbled, pushing past Roland into the center aisle.

"Come, young man," the preacher said, his eyes on me and his voice soft and beckoning, the people with the bowed heads swaying and murmuring. They knew someone was approaching the altar. And I don't know how to explain it, but there was an energy in the room. I felt it, like light at the base of my spine, urging me toward the altar. Years later, I've wondered over it, because in that moment, I heard the pain in the preacher's voice. He was hurting, too. He needed me as much as I needed him. As light calls to dark. Or dark unto dark.

I took one step toward him, my head down. My vision had gone blurry. I was terrified that one of the migraines I had begun suffering since the accident was coming on, but in that moment I wanted him to lay hands on me. I wanted to believe. I wanted him to lay hands on me and say, He is not dead, only sleeping.

Instead, I turned on my heels and lurched toward the front door. He didn't call out after me, instead addressing the congregation, moving on with his prayer.

Outside, a snarling wind bit into me. I felt the tears on my face freezing. A cold that torched my lungs. I kept on stumbling across the parking lot like some wounded animal until I made it to my car. Trembling, wrung out, I climbed into the Continental. I didn't deserve any forgiveness. I had failed to save a good person, helped steal a wife from a husband, a mother from her daughter. I had been an accessory to a crime that I didn't even know was being committed. Her husband had named my condition correctly. I was dead in my sin.

I didn't start the car up right away, but sat shivering

in the front seat trying to steady myself by gripping the wheel. When I glanced back at the church I could see Roland standing sentinel by the front door, watching me curiously. After another coughing fit, the engine turned over. When it sparked and rumbled to life, I peeled away.

Maura, did you tell me the truth about your husband? His violence? Were you really afraid of him? That man, back there?

I never saw any bruises, but I believed I had touched her wounds just the same. After she disappeared, I called the local police to tell them what I knew, to accuse Elijah Winters, but I had no idea if they followed through with any kind of investigation. I had believed Maura when she had no one else to turn to. No one in the world but me. She wouldn't go to a shelter. There was no place safe from him, she'd said. Not for her, or her daughter. I had to come back, had to let him know who I was, but I didn't know how I'd find the courage.

I had to see him again, but I no longer knew if I was the light or the shadow in this story.

Concerning the
Unkindness of Ravens

In one of the religion classes I attended, the prof talked about primitive tribes who believe that the fontanelle, the soft spot on a baby's skull, is a doorway for spirits. Through membrane where the brain pulses underneath, stretching and flexing like spongy muscle, spirits trickle in. This makes babies both holy and wholly vulnerable, attended by seraphim and spectra, until the bony plates grow over that fleshy place, hardening, and a world of possibility shrinks to the mundane every child must muddle through to reach a humdrum adulthood, where no spirits ever visit.

My car accident split me open body and mind. I'd broken three ribs in my left side, had four silicone screws stitching together a busted collarbone, and my left hip had been fractured. At the hospital, the attending surgeon told me he had expected to put me into a medically induced coma so he could drill into my skull to release the pressure, but my brain hadn't swollen. I was lucky, he said, to emerge from the wreckage without any lasting damage to my spinal cord and neck. After I recovered from the concussion, troubling migraines lingered, so I left the hospital with a serious arsenal of medication: Percocet for pain, sumatriptan for the migraines, Effexor after they diagnosed me with what they called "situational depression." While I didn't drink, partaking of this cocktail of pharmaceuticals played with my perception of reality. I hurt all the time and couldn't imagine a life beyond the hurt. My survival didn't feel like luck, but there is this: when my skull cracked like a clay jar, I didn't just become ultrasensitive to light and sound. I saw things I had never seen before and have not seen since. My damaged skull throbbed like a fontanelle opening unto a spirit world where most mortals cannot tread.

All these years later, even if this second sight has dimmed, the cracked places healing over, I can't forget what I saw. The Apostle speaks of powers and principalities at work in this world that are invisible to the human eye, a struggle beyond flesh and blood, a spiritual evil that lies upon the earth. I am not certain about any of what happened next—some of it feels so impossible—but I know this much. That winter of 1999, just before the turn of the millennium, I walked with angels and demons.

Following my visit to Rose of Sharon, the demons came for me first.

Ravens arrived the next morning, blown south from Canada as if by fallout. Big black birds with glossy wings and devil eyes. When I took Kaiser on his morning walk, I marveled at the storm of birds up in the barren grove, all bristly like wind in leaves. A hundred and then a hundred more, filling up the pines on the ridge. I heard anger in their croaky choir. So many, it was as if a seam had unzipped in the gray sky and out poured these birds, bickering in the branches like they had taken a wrong turn somewhere and couldn't agree on which way to go next. Kaiser made a whimpering sound, like he could sense something wrong in the ravens, both of us stunned by the confabulation of their caw, caw, cawing. I had never seen such a wonder, both beautiful and terrible.

Branches creaked and cracked under the weight of so many birds, ravens on every bending bough, painting the pines inky-black. A shiver scratched at the base of my spine. When the migraines came on it felt like an electric storm, fast-moving flashes of light and dark gathering at the corners of my eyes, my world shrinking to a trembling tunnel. If I collapsed in such a place, I was sure these birds would drink my eyes from the sockets.

"Don't be scared," I told Kaiser, my voice a little loud to be heard over the ravens. "They call it a 'murder' when so many flocks gather. No, that's not right. A murder is for crows. Flocks of ravens are called an unkindness. An 'unkindness of ravens' is the right term." I coughed into my gloves, because naming them correctly had not taken away any of their dark magic. "I know, I know. Ornithologists are major fans of understatement where ravens are concerned."

His hackles up, Kaiser turned back toward the house.

"Not yet," I called after him. The old dog had shat himself the day before, right at the door to the backyard, and I didn't want any more messes. It was only seven in the morning and I had meant to walk the dog and then get back inside and start working on my programming for *The Land*. The first week of my convalescence had passed and I had little to show for it. I knew if I had any chance of getting this project done, I had to establish a regular schedule: creativity only came if you made time for it. Let Kaiser finish his morning business and then we could take shelter. But the dog wasn't cooperating, spooked by the ravens.

I figured he needed some encouragement, so I unzipped my pants. The cold nipped at my nether regions, but I shut everything out, the ravens' sonic disturbance, my failures so far to make progress on my program, the sorry work I had done as a self-appointed detective investigating the mystery of Maura, the weeks I'd spent with my privates hooked to a catheter. The golden arc I managed to carve into the snow felt triumphant, but Kaiser only sat on his haunches, unimpressed. I quickly zipped my pants.

I shared the dog's unease. It wasn't just the sight of so many ravens massed together bothering me. I sensed something else stirring in those birds, a carrion cry up in their heads, a darkness that had harried them here. Inside my brain I picked up a vibration, a humming of fear and hunger ahead of the long winter night, joining with a sibling shadow inside them. These birds were only birds, I reminded myself, just animals, and so who knows why they do what they do, but I couldn't shake a supernatural sense of foreboding. What had Pastor Elijah called the devil? The Enemy. He was here. I sensed Him. He had come with the birds. In the trees I heard the steady splat of their shit dropping from the branches as they emptied themselves. I put up the hood of my parka in case any winged overhead.

Finally, Kaiser finished his business and the two of us were hurrying through the falling snow along a compacted path we had made between the back door and the grove. Flashes of color lit up the edges of my vision, dark approaching wings, the onset of another migraine. This one was going to be a doozy. I was jogging as quickly as my aching hip would allow when I slipped in the snow and went down hard, striking the back of my head. Before I could rise again, the migraine had me in its talons, pinching until it punctured through membrane. I cried out thinly, so intense was the agony, as I fell back in the snow. It was like the shadow I had sensed up in the birds' heads had overtaken me, pecking and shredding light and sanity from my brain.

I believe I went unconscious. When the pain finally released me, I believe I even dreamed, encased in the warmth of my parka. I saw Maura again, that first time at Bay City Mutual. I had known before I even met her that I would like her. Transferring from a branch in Duluth where I'd been living with a cousin and attending Lake Superior College part-time, to Aurora Bay where I was starting school at NMSU, I had read the list of names ahead of time and tried to imagine my new life there. Maura Cosette Winters stood out among the list of tellers. I remember putting my finger on her name, whispering the pure musicality of it aloud, all iambic pentameter, the same cadence as a beating heart. Maura. I already knew before I even saw her that she would be beautiful.

And Maura was. She had wild, gingery brown hair she tried taming in a bun, but wisps were forever escaping in a spill of curls down her neck or wavy strands she had to brush from her large, mercurial eyes. Her high cheek-bones and olive skin made her look foreign among the pasty white northerners that inhabited Aurora Bay, like she stepped from the pages of a story Scheherazade told to save herself from the Sultan's executioner. She wasn't like anyone I'd ever met before. Quiet and reserved at first, she shook my hand formally when we met, and something caught within me when I looked into her eyes. Her eyes shifted color in different lights, green one moment, then blue or brown. She slid her hand from my own and walked away. That day, she had hardly said two words to me.

Our small bank branch kept longer hours and a smaller staff than main locations. A few nights later we closed together for the first time. Near the end of a long day, I got stuck dealing with a rich old crank who was shutting down his checking account, angry it didn't pay him enough interest. I had tried getting him to keep the account open at least until he spoke to our investment specialist the next day, but he proved intractable. This would mean trouble for me in the morning when our manager came in. Harry Larkin hated losing accounts, especially premium, gold-star accounts. That this guy earned any interest at all on a checking account made it exceptional, but it wasn't good enough.

While I went through the procedures, the old man further treated me to a long harangue about how he shouldn't have to pay taxes for education because he already put his own children through school. By the time I had his account closed, a cashier's check for his substantial balance printed, I had heard an earful about the troubles with the world these days. I should have just let him walk away, but everything about this squat little man bothered me, even the clothes he wore: a turtle-neck with high-water golf pants and Italian loafers with no socks on. He had the hairy feet of a hobbit. I handed him the check, and the words "Good luck on your quest" just slipped out because I doubted he would find a better deal at any other bank.

With him halfway out the door, I thought I could get away with a little sarcasm, but his gray wattles flushed a dark purple above his turtleneck. His heavy-lidded eyes narrowed. "What'd you say?"

I shrugged. "I only meant to wish you well. Have a good night, sir."

One fat vein pulsed in his balding pate. Even if he was no longer a customer, he wasn't going to let this go. "You were mocking me."

I shrugged again, which further infuriated him.

"I'm going to let your manager know about what you said," he said, jabbing a finger at my tie. "I will be filing an official complaint."

"Sir," Maura said, stepping in. "I'm the Ops. Supervisor. I can help you." She locked her till and came around the counter, opening the half door that separated us from the rest of the lobby, empty of any actual manage-ment at this time of night. Maura guided him over to the desk and pulled out a chair for him. I couldn't hear what they were saying, because there were other customers in line to deal with, just the low murmur of her consoling voice as she scratched something down on a blank form. They talked for a long time — long enough that I was sure I was in trouble — before finally he left, Maura escorting him out the door, the guy glaring in my direction, muttering something about "this insolent generation."

Maura still had the form as she came back to her place. "Well, what do you have to say for yourself?" She looked prim and disapproving, her face not giving anything away. I still didn't have a firm read on her. Was she going to turn me in? "As your Ops. Supervisor," she went on, "this is the part where I'm supposed to bust your balls."

I blushed. "There's no such position at this branch," I said. I was pretty sure Maura was a Customer Care Specialist, level two, just like me.

Maura showed me the page, a blank loan application sheet where she'd printed OFFICIAL COMPLAINT FORM at the top and the name LUCIEN SWENSON underneath with details of my transgressions. She smiled and then dropped the form into the shredder. There were no customers in the lobby. She set one hand on her hip, shaking her head at the departing customer. "Good luck on your quest," she said, "Frodo Douchebaggins."

After that, we were tight. "So you're a student at Northern? What are you studying?" she asked during another lull between customers. I liked the sound of her voice, too, a little husky for a woman, tinged with smoke.

"Life," I said. If that sounds like a smug answer, I was

twenty. A dumb punk. I already knew then that I wasn't cut out for biology, though I had doggedly enrolled in calculus and anatomy that semester. I wanted to study English, but my dad ruled it out. It was pre-med or econ like him, so I could grow up and work for a bank, groom myself for management. That was my dad's deal for me. He would pay my tuition so long as I stuck to marketable majors. My job at the bank covered most everything else.

"Life studies must be one of the liberal arts," she said. "Something in the humanities?"

"It sure as hell isn't a science."

Maura just laughed. "No," she said, "it's more like a poem written by a drunkard, down in the ditch looking up at the stars."

"Something like that," I said, recognizing the Oscar Wilde reference.

I didn't know many people in Aurora Bay. My cousin in Duluth had moved to Sioux Falls and the rest of my family lived in Chicago. After the move I lost touch with friends from high school, most of whom had gone on to better things at the University of Chicago or Loyola. Northern had proved to be one of those suitcase campuses, a ghost town on the weekends, and I'd only made a few friends. Where Maura was concerned, I was doomed from the start.

And from the start, I idealized her. One time Harry Larkin held the monthly staff meeting at night to go over changes in procedures and projected growth in branch checking accounts along with new marketing pitches. Maura brought her daughter, Sarah, to the meeting, then just a baby. Baby Sarah had thistledown hair and the huge round eyes of an anime character, and she delighted the loan supervisor and other female tellers with her cooing charms, though Harry had been clearly displeased by the distraction. He was introducing an important new marketing blitz—No monthly fees! Automatic overdraft protection!—and tellers would now be expected to make cold calls during lulls in the day. I sucked at sales, so I ignored much of Harry's instructions and instead made faces at the baby, who had the trilling laugh of a bird.

After the meeting ended and everyone else skedaddled, another teller named Dorothy—a stout, matronly woman—and I were handling final closing procedures. Dorothy was the only female I've ever met with a mullet, which somehow suited her personality and her square face. She was already a grandmother at the age of thirty-seven.

Maura had not left with the others because baby Sarah needed to be fed and so she had discreetly rolled her chair over to one corner by the branch manager's desk to unbutton her blouse. She'd positioned the chair so it was facing away from us, so from behind the teller's station I could just see the crown of her head, see how she cupped the baby by the back of her head, both of them bathed in the soft green glow of the branch manager's lamp. In the quiet after closing, I could hear the baby feeding. They were held by the light, mother and child. I could see how much Maura loved her baby.

Maura, do you know what I felt most in that moment, what I still feel? I wanted to protect you. Even before I knew you were in trouble. I wanted you and Sarah to stay in the warm light and not have to step outside into the icy, outer darkness. I wanted to be the one who kept you safe. I didn't know how much pain this would mean for both of us, but even if I had known, I think I would have still done the same.

I hadn't realized I was staring until Dorothy nudged me. "She's sweet on you," she said.

"I'm good with babies," I said. But of course, she hadn't meant the baby and I knew that.

Dorothy gave me her cut-the-bullshit look. "Don't get any ideas," she said, patting me on my shoulder.

I WOKE, NOT UNLIKE Maura's man down in the ditch, but I wasn't looking up at any stars. Instead, I woke to a nightmare. I woke when Kaiser stuck his icy muzzle right into the soft of my neck and let out a snort. The pain softly thrummed behind my temples, but I could see again. I climbed unsteadily to my feet. I woke to the rage.

I stood up in the ringing din, in the falling snow. The reek and scream where ravens dark as bruises blotted the pines. Something must have torn up inside their heads. All these years later, I can still feel it inside me. A rip in time. Whatever tissue that had penned the boiling shadows inside their brains at bay disintegrated. Or, when I stood I snapped a branch, sharp as the report of a rifle.

All at once they lifted from the trees, flinging their bodies from the branches, screeching, rising into the sky and then diving with talons outstretched, one whisking right past my head. Still groggy with the remains of a migraine, I didn't even duck. At first I thought they were attacking me. I was about to be the first man in America to die by being pecked to death by an unkindness of ravens, or carried off like the scarecrow in *The Wizard of Oz*. The air whirred around me, a maelstrom of beak and talon. Then I saw one impale its beak into the chest of another. Those two plummeted to the ground, locked in their fatal embrace. I realized what was happening. They were killing each other, killing their own kind. Mothers and brothers and friends. Hundreds battling. Whirling black feathers and bones cracking. The thump and thwack of bodies smashing into the icy ground.

Kaiser and I stood in the vortex, stunned by their savagery, the birds' minds bleeding red, all pulsing shadows. The birds did not see us. They shuddered at each impact. They flew all around us, but we were not touched. What a terrifying thing a nightmare is when you stand in the midst of it.

How long did it last? How long? Time elongated.

When the battle was done, the shadow lifted, ascending like a breath, one last gasp before perdition. Around us lay the dead, dozens bleeding out in the snow. The Enemy gone. It had taken all morning for so many ravens to fill up the pines on the ridge, but they died in a few minutes.

The survivors, most of the birds, winged off north again, climbing vanishing ladders of snow into the clouds. Black feathers clotted the ice, pinkish streaks of blood and bird brain. We stood in the middle of it, untouched. A great silence spread and deepened. The pain in my mind quieted.

Kaiser and I walked back. A metallic taste burned in my throat. Blood spattered my coat and one long bloody streak marked one of the bay windows where a raven had struck in its madness. I shucked off my coat inside, let Kaiser in, and closed the door. Numb with shock, a shock nearly as visceral as I'd felt during the accident, I stripped off the rest of my clothes and wandered naked upstairs and took a sumatriptan and a Percocet and climbed under my sheets. Sleep is an inhospitable country if every time you roll over on your left side barbs of pain spike throughout your entire body, but I slept, and this time I did not dream. My sleep was like the snow, a whiteout, and when I woke it was as if the massacre had never happened.

I shrugged on a t-shirt and some sweatpants and wandered downstairs to feed Kaiser. The clock showed it was a little past three, so I had slept much of the day. Outside the bay windows, I saw a few wolves had appeared to drag off the corpses, at least three with maybe more circling deeper in the grove, ghostly shapes. The wolves should have thrilled me. Most people go their whole lives without ever seeing one in the wild, but I was too shell-shocked to wonder over their primal arrival, so intent on their feast they did not lift their bloody muzzles to see me watching them.

Near the birches, one fox, a splash of fiery orange, made a feast of his own, keeping a nervous eye on the larger predators. I felt sure watching that no one would ever believe me. In the years since, I have heard of ravens doing this up in Alaska when their flocks grow too numerous, driven by starvation or overpopulation. Surely, there is a natural explanation. Such rationality insulates us from suffering. I know I didn't just imagine my mind spreading out to touch the minds of those birds. I felt their hunger and pain. I sensed the drained emptiness in their bellies and in that emptiness, a place where shadows seethed.

In that moment I felt I had seen the Enemy and I knew now what he could do. And I knew he could do the same to the human heart.

Snow kept falling and falling. I was about to turn

away when I saw a fleck of black stir in a snowdrift near-est the bay window, a smaller raven struggling to rise. Alive, a lone refugee of the war. The fox and wolves hadn't noticed it yet, but they would soon. I didn't stop to think. Barefoot, I opened the back door and waded into the snow to fetch what I figured was a dying animal.

The door snapping shut behind me startled the preda-tors. A large gray timber wolf lifted its muzzle from the red-soaked snow. It had eyes like white fire in the dark, lit from within. Too late, I remembered old man Kroll advising me about the .30-06 in the gun cabinet. Could I make it back inside if they came for me?

Yet I did not feel that same sense of dread as I had caught up amid warring ravens. Her glowing eyes held my own and I sensed her intelligence, her rightness in this wintry world. She belonged here as I didn't. I write *she* even though I had no way of knowing for certain if she was the alpha female. In a fellow mammal I just remember sensing a distinct motherly presence.

"Mine," I told the wolf about the surviving raven behind me. "I'm taking this one." She huffed in dismissal and, with her tail bristling, retreated into the woods, tak-ing the rest of the pack with her. I watched her go and then turned to my task.

I took off my sweatshirt, wrapped the bird in it, and carried it inside. The sleek black body quivered as I cradled it to my chest, holding it against my bare, goose-pimpled skin. Its eyes were sealed shut, covered in a gray film, like it was sick with some disease.

I thought about calling animal control, but it was already too late at night and I would have to also tell them about what I'd seen in the woods, try to explain it somehow. The sheer savagery. I couldn't do it. Holding that breathing bird against my chest, I had this feeling it had been sent. A messenger from beyond. Wrapped in my sweatshirt, the raven made a muffled caw of protest, unhappy with the effort I had made to save it.

Unsure what to do next, I brought the wounded bird into the garage, found a discarded box, and made a nest of newspapers. I sat on the garage step and rubbed the glossy black body in my sweatshirt trying to revive it. The eyes never opened, but I could feel the tremor of its breathing in my hands.

I'm the caretaker, I remember thinking. And for the first time in a few months my life made sense, had some purpose. This is why I was put here, in the midst of this madness. I was here to care for things, and not just the house and dog. I had failed to take care of Maura. I couldn't fail again.

Winter Visitor

I drove the twenty-mile trip to NMSU on roads slick with freezing rain, hemmed in by jack pine, the tamarack in their sphagnum bogs shedding the last of their golden needles. The ride gave me time to think. On a good day, once I crested the last hill the looming trees should have dropped away to reveal a vista of Aurora Bay, glowing green as a gem below, but in the storm the bay glowered, the same leaden color as the lowering sky. The vast inland sea of Lake Superior brooded beyond. I had been longing for a view of open water, for the clarity I hoped the sight might bring, but the choppy waters below frothed with whitecaps.

I had driven here because I desperately needed some normality in my routine. At school I paid for my standard coffee at the Commons where I searched out a class to attend from a crumpled semester schedule in my backpack. I hadn't slept well the night before. Hell, I hadn't slept well in months. I needed something else to occupy my mind, to keep it from returning to Maura's vanishing and the accident. The brutality of the ravens and the lone survivor I'd pulled from the snow. The carrion bird of my brain circling bruised skies.

While I was scanning the schedule, I spotted my buddy Noah just coming in. Noah was one of a few people of mixed race on campus, athletic and good-looking in an all-American way, with dark, coppery skin and long-lashed green eyes he'd inherited from his white mother. A goalie for the Voyageurs' hockey team, Noah happened to be one of the nicest people I knew. This morning, a blonde walked by his side, her extravagant hand gestures indicating they were in some kind of debate from a previous class. Instinctively, I ducked my head. Noah would have questions. He would want to know if I felt better, what progress I was making on *The Land*, when we would hang out again. Why did I feel separate from him since the accident? I can't explain why I didn't want to talk to him, except this: I didn't want anyone's pity, and there are few things athletes pity more than a cripple. For all these reasons, I slunk out of the Commons before he spotted me.

I ended up in my old anatomy class. Before I dropped out, I had a capable lab partner, Naomi, who wielded a scalpel like a talon, peeling back the leached skin of a fetal pig to expose a universe of sluggish gray organs that I dutifully mapped out in my notebook. "Poor Oliver," I had said at the time, pretending he had been our pet, recently perished after a mysterious illness. "You poor, poor bastard."

"You're not supposed to name dead fetal pigs," Naomi said in a flat voice, clearly repulsed by the notion.

The coursework varied between lab and lecture days, and today was one of the lectures so I could slip in a little late and find myself a place at the back. Professor Rhone was already busy lecturing by the time I snuck in. I waited until his back turned to the board, where an invertebrate had been neatly diagrammed, before I searched for a seat. I kept my head hunched, not looking to see if Naomi was in class that day, until I found a spot at the back. I unzipped my backpack and cracked open a Mead notebook and began to take notes. *Hadean. Archean. Proterozoic.* The words singing out from the professor as they had from the preacher's mouth. I wrote as fast as he talked, my pen scratching out furious patterns, copying diagrams from the board, faithfully at first before my attention wandered and in the margins I began to animate a war between amoebas. All of life a struggle, from the dawn of time. Ravens warring in the snow. Our bodies at war on a cellular level. High up in the lecture hall, alone in my row, I heard the professor's drone and the hum of the generator and the ice striking the glass of the sky-lights, a gust of wind bringing slanting sheets of freezing rain. My head felt heavier and heavier. There is nothing better than a good lecture-nap. I slouched in my seat and let my heavy head do the rest.

I slept so deeply I dreamed. In my dream the devil was chasing me. I was not sure how I knew it was the devil. There was something about his very ordinariness I found terrifying because no one but me knew who he was, his face both familiar and unplaceable.

In the dream he stood on the shores of the Wind River and he called to me again and again. In the waking world, I didn't believe in the devil or Hell, but in the dream it was some freaky shit. In the dream I knew that Hell was real and it was here on earth and in our brains and in our DNA. Even animals like those ravens knew Hell. I knew there was a great spiritual evil hovering over the world, clouds of wings occluding the sun.

A stranger in the kingdom, the devil looked lost, a stray piece of dark, unloved. This, too, seemed so ordinary, his longing tucked inside so much rage and violence. He wanted to be loved for his power. I sensed this power as well. He would give me some if I let him.

I was not alone in the dream. I had something precious. He cried out not only for me, but for a baby I held in my arms as I stood in the knee-deep rushing current of the river, my teeth chattering. I was covered in blood like I'd just come from the accident. It spilled out of my shattered skull.

"Bring it to me," the devil said, "and I will let you live. A life for a life."

The baby squalled in his loose bundle of cloth, a sound that filled me up. I knew exactly who this baby was. The child Maura and I were meant to have together. Our baby. It was ours and now the devil had come to claim the fruit of our sin. I knew that if I obeyed the devil both the baby and I would be lost forever.

Farther out in the river the waters deepened, but there was no way to make it to the other side. Downriver, the rapids ripped along. I walked along the shallows as the devil shadowed me on shore until we reached a bend in the river and he stepped into the water. I could walk over to meet him or give myself to the river.

(I could choose death. I would choose death rather than give the baby to the devil or learn the Name he had for me. I would choose to be split open once more. Let the hurt come.)

I went deeper into the current, the bundled baby wrapped tightly in my arms, and the surging water swept me from my feet. We raced along between boulders that were sure to crush us, the devil screaming after us. "The baby is mine! Mine! Mine!" He screamed a name over the rapids, claiming me. I heard it in the roar. Jagged rocks loomed in the torrent as I spun out of control, heading right for a collision that would wreck me and the child I could not save.

The next thing I knew, I was standing up in the middle of Professor Rhone's lecture, my ears still ringing from the shock of impact with the boulders. I must have cried out in my sleep. I barely knew why I was standing up, my pen gripped in my fist, sweat soaking my shirt. The same heat in my throat as when the preacher beckoned me closer. I was shaking and my mouth tasted of blood. I must have bitten the inside of my cheek during the nightmare.

"Yes?" Professor Rhone said. He had shaggy eyebrows, a permanent five-o'clock shadow darkening his jawline. Students whispered about his three tours in Vietnam, what he'd seen over there. Before class, Rhone stood outside chain-smoking cigarettes and tossing the burning butts into a snowbank. Known for his temper and for sprinkling his lectures with unexpected profanities, Rhone didn't like interruptions. He didn't look pleased to see I'd returned to class.

My mind felt full of noise, the icy rain falling inside me. I swallowed and tried to get my bearings. I was not dead. The river had not broken and drowned me. The devil had only been a dream. The baby. The rest of the class turned to look at me. I could see Naomi now, up near the front, scrunching down in her seat.

I had to say something, so what came to me is what

I had been wondering about all semester when Rhone talked about evolution, but hadn't dared speak aloud. I cleared my throat. "There are something like six million species on the planet," I said, my voice cracking. "And I was wondering how it's possible for so many variations to have evolved from single-celled bacteria. Or whatever?"

My question trailed off. Professor Rhone's jaw worked while he massaged a stick of chalk in his fist. "Well," he said, "given enough time, anything is possible." He gestured for me to sit down; clearly he felt he'd answered the question definitively. Time. Like millions and billions of years. Eons. Time. Gobs of it. Time was the solution to everything! His frown deepened when I remained standing.

"But how is it possible when the Second Law of Thermodynamics says that all things decay and break down. Entropy. This is one of the central principles of energy that governs the universe. How does life evolve faced with chaos and decay? How does anything?" I was losing the thread of my question. The other students in the lecture hall shifted uncomfortably in their seats. They must have all thought I was some kind of religious nutcase.

"What are you asking exactly?" The chalk in his fist had been ground to a nub, a white snow coating his loafers. I bet this guy killed a lot of people in the Nam.

Why life? is what I thought. How does life go on when

the world itself seems so hostile? "It's just . . . I've been thinking, why not God?"

"Why not God?" he repeated, and he shook his big, shaggy head slowly and sadly from side to side. "I believe you're in the wrong fucking class."

I WENT HOME AND didn't go back to Northern for a few days. I didn't think I'd go back to school ever again. When I got home, the first thing I did was check on the rescued raven.

I hadn't expected it to live through the night and left without checking in on it earlier that morning, not wanting to deal with a corpse then. So when I returned from my failed trip to Northern State and opened the garage door that afternoon, I was sure I would find the body stiff with rigor mortis. Instead, the box was empty. I went down the steps and checked all around it. Not a single feather nestled amid the shredded papers, not a trace of blood. This worried me even more than a dead body.

I half-wondered if I had dreamed the moment, the great battle in the snow, the lone survivor. My grasp on reality so tenuous I moved in a waking dream. Then I heard it squawk from up in the garage rafters. Ten feet away, half-obscured by shadows my eyes couldn't penetrate, it called to me in its harsh language.

"You're alive," I said, a sense of relief flooding through me.

In answer the raven fluttered deeper into a loft area amid the rafters, hiding from me. I didn't want to frighten it further so I left it alone and carefully shut the garage door. I was going to have to figure out what to feed it.

I ended up feeding it Kaiser's dog food, pounding the nuggets into smaller pieces and placing them in a trail leading up to the stairs. When I returned a few hours later, the food was gone, the bird back in his hiding place.

The next couple of days I settled into my habits, caring for the raven, walking the dog in the snow, visiting the koi pond, which looked frozen over completely now, and digging into old man Kroll's impressive collection of movies on Betamax. So far I had made little progress on the programming I had left to do for *The Land*, but I had all winter ahead of me. An insomniac with access to enough pharmaceuticals to rewire my brain—I stayed up most nights watching the classics. *Chinatown. The Godfather. The Bridge on the River Kwai.*

The lower level had another sunken room that was like a bunker. No windows. A dusty mothball smell mingled with stale popcorn grease. A vintage movie projector, an eight-millimeter, occupied the center and there were two plush La-Z-Boys on either side in front of a big screen. The eight-millimeter collection was "off limits," he had explained to me while giving me a tour of the house, so I stuck to his Betamax shelves. Here in this windowless place, while the mirage of images flashed on the screen, I felt safe enough to sleep. I didn't so much sleep as catnap for a few hours. I think I had the best naps ever in my life in that La-Z-Boy recliner, under the spell of my meds and Hollywood.

I was just getting into *The Exorcist* when the doorbell rang. The sound jarred me from the dark dream of the movie. Who could possibly be here? This house was in the middle of nowhere. I paused the movie and climbed the spiral staircase. I opened the door to reveal a skinny girl who appeared to be about my age and was dressed in a pea green army coat, a duffel bag slung over her shoulder. Her dark hair was chopped short, her features sharp and hawkish, her eyes brown and almond-shaped. Her coat appeared too thin for the weather, her face pale as the clouds dropping snow behind her. She tilted her head, birdlike, as if I was the mystery here. "Who are you?"

"Me? Lucien. I'm looking after this place for the Krolls."

"Lucien?" She frowned as if she disapproved of the name.

I considered explaining how I'd been named after a cherished grandfather, but truthfully I'd never cared for my name. I thought maybe I really should change my name to Meshach.

The girl peered past me into the foyer as if looking for someone. "Where are my parents?"

"Uh . . . parents?" Neither Kroll had mentioned any

daughter. Rambling through the house, I'd seen no pictures of this girl, no toys or dolls or any sort of evidence that any child had ever lived here. The only framed photos mostly featured Mr. Kroll in blaze orange or camo posing with recently slain animals, elk or bear or some other luckless beast, blood freckling the leaves about him.

She hugged herself with her arms and let out an exasperated sigh. Her lips had a bluish cast from the cold. "Listen, I don't know who you are." Her tongue darted out to touch her lips, and her eyes locked on mine as if she had made some vital determination. Without another word she pushed past me, tracking snow into the foyer.

I snagged her by the elbow. "Hey," I said. "I didn't say you could come in."

The girl looked thin and bony, but she shook out of my grip, dropped her duffel, and jabbed one finger right in the center of my chest. She smelled like she hadn't bathed in a month, a musky animal odor overwhelming in tight quarters. "What have you done with my mom and dad?" she said, advancing on me until she had me backed against the wall.

"They're in Texas," I told her, still not sure what to believe. I squeezed past her to the open door, taking one fresh gulp of cold air before shutting it and turning back to her. "South Padre Island. At least until March or April. I'm caring for the house and dog while they're gone."

"Kaiser?" she said, her nose twitching. "And they're gone all winter?"

She made it sound like they had never done it before, which had not been my impression. "They couldn't wait to escape the cold."

She quirked one thin eyebrow, as if she knew there was more to it than that. I hadn't mentioned any of the Y2K talk. I considered it vaguely reassuring that she knew the name of the dog. "They'll be back when the snow melts," I continued. If the world doesn't end on December 31st, I didn't add.

"And you're in contact with them?"

I massaged my sore hip, which ached from the cold the girl had brought into the room with her. "I have their number in case something goes wrong." Such as a stranger forcing her way into the house.

"Are you hurt?"

"It's nothing. So, you're . . . their daughter? You think they would have mentioned something like that."

She spread out her hands, palms up. "Why would they? We've been estranged . . ." She lingered on that word, her small, sharp face tightening at some unpleasant memory. "They wouldn't expect me to come home for the holidays."

"There aren't any pictures of you anywhere," I said. Not a single room bore any girlish trace, like a stuffed bear or a pink quilt, but then again she didn't seem the girlish type. Thanksgiving was little more than a week away. How long was she planning to stay? I resented this intrusion on my peace.

"We aren't on speaking terms. My dad wiped his hands of me." She made a gesture, a flat, slapping sound as her palms came together. I could picture Mr. Kroll doing the same.

"I'll call them," I said. "They'll want to know you're here."

She shook her head, her brown eyes huge and pleading. "Don't," she said.

The pain in my hip jogged up into my skull and started to party there. Starbursts began to pop and flare at the corner of my vision. Not again. Not now. I didn't feel so hot. Fuck. After the accident migraines came on when I was stressed, thunderclouds boiling up inside my brain, a roaring wind across the plains.

"I wasn't expecting a happy homecoming," she said. "I just need a place to stay for a while. I took the bus from Bellingham and then walked the rest of the way."

Bellingham? I pinched the skin between my eyes. That was halfway across the country.

"Heh? What's wrong with you?"

"I just need to sit down for a minute."

The girl led me into the kitchen by the elbow and sat me on one of the chairs. She banged around in the cabinets before finding a glass she filled at the tap. Shaking,

I accepted the glass, stood again, and started walking away. My sumatriptan was on the nightstand in my bedroom, and I needed it now. The girl tailed me. I still didn't know her name, thought there was something off about her story, but I had pressing physical concerns of my own, a monsoon drumming behind my temples.

In the bedroom, pain walloped me. I nearly dropped the glass I was carrying. It felt like I had a whole fraternity inside my skull, all of them drunk and hurling bottles and shit at the walls inside my head. I managed to set the glass down and reached for my medication, but I was shaking so badly by then I couldn't get it open.

"Here," the girl said. She took it from my hands, unscrewed the cap, and fished out a pill. "Open up," she commanded, so I did and she set the pill on my tongue gingerly, like she was doling out a Communion wafer. I chased it with a gulp of water, but the migraine had me in such a fierce grip I couldn't even see straight. The girl guided me to the bed, pulled back the covers. I felt her take my shoes off. I no longer noticed the intensity of her odor. Her voice was soft as she laid a cool hand on my forehead. A winter priestess attending her parishioner. "It's going to be okay," she said.

I shut my eyes, unable to respond. Hadn't I promised Maura the same thing? She shut off the lights and left me in the dark, where the pill warred with the fraternity of pain and eventually won out. I was so tired. How long had it been since I had a full night's rest, undisturbed? The medicine made me so woozy that I shut my eyes to rest and soon slipped into sleep.

The Land

"I never slept easy there," Maura told me one rainy night when the bank was largely empty of customers. When she talked about The Land — a steep slash of hillside where Airstream and Scottie trailers squatted amid the jack pines, the foundations propped on hewn logs to keep them from sliding downhill — her eyes grew distant as though the place spread out right before her. "When it got stormy, rivers of mud ran under the foundation. The trailer swayed like a ship at sea. I could feel it shifting. Those nights I dreamed of it giving way in a rush of water, saw us sliding down through the pines all the way to the Wind River. I always woke before we went over the falls."

"Sounds awful," I said.

"He'll take us back there one day. Sarah and me." Maura glanced my way as she unpinned her hair and let it down, a nimbus of curls framing her face. Maura wore just a touch of makeup, lipstick, and eye shadow she wiped away with a handkerchief before she left the office. Her husband considered makeup a vanity in a world that was ending. At home she answered to his demands. At work she could be herself.

"You don't have to go."

"Eli only agreed to leave after I fainted and fell down the metal stairs of our trailer. I fell hard. I was pregnant with Sarah at the time. Both of us so scared we were going to lose her." Maura dropped her gaze. "Pregnancy does crazy things to my blood pressure. The doctor put me on bed rest. We moved to town. Got the apartment for the baby's sake, so we would be close to the hospital. But now that Sarah's getting older, he'll take us back."

I loved these stories, loved watching her face while she told them. "But you don't want to go, right?" I knew that Elijah wanted her there so he could control her, maybe even force her to quit her job. How could I help her see that she didn't have to go?

Maura didn't answer right away. She bit down on her lower lip. "It's not such a terrible place. When we first lived there, Eli had just gotten out. No one would hire him, not with his record. We needed a home and Mother Sophie took us in. In some ways that place made us."

I knew about Mother Sophie from past conversations. A blind old woman whose forebears had made a fortune in the timber industry, she used her windfall to buy the property and the trailers, leasing them to members of her Christian Identity church, a motley bunch of outcasts, criminals, and dreamers. I knew The Land was meant to be a refuge against the apocalypse, that Mother Sophie had paid for the correspondence courses Maura's husband had taken from a seminary back east before bringing him in as co-pastor for the church, and that she'd even helped him finance the loan on his tow truck.

"We owe her," Maura continued. She opened the upper cash drawer and started counting out twenties to band in a stack of five hundred and tuck in the lower drawer for safekeeping — most robbers wouldn't know about the second drawer — her long, elegant fingers moving with a card sharp's dexterity. "Besides, Eli really does believe all that stuff about the Great Tribulation. He honestly thinks we're going to be safer there."

"You don't?"

Maura's face hardened, the light in her eyes flattening. "From what I've read of history, it seems to me that the world is always ending. And it's always beginning again."

"Martin Luther once said that if he knew the world was going to end tomorrow he would plant an apple tree today."

Just then a man entered the lobby and set up at the kiosk to fill out his deposit slip. Maura lowered her voice.

"Hush with your heresy. Let's talk about happier things the rest of tonight. Deal?"

Those late nights closing with her, I talked to her as I'd never spoken with anyone else. There were no secrets between us, and I could see why she longed for happier stories. Maura told me how after her mother died of breast cancer, her dad lost it and ran off. She spent her teenage years as a foster child growing up with different families on the Iron Range. One of her foster brothers could hot-wire any car in town and would drive her to a nearby ghost town where they would have midnight picnics outside an abandoned mine, sitting on the warm hood of the car, the engine ticking. I heard about another foster family getting involved in the Christian Identity church, where Maura would later meet Elijah when they were both just sixteen. Stories from my own life paled in comparison: my parents' divorce, my dad's subsequent remarriage to a much younger woman, Barb, a loan officer from his branch—that old song—his transfer to Milwaukie where he started up a brand-new family with bratty twins named Colleen and Connie, my half-sisters, now four years old. My mom got the house, full custody of me, and weekly AA meetings.

Girls my age I found mystifying, but I had an easy time talking to the married tellers I worked with. They enjoyed joshing me over my presumed virginity, or to see if they could make me blush by talking frankly about sex or reading aloud from some article in *Cosmopolitan*. Maura didn't join in the teasing, but I felt her eyes on me, amused by the sport.

When we closed together, she was always humming something under her breath, like she couldn't contain the music inside her.

"What're you singing?" I asked her one time.

"Nothing," she said. She feathered her hair behind one elfish ear. I liked her even better for the parts that weren't perfect: her ears too pointy, her eyebrows too thick for a woman. "Just a little lullaby I made up for Sarah."

"Go on," I encouraged.

She shook her head, but I kept pestering, so eventually she drew in a deep breath, her eyes fixing on that distant point again, peering beyond the lobby. She started low, her smoky voice gathering urgency:

Heed the song of meadowlark,
A mother's voice warns in the dark,
While the fox hunts for her nest,
Her song lures it closer to her breast,
Heed her well, her sacrifice,
How mother sings of paradise,
Her children asleep in downy bed,
She calls the fox to her instead,
Heed her well and hush until light,
Mother's song reaches into night.

An old woman had wandered in and stood listening at the kiosk. She clapped for Maura, who blushed in response.

"You wrote that?" I said.

Maura shrugged. "There's not an original word in it. Sarah's really colicky some nights." She lowered her voice so the customer wouldn't hear. "Eli can't stand it if the baby carries on. But if I sing, it does something for both of them."

I understood. Those songs, pitched in her smoky voice, did something for me as well. "You should write it down."

Maura shooed me away with a brush of her fingers. The old woman had finished filling out her deposit slip at the kiosk and waddled over to Maura's slot. She studied us both, a woman with a cloud of silvery hair and periwinkle-blue eyes. "Strange how there is so much darkness even in old nursery rhymes," she said. "The farmer's wife with her carving knife? You ever wonder what happened to the farmer in that song? She already did a number on those poor, blind mice."

Maura laughed. I leaned into the conversation. "I read once that 'Three Blind Mice' is actually about Bloody Mary. I guess she had three bishops burned at the stake."

"Watch out for this one. He's full of history lessons," Maura said. "So what about them being blind?"

"Their blindness likely refers to the fact that they were Protestant and Bloody Mary was Catholic."

"Why sing of such things to babies?" the old woman asked.

"Mockingbirds and diamond rings," Maura answered in a singsong voice. "Rocking cradles left in the trees." Her voice softened and she sighed. "I think mothers sing to warn children of the world that waits for them. And they sing for themselves. For their own mental well-being."

Maura finished the transaction and handed the customer her receipt.

"And they sing for handsome young men," the old woman said, and tittering, wobbled away.

It was my turn to blush. "Well, that was embarrassing." I had been thinking of something else. If Maura was singing of herself. Drawing the fox away.

"She does raise an important question. Why hasn't some girl snatched you up?"

I swallowed, my blush deepening. She found me attractive? Me, the skinny high jumper on the track team, the goof who played second board on the chess team in high school, so incredibly shy he had gone to his senior prom solo? "Girls want someone with confidence," I said.

"Then get some confidence," she said, like I could just pluck it from the air. "You should be dating. Tell me about the prospects in your classes."

This, I figured, was a good way to avoid talking more about her music. I shrugged, looking around for another

customer to interrupt us and rescue me from this interrogation, before I told her about Naomi, my lab partner.

"Naomi. That's a good name. Biblical. Not marriage
material, because she's a bitter woman in the Old Tes-
tament, but someone to date before life turns her sour.
What kinds of things does she like?"

"No idea," I said. Naomi already seemed sour and
taciturn as a young person. "The smell of formaldehyde
makes conversation difficult."

"Well, find out then. Figure out what she likes. Start
asking questions and show an interest in her. Then we
can figure out a strategy. I'm going to help you woo her."

"Why?"

"Aren't you the guy studying Life?"

The next time we closed together I brought in the
schematics for my video game, *The Land*, which I kept in
an old portfolio tote I had once used for art classes. I had
named the game for the secret place she told me about,
the refuge. I wanted to share it with her since she had
shared her music with me. Just that one song caused me
to make changes in the basic story line. She had sung her
lullaby low and sweet, but I had heard the danger in that
lurking predator. The fox wore a human face. The Land
didn't sound like any true refuge to me.

By then I was already in love with her. Whenever I
sat down to study for my classes she constantly occupied my thoughts. Daydreaming the kind of fantasies a

twenty-year-old young man daydreams when he thinks a woman needs to be rescued. I fantasized about us being together. I would be a good dad for Sarah. Maura could come with me to Chicago or some other big city where Elijah couldn't track us down. I just needed to tell her how I felt. I thought the game offered the perfect chance. I wrote it for her, after all.

I had to work up the courage to tell Maura about The Land in my game. The story featured a queen married to a wicked king. The queen knew magic in a world where witches burned, so she had to hide it from her husband and his advisors. One night she overheard him plotting a war against a neighboring kingdom—innocent allies—to gain power and land, but he caught her listening in. When he found out about her magic, he realized he could use her as a weapon. So she fled into the woods, a place where monsters dwell, with the court fool as her lone companion. They were separated by a tangle of trees. If the kingdom were going to survive she was going to have to find allies in this perilous forest and the fool was going to find her before the king and his men. He would have to learn to fight. This was my opening montage, a cutscene of a man and woman hunted, the king's hounds closing in, the dark woods spreading into the unknown.

I had to describe all of this for her because the program was stored in files on RPG Maker, the game engine I was using to program it, along with my own artwork imported through Adobe Photoshop and MS Paint for the backdrop and cutscenes. None of the computers at work, dated systems with green-tinted monitors, could run files saved on floppy discs. I'd drawn maps and illustrated characters and scenes in several spiral-bound sketchbooks. I was a passable artist, a Sunday watercolorist who didn't have the talent to major in art even if my dad had approved. Since I was using a game engine instead of programming the game from scratch, the art and the music files I was importing to create a fully immersive experience were what would make it original. I even hoped to record a few of Maura's folk songs and upload them to the game.

Maura touched the drawing of the queen. "There's something familiar about her," she said, the corner of her mouth turning up.

I said nothing. Of course the drawing looked faintly like her. What I lacked in subtlety I hoped to make up for with daring.

Her eyes were shining, specks of mica flickering and mercurial in the pupils. She touched her breastbone. "I think it's lovely," she said. "And I hope the queen gets away."

In that moment I wanted so badly to hold her, maybe let my hand rest above her waist, near the small of her back. With the drawings spread out, our elbows nearly brushed together, we stood so close. I was keenly aware of her smell, an undercurrent of sandalwood or lavender, the scent of the forbidden. I so ached to touch her that I let my hand graze the sleeve of her cream blouse, felt the thrill of static electricity in my fingertips, the heat of her skin beneath. "She will," I said. "This queen is a very resourceful person. And she has help. Someone who cares for her very much."

Maura pulled away, stepping back from the counter. She glanced toward the lobby to make sure no one else was around, then back at me. My heart grew wings and lifted in my chest. My head felt airy and light. The secret was out. I had just done something brave.

"Lucien," she said. "I would feel terrible if I've given you the wrong idea about anything. I hope I haven't. I'm married."

One single sentence took the wings in my chest and snapped them. I inhaled sharply as though slapped. "I know that," I said, and I couldn't help hanging my head, like a kid being chastised. I couldn't look her in the face. Shame flooded me. All my idiotic fantasies.

"I'm flattered that you think such things about me. Really. And I think highly of you. But I'm married, and I have a daughter." She spoke in a quiet voice. Her words were kind. She held my heart and its broken wings in her hands and handed it back to me gently.

"I'm so sorry," I said. There were actual tears in my eyes when I looked at her.

"Don't be sorry," she said. Even in this moment, she was radiant somehow, the color high up in her cheeks, her eyes glittering. She liked me. "I value our friendship so much. I wouldn't want anything to change between us." She held out her hand. "Okay?"

I took her hand, felt how warm it was in my own. The charge of energy between us. Skin to skin, it felt right. Such secret mercy. "Okay," I agreed.

I WOKE TO THE smell of bacon frying. Wintry light leaked through the curtains, so I knew it was morning. I couldn't remember the last time I'd slept the whole night through. The inside of my mouth tasted of ashes. I had been dreaming of Maura and I wanted to linger in that place of dreams, but there was a stranger in the house. The t-shirt I had gone to sleep in smelled a little stale, so I climbed from bed and fumbled around for the freshest one I could find on the floor, tugged it on, and wandered down the hallway while I considered what to do. I should at least ask for identification, get some kind of proof.

In my groggy state, entering the bathroom was like walking into a sauna, the mirrors still partly steamed. Some of her stuff already occupied a spot near the sink, a purple toothbrush and a Ziploc bag with Tom's of Maine toothpaste and floss and other incidentals. *I'm here to stay awhile*, her things said.

Should I call the Krolls or not? Some random girl

claiming to be their daughter didn't factor into any of the instructions they had left me with. But she had known Kaiser's name, seemed familiar with the place. Still, the right thing to do was to call them. I was the caretaker. I resolved to dial them up first chance I got.

The girl was already busy in the kitchen, a plush purple robe wrapping her, her feet bare, her damp hair pulled back in a ponytail. She'd let Kaiser out of his kennel on the lower level, and he sat obediently next to her, tail thumping the floor. She turned when I padded into the kitchen and smiled shyly. "I hope you don't mind your eggs cooked right in the bacon grease," she said, turning back to the stove to crack another one into the pan. The bacon waited beside the gas stove in a paper towel she must have been using to sop up grease. From the thump of Kaiser's tail on the linoleum, I could tell he'd already been properly bribed. Whether she was a stranger here or not, the German shepherd belonged to her now. While the eggs sizzled, her hips swayed faintly under the robe. It looked too big and frumpy on her, too old-ladyish, so I figured she must have raided Mrs. Kroll's wardrobe while I slept. "And there's coffee, if you want it. You feeling better?"

"I could use some coffee," I said in a froggy voice. "And I'm feeling fine." I sat at the table without getting myself any since she'd used the percolator on the stove and I didn't want to mess with her preparations.

A minute later, she switched off the burner, ladled eggs on plates, adding bacon from the paper towel and a slice of sourdough from the toaster. She carried both plates over, expertly balancing them, and set them on the table. Then she held out her hand. "My name's Arwen. I thought we could start over on the introductions part."

Arwen shook hands just like her old man, if it was true: she didn't let go right away. She peered down at me, a blue vein ticking in her pale throat. "You gonna call my parents?"

"I don't know," I said. "Seems like I should. I need to do right by this place. My old boss got me this job. He's counting on me."

"Just give me a little while. A few days. I'll pay you back for this food. You won't even know I'm here."

The last thing I needed in my life was more trouble. I didn't know much about the world, but this girl here, she looked like trouble. And I knew how a few days could turn into a few more. Yet I heard myself mumble, "Okay."

"Okay," she said. Arwen let go of my hand. She went back over to the stove where the percolator bubbled over, spilling a dark caramel liquid onto the blue flames beneath. She shut off the burner, poured a mug for each of us, and then sat with me at the breakfast table. Sunlight rinsed through a skylight above us. Arwen watched while I picked up a fork and split the egg, yolk bleeding yellow, and then shoveled it into my mouth, surprised by my hunger. We ate in a companionable silence and I could tell she was as famished as I was. The hollows scooped under her brown eyes told a story of hard traveling. It seemed my winter aubade here in this house was turning less and less restful each passing day, but in that moment I happily traded in my peace for good coffee and eggs cooked in bacon grease.

Once we'd emptied our plates, we sipped our coffee, Arwen doling out bits of bacon to Kaiser under the table, and she talked about a place called Fairhaven in Bellingham, where she'd come from, explaining it had once been a hippy enclave before it became yuppified. She told me she'd been a kayak-activist out West in Seattle, part of a Greenpeace protest broken up by the Coast Guard, and she arrived in Bellingham afterward, hoping to find a safe spot.

The Greenpeace protest had landed her in jail for a short time, but she told me why it was worth it: "This one time an orca came right up to my kayak. Must have been three times the size of my boat. I should have been scared out of my mind. It turned over in the water so this one huge eye stared up at me from below. I could sense the intelligence. It was curious, you know? Out there on the saltwater I was the alien. The trespasser. Yet it welcomed me like a friend."

I could tell she had told this story many times because her voice had a reverent quality. She was describing a holy experience, so I just listened and tried not to notice how her expressive hand gestures caused her robe to part. Apparently, she wasn't wearing anything beneath it. Arwen must have seen where my eyes had wandered because she tugged it closed at the throat.

"That's what I thought we were fighting for," she finished, and she looked at me as if to measure the impact of her story. For a moment, I wanted to tell her about the ravens, the battle in the snow and the wolves that came after, but for some reason I couldn't. Her story was sacred, mine was about brutality. Both were true about Mother Nature, but to speak the story aloud would mean giving away some of its dark magic, stealing away the impossibility of it all. It wasn't a story meant for her. "I haven't ever seen anything like that," I said.

She nodded, sipped at her coffee. "If you're from Chicago how'd you end up way the hell up here?"

This was a story I could tell. "When I was thirteen I camped with my church's youth group up in the Boundary Waters. We had a miserable time. It rained every day. The mosquitoes were relentless. But our last night there, the clouds broke. Just after sunset we saw the aurora borealis. I've never seen anything so beautiful, the whole sky above us spread with green fingers of fire. Our guide told us that the Inuit feared the northern lights could reach down like a burning hand and pluck them into the stars. The other kids didn't seem to care, but the story thrilled me. This idea that you could be lifted into another world."

Arwen smiled softly. "You found a place worth protecting. Something worth fighting for."

I nodded, though I wasn't sure how much of a fighter I had become. When I got home from that trip my dad had already moved out, so I had come home to a different world. Returning here meant coming back to a place where a hand might lift me into elsewhere, set me on the path, show me the way? Long before I met Maura, long before I heard about Y2K, I was already beginning to plot the story of my vanishing.

Arwen asked me something about Chicago and we both agreed that we didn't care for cities. My mom's place, a ranch-style house in Mount Greenwood, wasn't much to look at from the outside, but it sat across the street from the cemetery, so at least the neighbors were quiet.

In the Fairhaven section of Bellingham, Arwen told me, they were still trying to dream themselves back to 1968 and a world that didn't exist anymore. She didn't look like a flower child who had left a utopia, her eyes too flinty. She looked haunted or hunted. I had the feeling she was running from something. Her story about the killer whale? I couldn't put my finger on it yet, but there was something she wasn't saying. "Why leave such a nice place?"

"I never said it was nice there," Arwen said. She looked even more hawklike with her hair pulled back. "Maybe it was for a time. I was in a relationship that wasn't healthy and didn't end well. I needed breathing room." She didn't look down or away but watched my face while she spoke. "I had to get away, but I didn't have money or a place to stay. So that's what led me here. With my tail between my legs. Only there's no Mom or Dad to greet the prodigal daughter."

"How'd you get here if you took the bus halfway across the country?" I couldn't recall hearing any car outside, though I'd been down in the basement. Just the sound of the doorbell.

"Hitched," Arwen said, like she did it all the time. "Then I hiked from the main highway."

A FEW HOURS LATER, after we washed the dishes, I showed Arwen the raven I'd rescued, telling her that it had struck the glass of the big bay windows.

"I hate those windows," she said. "They're hell on the local bird population."

The raven watched us from his spot high up, his neck swiveling, pebbly eyes glittering.

"Albert keeps his golf clubs up in that loft. That bird is going to shit it full."

"Sorry about that." I noted how she called her old man by his first name.

"Don't be. He has it coming."

I didn't know what to say to that, so I led Arwen down to the basement where I'd rigged together two computers by a LAN cable, one a Dell that my dad bought for me when I started college, the other a base model I'd built from the motherboard up, loading it with the latest equipment, a geeked-out Nvidia GeForce 256 graphics card, Soundblaster Live for audio, and a Pentium III processor that hummed with 750 MHz of power. I fired up the system until the flickering screen awaited my DOS commands.

Arwen didn't care about my flunking out of college, which she said was for "future corporate burnouts," but after I told her about *The Land* she wanted to see it in motion. It was nice to have someone to talk to for a change. I hadn't realized how lonely I'd been.

After a few minutes the screen filled with the new opening montage, a cutscene that showed a dragon's-eye view of a three-dimensional castle, skulls impaled on poles and ravens swarming in great clouds as a dark figure paced the ramparts, his cloak flapping out behind him. The speakers throbbed to a moody soundtrack, heavy on synth, uploaded from Napster. Flickering, the screen now showed a new scene: a lone man fleeing through the trees, his belled fool's cap bobbing as he runs. He twists his neck, straining to hear the distant sound of hounds baying, and then he flees deeper into shadowy woods.

Kaiser barked from his kennel in the next room, disturbed by the tinny sounds echoing from the speakers.

"You did all this?" She sounded genuinely impressed. Maura hadn't ever seen the actual thing in motion.

I swiveled in my desk chair. "It's not finished yet. Watch this." The montage had given way to a top-down, isometric scene. To get an isometric view instead of the traditional 2D offered by the game engine had taken additional scripting and programming with eight-directional pixel movement, but the work was worth it if I could make a world a gamer could get lost in.

A black mouse-controlled arrow hovered god-like over the fool in the woods. I clicked on him to move him deeper into the trees as the hounds bore down on him, baying through the speakers. He didn't get far before they caught up to him. I clicked one hound and the fool slashed out with his clumsy kitchen knife. It howled and fell, but the others closed in, lunging. Then the king's hunters followed and their arrows whipped thick through the leaves. The screen flashed light and dark once more before showing the man's head, his belled fool's cap now blood-spattered, mounted on the ramparts, a raven pecking at one eye socket. "Game over, man," I said in my best Bill Paxton imitation.

"Yikes," said Arwen. "But what happens if he gets away?"

"That's the thing. He's supposed to find the queen. He

was the one who helped her escape. Everyone else who was part of the plan is dead. He doesn't know where she is or what's happened to her, but if the king finds her before he does he's going to use her magic to bring about Armageddon."

"I've never been much of a gamer, but this is really cool." Arwen leaned over the top of my chair. She smelled, not unpleasantly, of clove cigarettes. "It's like an interactive movie. Why'd you sound so bummed earlier?"

"The beta's so filled with bugs that it's unplayable. No matter how hard I try, no matter which direction I send the man, he always dies. Always. The hounds find him and then the hunters. I've made the first game where the hero dies every time. He's doomed no matter what."

"Like Max von Sydow," she said. "From *The Seventh Seal*," she added. "It's an old Ingmar Bergman flick. Max von Sydow plays a knight hunted by death."

I swiveled again in the seat to face her.

"You should see it," Arwen said, raising one eyebrow. "Seriously. For research and all. Albert has a copy on eight-millimeter. We could watch it, if you wanted."

Keep Your Lamps
Trimmed and Burning

I had to walk Kaiser before joining Arwen in the den. After a week here I no longer bothered with snow-shoes since we'd tamped down a navigable path through the pines on our rambles. A flurry of snow spin-drifted through the bare birches. We went as far as our aching bodies would allow us, pausing to pay homage to the koi goldfish, entombed in their icy pond. The big grandfather pines shrugged off sleeves of snow as we walked under the burdened boughs, but otherwise the woods were hushed and whispery. The quiet made me nervous. A shadow waited out here in the trees, beyond the furthest edge of my vision. I sensed it, a residue linger-ing from the carnage of the ravens. These had become the woods of a Hawthorne story, I thought, where a wanderer might encounter the devil out seeking new converts.

One night at the bank I remember asking Maura why

she thought the original settlers had named so many places in the wilderness after the devil. The Devil's Spine. The Devil's Backbone. Even our own Wind River flowed out of a gorge called the Devil's Maw. "Some of the most beautiful places in the country. Why pin a name for evil on them?"

"Lucifer was the most beautiful of the angels," Maura had said, musing as she brushed a lock of hair from her eyes. "Those places are breathtaking . . . but they might also kill you." In the deepening cold, I remembered how beautiful Maura had been to me and thought about the Rose of Sharon and Pastor Elijah. My unfinished business. I didn't feel nervous or afraid about confronting her husband, only a sense of urgency. Sunday couldn't come soon enough.

These long walks hurt, but I needed the exercise. I had to rebuild the muscle in my legs and hips, especially since I'd been skipping my physical therapy sessions. I was done with doctors and traction machines. I wanted to keep going, but Kaiser's breathing had grown ragged. Fearing the dog's great heart would burst in his chest, I led him back home. By the time we reached the grove, I smelled wood smoke. The Gingerbread House loomed over the birches, a fairy-tale vision, smoke spiraling from the chimney. Arwen must have kindled a fire in the big stone fireplace. In just a couple of days, she had made herself at home, the banished princess restored to her realm.

In the mudroom, I stamped my boots and Kaiser shook snow from his fur. We ambled into the den with its high, arched ceilings and bay windows, enjoying the heat of the stone hearth. She'd brightened the place already. I didn't see her right away, not until I looked in the bunker room that adjoined the den. Along with his massive movie collection, old man Kroll kept many of his books there, locked away behind glassed-in lawyer bookcases. These, too, were "off-limits" he had explained, though it seemed strange to me, to give a person keys to your gun cabinet but lock away the books. Arwen sat legs-crossed on the wood floor, coffee-table-sized tomes spread around her. She didn't even look up, not until I knelt beside her and picked up one of the books she had taken from the shelf. The leather cover read *Gemäldegalerie Linz,* and the pages inside, yellow and filmed by age, featured large sepia photos of artwork.

"Do you know what it is?" she said, setting aside her own book.

The leather cover was soft and green-skinned. The book felt eerie and alive in my hands. I shook my head.

Arwen scooted closer and took it gingerly from me. "This is his favorite," she said. The high gloss of the photo in its casing showed a Renaissance scene, gaily dressed couples preparing for some feast or dance, the hounds a blur of movement at the edge.

"Looks kind of ominous," I said.

"No kidding," she said. "It's about death. Well, sex and death. But that's what all art is about."

"Okay," I said, though I didn't like these kinds of pronouncements. Everything seemed to be about death these days, even my anatomy class. Even what little I'd learned about sex turned out to be about death. I was ready for a change of subject.

"There's a movie about it, too. Albert owns one of the last eight-millimeters. Maybe the last." She put her finger on the page. "This one's a silent film. It's about this evil, witch-like woman who seduces a father and son. The son kills his own father and then turns all the churches in town into whorehouses and places of devil worship. Then, death himself . . ."

"To think I had him pegged for a rom-com sort of guy."

"Funny," she said, without smiling. "So, death—"

"Wait," I said. "You're not one of those people who talks during movies? Who gives away the ending?"

Now Arwen laughed. "Sorry. I get carried away when it comes to old movies. But no talking is a good rule."

"And that old projector. It really works?" The old man had forbidden it.

She folded the book closed and smiled. "You're not too busy with your studies?"

I shook my head. "What's the title on the album mean?"

Arwen turned away and caged the book back on its shelf, locking it away behind glass. "These photos were intended for an art museum. It was to be built in Linz, Austria."

Linz? I searched my mind for the significance of the place. "Was to be built?"

She looked at me over her shoulder, quirking one eyebrow. "If I said any more that would be giving away the ending. I'll get that projector going."

Late afternoon into evening we watched movies, me dozing in and out in the La-Z-Boy beside her. I admit to sleeping through much of *Die Pest in Florenz*, but Arwen didn't seem to mind. We took a short break for summer sausage sandwiches with German mustard and to make popcorn and then settled in for *The Seventh Seal*. A double matinee with gothic movies featuring scenes of Armageddon. It was a way to pass the time.

While the projector rolled, I snuck peeks at Arwen. I liked her silhouette in the flickering light of the eight-millimeter, the spectral shine of her sharp profile, the intense way she loved these movies. Her face lit up by the screen, her hair pulled back, she looked like a dark version of Mia Farrow from *Rosemary's Baby*. The second movie, *The Seventh Seal*, fascinated me: Max von Sydow's chess game with Death in order to forestall his own demise, his longing to accomplish one meaningful thing before his time was up, the plague and the mad witch burning at the stake, the picnic that is the closest vision to any kind of heaven, one found on earth and not in the hereafter, and the final danse macabre as Death sweeps him up. I loved it, though I knew it would follow me into my dreams. The fool in the game I was designing would have a face now: Max von Sydow's.

I ducked out with a quick good night when the credits rolled and got ready for bed, knocking back a Percocet along with my migraine med and anti-depressant, so I could float off to sleep in a warm, narcotic haze. "Maura, where are you?" I said softly after turning off my lamp. I climbed under the covers and squeezed into my pillow, trying to conjure her face as I had earlier in the snow. More than anything, I wanted to dream of her again that night. Such longing only carried me into nightmare.

When I slept there was a woman screaming in my dream. At least I thought I was dreaming at first, because it felt like I was inside one of those movies we had just watched. Her strangled cries shocked me awake. Maura? Was it her? How did she get here? I remember wandering down the hall. Awake or asleep? All these years later, I'm not sure. The fabric of my reality, between narcotic dream and cloudy waking, felt tissue-thin.

I stumbled down the hall, following the calls, not knowing what was happening. The voice led me to the garage door. I remember the cold seeping under the door, how I paused to wonder if I should be feeling such physical sensations in my sleep. I didn't want to open the door.

I knew I didn't want to see whatever waited for me on the other side, but I didn't have any choice. The doorknob like a hunk of ice in my palm, I twisted it open.

Arwen, clad in a long black dress, sat on the concrete steps. She held the raven in her lap, wrapped in a bloody towel. How had she coaxed it from its hiding place? Her other hand, red with blood, clutched a hooked knife dulled by rust.

"What're you doing?" My voice sounded tinny and faraway, echoing as if from speakers.

She turned to look at me with her dark, almond-shaped eyes. "I split the tongue," she said. "So it can tell us the message it has brought."

The swaddled raven gasped for breath in her grip. The pink tongue that flicked out from the glossy beak was cruelly forked, a devil's tongue. And when it cried out, it spoke in Maura's frightened voice, "Help me. Lucien, please. You have to help me."

I woke in the clean wash of sunlight, my heart pulsing in my throat. I knew the folklore about splitting a raven's tongue so it could talk. I felt sure that the shadow that had fallen over me after the ravens killed each other had followed me from the woods. I worried that it lived inside me now and would the rest of my life.

Sunday morning, I arrived at Rose of Sharon early. Deacon Roland shook my hand and greeted me by name.

He ushered me inside and introduced me to an elderly white-haired woman. Mother Sophie, the fabled woman from Maura's stories. I hadn't seen her at the previous service.

Wearing a long dress of yellowing ivory, the old woman held out both arms in greeting, pressing her large, soft hands over my own. My palms were sweating, even though I'd just come from the frigid outdoors. She seemed to take notice of how this place made me nervous, squeezing my hands briefly before releasing me. "Meshach," she said when she heard my name. "You have a lot to live up to with a name like that."

"My parents got used to disappointment early on."

She frowned. "You are a child of God. Don't shrink to fit yourself to the world."

I didn't say anything, afraid of further betraying myself. There was something both magisterial and elephantine about her, a giantess with sharp blue eyes and a sonorous voice. I wouldn't have even known that she was blind if Maura hadn't told me. The usual Lucien might have said something mocking in response to her, but the words wouldn't come. Here I was Meshach. Here the words froze in my mouth because sometimes Maura said similar things, her hands at the nape of my neck, touching the curls above my collar. *You are going to do great things, Lucien. One day you're going to make someone very happy.*

"Where's the preacher?" I said when I found my tongue, because I hadn't spotted Maura's husband yet or her daughter.

"Mother Sophie *is* the preacher," Roland said, stepping in. "She's the senior pastor and Pastor Elijah is her associate. He has some private matters to attend to and will be gone the next couple of weeks."

"Private matters?" Mother Sophie said. "There's no reason to be elliptical, Deacon. Eli is getting The Land ready."

"Oh," I said, because that also sounded fairly elliptical. I tried to keep the disappointment out of my voice. I had no idea yet where The Land was. I needed to find my way into their inner circle if I was to ever discover any ideas about where Maura had gone and what had happened to her. This would be harder to do without her husband around. I already felt a little foolish for forgetting that Mother Sophie was the senior pastor, an odd arrangement for a right-wing church.

"You will stay for coffee, Meshach," the old woman said. Her voice was pleasant, but it was not a question. "I would like to talk further with you." She turned and walked away, her long dress sweeping the shag carpet.

This time I sat far away from Roland and his Saturday night special. People filed in and filled the rows, though none sat right by me. I saw a few families, the children squeezed in between the adults. Some of the men wore blazers like Roland, though they often had sweatshirts on underneath, big belt buckles and blue jeans. The women, who were mostly white, all wore dresses, but a few had raven hair they wore so long it hung to their hips. These women had the high cheekbones and darker skin of Ojibwe from a nearby reservation. This also took me by surprise. I had not thought Indians would be welcomed in a white supremacist church, but then again, Rose of Sharon didn't advertise itself as such. No more than thirty strong, they were a younger congregation than I expected, and not skinhead punks in black shirts and jeans or bearded Unabomber loners like I had first pictured.

I picked up fragments of their conversation, mostly ordinary things about the weather, the coming snow. They stole glances in my direction but didn't engage me directly. So far as I could see there were no clocks in this room, but they were ready when Mother Sophie raised her arms and called them to worship with the hymn "Keep Your Lamps Trimmed and Burning."

"For the world is overcome," goes one line in the hymn. Someone forgot to tell the world, I remember thinking. After the opening hymn, Mother Sophie led us in a short prayer before starting into her sermon. If I had been disappointed by the ordinariness of my first visit here, she more than made up for it.

Gray wattles swung from her neck and arms as she

gestured and called for us to take up our Bibles and turn to the Book of Revelation. I didn't know my Bible well, those few years of Sunday school mostly focusing on kid-friendly stories, Jonah getting swallowed by the whale, Noah's Ark, Moses parting the Red Sea. That kind of thing. So I had little idea what I was in store for. She started by talking about current events and described the turmoil in the Middle East (when is there not turmoil there?), saying this was but one sign fulfilling the prophecies. She spoke of a star named Wormwood that was going to fall from the sky and contaminate the waters of the earth. Then she began to read from the chapter, speaking of dragons with horned heads rising up from the sea. Strange chimera, half-leopard and half-lion, scarred by past wounds. How the people bowed in wonder before the beast.

"Who has seen the beast?" Her eyes gazed out over the congregation as if looking beyond into a world where such things roamed. My fingers itched as she spoke. I wanted to draw the bestiary of the chapter. I knew that I was going to add these creatures to the game I was designing. The evil king in my story would send four horsemen in pursuit of his queen. And she would be pregnant.

"The beast is here," she said. "He is of our own making. He has risen from the seas inside us. Born of our sinful nature and wandering minds." Mother Sophie began to describe the world as she saw it. Women dying of overdoses and leaving their children motherless. Gangs knifing and raping. The epidemic of suicide among the young. Aborted babies stuffed in garbage bags and dumped in fields. A tide of mud people at the border, bringing crime and disease. A church she called "the whore of Babylon." A government run by Jews that conspires against its own people. "Even now they are watching," she said. Her gaze glanced over me without landing, but I could feel eyes boring into the back of my head from the congregation behind me.

Maura, is this how you felt every Sunday? A great pretender? Did he hurt you because you didn't share in his beliefs?

Mother Sophie held up her own swaying arms as she spoke of Y2K and the coming days. Nuclear meltdowns and jumbo jets falling from the atmosphere, the computers dead inside them. The four horsemen riding roughshod over the sodomite cities of this earth.

"Will you receive the Mark of the Beast the One World Government sets upon you?" By this point, the room vibrated with tension. Mother Sophie had led us to a terrible place. It seemed so fantastical, so impossible, but I had read articles in respected publications that posited how Y2K could happen. I had not thought much about it before now, but here in this room, she made it a tangible reality for her listeners. I wasn't sure what to think.

Tears jeweled the corners of Mother Sophie's eyes. In the years since, I have not thought of the Book of Revelation as a particularly hopeful chapter, but it became so now in her rough, homespun retelling. She recited to us this passage from chapter twenty-one: "He will wipe away every tear from their eyes, and death shall be no more, neither shall there be mourning, no crying, nor pain anymore, for the former things have passed away." And when she finished, such a note of pure longing in her voice, there were tears in my eyes as well. I was not the only one. Behind me, a man blew his nose. One woman wept openly.

I'm not sure how long Mother Sophie spoke, but my bony posterior ached on the metal chair, so I figure she'd been talking for an hour before she mentioned Pastor Elijah. "I know some of you have heard he had a breakdown. But the Lord has his finger on that one. All you need to know is that Pastor Eli has gone ahead of us to prepare the way."

The congregants murmured in sympathy.

She called for us to bow our heads in prayer. I thought we'd come through the strangest part of it, but in the midst of one moment of silence, a woman at the back stood up and growled in a low, gravelly voice, a sound that didn't seem to come from any human being. The words, both foreign and unknowable, raised the hairs on the nape of my neck. It was like a dead tongue come to life, the cry of some terrible angel. Her voice filled the room with a dire, ancient chant. It reminded me of the nightmare-sound of Arwen's raven, calling out with its split tongue.

I turned around. One of the Ojibwe near the back stood swaying in her bright blue dress and patterned shawl. She wore a beaded necklace that clinked like finger-bones as she swayed. Her entire body quivered, shot through with invisible electricity. The moment did not feel fake or forced. I felt like I was in the presence of some Other greater than myself. There was no translation for the words that rolled from the woman's slack jaw. Yet, I discerned a story there.

I shut my eyes and let her words wash over me. And when I did, ravens whirled out of the snow, screeching in their harsh tongue. They flew past me, their black wings whisking near my ear. There I was again, in the midst of the maelstrom. And the Enemy was there, too, whispering of anger and famine. A story of blood and starvation. His chanting strung them together, like chords of music from a hidden conductor. And the Enemy was trying to reach for me as well, reaching for my mind.

Then the woman at the back of the room gave a great sigh, collapsed into her metal chair, and slid to the floor where she lay trembling as if her body was being squeezed by a great hand. She was quickly surrounded by other women, fanning her with pages of a prayer booklet and speaking in rushed, excited voices. I also slumped in my seat, released from the vision. I had to swallow down my sick.

"Tell me, children, who here knows what she was saying?" There was a querulous, uncertain ring in Mother Sophie's voice. Maura had also told me about this. Someone else from the congregation, guided by the Holy Spirit, had to translate what the person had been saying. Sometimes, there was no translation.

Did what I saw count? I felt a quickening under my skin, sweat trailing down my spine. No one answered Mother Sophie's question. Except for the ring of women surrounding the one who'd collapsed, the others in scattered places glanced around the room nervously or studied their hands in their laps as if afraid of being singled out by the Spirit next.

"Surely someone here felt the tremor of the Holy Ghost." Mother Sophie's gaze passed over the top of our heads, her eyes filming over with a deep disappointment.

More silence. Someone carried a glass of water up from the basement to the woman at the back. There was a ringing in my ears, like an explosion had gone off inside me. My own voice sounded so far away, but I heard myself say something. A rough question before I coughed out this sentence. "They came in the storm," I began, my voice quavery at first.

"Go on, Meshach," Mother Sophie said, her eyes finding me. "Go on and tell us."

I told of my vision and what I had seen that day, how it came back to me when the woman had been speaking. I stumbled a few times, but my voice picked up in strength as I spoke. A certainty that this was meant to happen. I had been chosen. At one point I even closed my eyes again so I could see it better. I swayed in my chair as the woman had swayed. "They were starving. They were scared. I could see a darkness swirling inside them. The one you call the Enemy."

I paused and opened my eyes. Mother Sophie's eyes were shut as if she were in a vision of her own. Everyone staring at me. I told them about the birds massacring one another and the wolves that came later to feed upon them and the snow that covered up the blood. How after a day it was as if it had never happened, but the woods still scared me, like the earth itself had been stained.

A long silence followed. Mother Sophie opened her eyes and drew in a deep breath. She thanked me and turned back to the congregation. "You are wondering what this means?" Her voice subdued, her hands folded in front of her. "What this young man saw has no ordinary explanation. Do you doubt that the world is broken? Do you doubt that it is a sinful place? The reckoning is coming. The carnage Meshach saw is but a physical manifestation of the trials in the world to come. A demon moved in those birds. Meshach here today bears witness. But evil is powerless against the name of God. I say again, only Jesus has the power to command the darkness. The only thing that redeems this fallen world is love. God's love. The things of this earth are passing right before our eyes. This old earth is dying. The things of the earth are but a pale shadow of the Maker. A shadow cannot command another shadow, that is only for the Son of Man. Oh Lord, send us Your light so we know the way. Send Your Holy Spirit to lead us out of this valley of shadow."

She continued like that a long time, half-prayer, half-incantation. I should have felt wrung out after seeing the vision, but strangely I felt elated, like sharing what I had seen had lifted a burden from my own spirit.

A few members of the congregation came up to talk to me after the service was done. I didn't know what to make of any of this yet, except that it felt nice to be at the center of attention, even if it wasn't deserved. Even if I was here under false pretenses. Down in the church basement, chewing on a crumbling old-fashioned doughnut and sipping black coffee in a Styrofoam cup, I tried to feel like I belonged.

Mother Sophie came up behind me where I was seated at the table. She leaned over me, her skin smelling faintly of talcum powder. "Can I pray over you?" she said.

She began to pray, placing her hands on my head. I don't remember the words exactly, but the feeling has not left me all these years later. It felt like she held fire in her palms, a healing heat. She finished her prayer, leaned over, and kissed the top of my head. "You will do great things for God," Mother Sophie said. "You will stand in the fire, Meshach." She thanked me for my words and went off to talk to someone else. I hadn't even had time to process the encounter before Roland stood beside me. He set his hand on my shoulder and said, "There's a prayer meeting this coming Tuesday morning at ten. At a place we call The Land. Care to join us?"

Roland drew me a map on a napkin.

Hymn of the Hunt

By the time I made it home my bladder felt ready to burst. I rushed inside the house and opened the bathroom door to find Arwen naked, perched on the edge of the bathtub, a razor poised at one ankle, the leg above lathered in cream, her breasts swaying. In shock, I stood there gaping like a fool. So intent I'd been on my mission, I'd forgotten that a stranger was now living with me. With the draining tub gurgling behind her, Arwen must not have heard the door open when I came in, but now she looked up, her eyes widening before she covered her breasts with her left arm. "Out!" Arwen snapped, and I hurried to obey.

I relieved myself in the downstairs bathroom and splashed cold water on my face before trudging back to my own room and shutting the door. From the bedside table I plucked up a fist-sized agate geode, a gift from

Maura. I sat on one corner of the bed and squeezed it in my fist until it hurt, until the stone pulsed in my palm like a dark, beating heart.

He had entered the bank shortly before closing, a twitchy young man in a red ball cap, the brim pulled low over his eyes. When he hunched over the kiosk to scratch out a withdrawal slip, I could see the ridges of his spine through his white t-shirt and the glint of something black-handled poking from the waistband of his baggy jeans. The lobby was empty except for him. I glanced at Maura, saw her take notice. He wasn't one of our customers, so far as I knew. A minute later the young man headed to my slot, his head down, his face unreadable. When he did look up his eyes were a jaundiced yellow and they registered surprise to see me on the other side of the counter. I would wonder later if he meant to target Maura.

The folded withdrawal slip he passed me had these words scrawled on it: *All your money. Don't hit alarm. Not a word. No die pak or I will kill you.* The misspelling in the last part—he knew about the dye pack hidden in the midst of one stack of twenties, rigged to explode if it left the premises and coat the money in red ink to render it un-spendable—is what made me glance again toward Maura. This was a mistake. The young man lurched, snaking one bony arm across the counter to snag me by the tie and yank me closer to him. I gagged, my tie turning into a noose that cut off my windpipe. I felt something cold and metallic poke into my temple. Close up, I smelled the ammonia reek of his breath when he hissed, "The money. Pronto, pretty boy."

When he released me my hands went to my throat and I drew in a raspy breath. "Pronto," I muttered dizzily. I wasn't afraid, but my mind had gone absolutely blank. A whirling void in my head. I fumbled through my upper cash drawer and shoved bills across the counter. I didn't even realize until after I'd passed him the money that the dye pack was still inside. From the crotch of his jeans he wrenched out a wadded-up pillowcase, stuffing the money in one-handed, some of it fluttering to the floor.

"Yours, too," he growled at Maura, waving the pistol in her direction.

Maura was opening her drawer when a customer entered the branch, a pregnant mother carrying another child in an infant car seat.

The robber turned and screamed, "On the floor! Now, bitch!"

The woman froze, one hand going to her swollen stomach. Her mouth fell open, but no words came out. He lunged in her direction, bringing up the pistol.

"Sir," Maura called in a clear and commanding voice. "Sir! I have your money right here." She slid it smoothly across the counter, as if this was an ordinary transaction.

He turned back to Maura, stuffing the pistol in the back

of his jeans. At her slot he grabbed for bills and tucked as much as he could into the bulging pillowcase. His head down once more, he scurried out without another glance at the pregnant woman, who was still standing there with her mouth open, too terrified to even follow his directions.

I remembered a strange sense of serenity in the immediate aftermath, recounting the story to the officers and to our manager, Harry Larkin. A bank robbery always involves the Feds and they catch about eighty percent of them. They would catch this guy—a tweaker skinhead named Milosz Jarowski—after the dye pack exploded, coating his hands in red, and his own mother turned him in.

Only later, after the cops were gone, only after Harry Larkin left Maura and I alone in the break room so he could fetch his bottle of Jameson from the glove compartment in his car, because he said we needed a shot to steady us and send us home, only then did the shakes come over me. I stood up too quickly from one of the swiveling desk chairs and a wash of dizziness made the room spin around me. Maura must have seen me reeling. "Oh," she said as she caught me in her arms. "Careful."

Since I'd been losing my balance, I ended up with my face pressed against her breasts, so close I heard the rush-rush-rush of her beating heart. She didn't seem to mind this intimacy, her blouse soft against my cheek. The feel of her body against mine righted me at once. We had been through something frightening together, so it felt so natural to hold one another. I had never touched a woman like this before. My hands naturally looped around her waist, drawing her closer as I steadied myself and the wave of dizziness dissipated. Her eyes were shining when I looked up, her cheeks flushed. Maura just shook her head. "Did the robber really call you 'pretty boy'?"

I nodded, too overwhelmed by the feel of her body against mine to speak at first. "'Pronto, pretty boy,' is a hard command to ignore," I said.

The bell in the outer lobby dinged to announce Harry Larkin's return with his bottle of whiskey, and Maura squeezed my arms reassuringly and stepped away. Harry didn't even seem to notice how close we were standing as he opened the bottle and poured a tall finger for each of us into Dixie cups from the watercooler. He held up his own for a toast. "Robberies are terrible, but I'm glad no one got hurt," he said. "Your first one is always a hell of a thing. Hell of a thing."

How Maura had watched me as we toasted with our Dixie cups. Her lips parting, the good burn of the whiskey in my chest, the laughter in her eyes.

Maura had given me the agate for my twenty-first birthday, a couple of months after the robbery. She pressed it into my palm along with a note folded into a crisp triangle. "Happy Birthday." We were alone together again in the back break room, next to the vault, standing so close our heads nearly touched. I only had an empty apartment to go home to. I wanted to stay here with her as long as I could.

Six months had passed since I clumsily confessed my feelings for her. Rather than putting distance between us, our relationship had only deepened since. I was sure Maura was in love with me, too. Things had also grown more intense because Elijah was pressing her to quit. He wanted another child. He had forced her and Sarah to move back to The Land, and Maura was trying to figure a way out. She hated it there, smothered by a belief system too heavy on wrath and fear. She told me if things were different, if she didn't have a daughter. If, if, if . . .

Her fingers pressed down on the gift, my skin thrilling where it touched hers. "You wrote a song for me?" So far she had resisted writing any of her music down.

"It's more like a prayer or poem."

I didn't like the sound of that. I folded my hand on top of hers, felt the smooth weight of the gift and wondered over it.

We had rarely touched before the night of the robbery, our connection purely emotional, wanting what you couldn't have, loving what you could not hold. The robbery broke whatever physical barrier had been between us. One night closing, Maura traced the love line of my palm with one finger as though she could discern our future there, and the rest of the night I felt the pulse of my blood beneath, a fissure or fault line that ran from my palm to my heart. Once in this small, enclosed room, I pressed my hip against hers, a dangerous dance, while we counted out twenties from the vault, her sandalwood scent blending with the smell of new paper. The other female tellers were starting to notice, Maura told me. She didn't have to tell me what they were noticing.

This night Maura didn't pull away. When I looked up she was watching me, the pupils in her hazel eyes dilating under the flickering fluorescent.

We had closed the bank a few minutes before, bid good night to the assistant manager, Toby Wilkes, and locked the front door behind him. Our tills had been balanced and we just needed to count the money from our cash drawers for the vault and then run a security sweep to make sure all the machines were shut down, all transaction forms tidied and stowed away. What nightly cash we counted would be zippered into a mesh envelope and dropped into a chute leading to a locked slot outside, where the armored car company would pick it up later that night. All was as it should be.

I grazed my fingers over the top of Maura's hand. She glanced away from me to the security camera that monitored the lobby and outer parking lot, where Toby's Fiero spewed exhaust under the lamps.

I turned, wondering why she was bothering with the

camera, and saw him pulling away. "I didn't think he'd ever leave," she said, and put her other hand on my chest where my heart knocked against my rib cage. "I want to do something else for you."

In the year and a half we had known each other I had daydreamed this moment over and over, but still when it happened it took me by surprise. She leaned in, her eyes closing, and kissed me on the mouth. That kiss broke me in half. It was like walking out of the dark, silent movie of my life into full sunshine, split open by light. Urgent and forbidden. I was too startled to even close my own eyes. I don't know how long we kissed before she reached down, her hand stroking my erection through my slacks. Her hand at my belt, her voice a husky whisper, she said, "Pronto, pretty boy."

I could hear Arwen stomping down the hallway in a huff, and I was afraid she was going to knock at my bedroom door. I squeezed the stone one last time in my fist. After Maura vanished I learned that an agate of this size is worth hundreds of dollars. I stuffed it in my nightstand drawer and went to apologize.

"Forget it," Arwen said over her bowl of cornflakes. "You're not a perv, are you?"

"What? Of course not. I'm safe as houses." Whatever that meant. This house no longer felt safe. Nothing in my world did.

"That's good, because we each need our own space."

She ate another spoonful and gestured at my formal wear, my Oxford shirt, navy blue sports pants and shiny wingtips. "You have an interview this morning?"

I shook my head, though it had felt good to dress formally, like I was heading into the office. I had spent most of these last weeks in a hospital gown or sweatpants. In truth the question about the interview rankled me. The enormous hospital bill had eaten up most of the insurance money. I was going to need to find work soon, or move back home at the end of winter. These were things I wasn't ready to think about. "I went to church."

Arwen frowned. "I didn't know you were religious." She said this in the same tone of voice she had used to ask me if I was a pervert.

This would be a good time to bring up how she had said she would only be here for a few days. Those days had passed and she had settled in and showed no signs of leaving. Yet, because I had walked in on her in the bathroom, I felt on the defensive. I had longed for a winter of quiet, but instead I had been beset by strange wonders and dark strangers. I thought of an old story by Saki I'd read in high school, "The Open Window," about a young man who heads into the country hoping for rest, but ends up being tormented by a girl who tells spooky lies. Arwen looked like she carried around her share of ghosts. I needed to get at her story. "So what if I am?"

"I just didn't think you were one of those people."

"One of *those* people?" I couldn't keep the irritation out of my voice.

"Bandwagon people."

"Oh, well it's not like I ran off and joined a commune of hippies or anything."

Arwen picked up her sloshing bowl of cereal and carried it to the sink. I took Kaiser for a walk, and when I got back, Arwen was gone. I searched the house, but didn't find her anywhere. The glass lawyer bookcase had been left open, the *Gemäldegalerie Linz* lying on the floor, open to show a copper broadside of a couple picnicking in the Alps, a brunette feeding strawberries to a man in a fedora, everything in black and white, except her hands were painted red, as were his lips. Her red-stained hands and his glazed mouth gave what should have been a bucolic scene an aura of the grotesque. I clapped the album shut and stored it in the glass prison the Krolls had made for it, as if it were a creature that needed to be locked away.

There were no new dishes in the kitchen sink, no sign any coffee had been brewed. I knocked several times at the locked bedroom door where she'd taken up residence, hoping to apologize, but there was no response. I was fairly certain I sensed her presence on the other side of the door, but I wondered if she had really left. Without her around, the house felt emptier than ever. Wrong somehow.

I stopped in the garage to fill the raven's dish with

crushed dog food and freshen the bowl of water. It watched from its silent perch in the rafters. "If I split your tongue what secrets would you tell?" It cocked its head, studying me with glossy black eyes. I thought for a moment about leaving the garage door open and letting it escape. Was it healed enough? Did this dark garage feel as much like a prison as my hospital room? "You need a name," I said to the silent bird. "How about Edgar?"

The raven stared. I left it alone to feed.

Arwen's apparent disappearance bothered me. I took Kaiser out on another walk, looking for traces of Arwen's small prints, but other than the tracks my Continental had made coming down the long driveway earlier that morning, the snow was undisturbed. After a half hour of stumbling around, a bitter wind drove us back inside.

I spent much of the rest of the day in the basement, sketching a menagerie of creatures from the Book of Revelation in a notebook first and then digitizing them in Adobe Photoshop before I could set them in motion as sprites in the RPG Maker program. I had not realized before this that the queen in my story would be pregnant and that the child she carried had a special importance, a child that might save the world if she could get away from her evil husband. Maura's child, brought back to life in my game. Powered by a fresh pot of coffee, I fell into a familiar fugue state that came over me whenever

I dove deep into coding, still trying to save my Max von Sydow stranded in his maze of trees.

By the age of twenty-one I'd been working with computers for a full third of my life, starting at fourteen when my teacher, whose real-life name was Mr. Drudge, acquired a host of brand-new Zeos 386sx computers and promptly banned students from playing any games in the lab, unless we programmed the games ourselves. I quickly learned BASIC and MS-DOS coding, which I used to create simple copycats of classics such as *Pong*, *Space Invaders*, and *Joust* for myself and other students.

A year later, after being stranded at a bus stop for a half hour in below-zero windchill, I used a maze algorithm program I'd created to plat out the streets of my suburb and map more efficient routes for drivers, a program I sold for eight hundred dollars to the district. This windfall bought my first desktop, a Commodore Amiga 500, the best gaming machine out there at the time. Buoyed by early success, I started programming games in BASIC and Easy Amos for the system before taking on the Amiga's actual assembly language.

The creation of *Frankenstein's Dream*, a *Zelda*-style RPG, absorbed the next two years of my life. As the lonely monster, you roamed high mountain villages in 8-bit glory, avoiding the torch-bearing villagers while seeking out food. If cornered you could kill lone villagers easily, but doing so cost you soul-damage, and if you sustained too much you lost any control over the avatar and could only sit and watch as Frankenstein rampaged through the land until enough villagers gathered to burn him alive. I worked on it until I couldn't do any more solo with the program without a publisher, which you could only find through copy parties in those days. I talked my parents into investing in the scheme, and together we did market research, created promotional materials, and when it came time my dad and I flew all the way to Stockholm for a copy party where we pitched the game to Niflheim Publishing. The game was accepted and scheduled for publication in late 1993. This should have been the realization of a dream, but I'd made a major mistake in programming the game in a closed-assembly language for the Amiga. In 1994, after a series of missteps, the Amiga's parent company of Commodore went bankrupt, which caused Niflheim to fold a few months later. Not a single copy of *Frankenstein's Dream* was ever distributed. My parents lost several thousand dollars and I lost a couple years of my life.

In the first cutscene I ever created, the lonely monster confronts his maker, and it's not the mad scientist you expect, but a woman, the author of *Frankenstein* herself, a digitized Mary Shelley. "Why did you make me?" he asks in the scene.

"So that I would not be alone," she says. "We are not meant to be alone. You must live."

As a teenager, I had been a little in love with Mary Wollstonecraft Shelley. *Hear my tale,* her creature called across the centuries. A ghost story, written by a woman haunted by the death of her own child, by the death of Percy Shelley's first wife, who drowned herself after her husband ran off with Mary, then only a teenager. A ghost story written by an adulteress weighted down by guilt in the "Year without Summer," when a volcanic eruption caused the skies to rain ashes over Europe and her nightmare vision became a living, breathing thing. *I saw the pale student of unhallowed arts kneeling beside the thing he had put together,* she would write. And this is what I must do, I thought. My nameless fool must find a way to live.

I could not fail. I had to finish this game. One day, Maura, wherever she was, might see it in motion. One day my parents would see it as well. And no matter what happened, they would see they had not been wrong to have faith in me.

I worked past dark, stopping now and then to listen for Arwen's return. She didn't have a car or any mode of transportation. Where had she gone? Or was she still in her room? I had just leaned back in my squeaky desk chair when the power went out.

In the pitch-dark, I fumbled my way to the outer room. Even standing before the big bay windows there was little light, the moon hidden behind clouds. A cold wind pressed at the glass from outside. Kaiser slept through it all on his dog bed, his snoring loud beside the door.

In the faint light coming through the windows I picked my way up the spiral staircase and searched in a drawer near the phone, where I'd spotted a flashlight after first arriving here. Once I found it and clicked it on, the first thing I noticed was the pad next to the phone — the pad where the Krolls had written down their phone number and address on South Padre Island — was no longer there. Arwen must have taken it. Where the hell was she?

I felt a migraine coming on from spending all day staring at a glowing screen. I went back to my bedroom and took a sumatriptan and Percocet, shut off the flashlight, and waited to float off on the dreams of Lethe, hoping for a vision of Maura. Yet, tired as I was, I couldn't sleep. I cursed myself for drinking coffee past four o'clock; too much caffeine still coursed in my veins.

This was why I was still awake when the wolves came, as old man Kroll had promised they would. As if they sensed me vulnerable in the house, in the dark and creeping cold.

I heard them long before I saw them. Since I couldn't sleep anyway, I got up and traipsed down the hallway in my boxer shorts and t-shirt, passing Arwen's locked door, noticing light spilling under the sill. She was back and she must have found a candle. Or she had never left. I didn't know what was going on, but I left her alone and followed the sound of the wolves, as if summoned.

In the moonless dark they were a sound rather than a shape, a sibilant question voiced in the night, their barking rising in pitch until one of them loosed a wail, as if pierced. I didn't hear anything sad in their singing. It seemed more celebration or greeting. They were calling out not just to the night or the cloud-shrouded stars but to Death himself. The night was their church, and this was their hymn of the hunt. They knew Death and walked with him and brought it to other creatures of the wood, and they knew he stalked them as well, but they were not afraid. They sang, rejoicing in their sleek coats against the long night.

I couldn't imagine taking up the .30-06 as Kroll had instructed. I listened and I heard the hunger in their song, but not the shadow as I had felt with the ravens. When they drifted away in search of prey, I went back to my room and crawled under my covers. With the power out, it was already chilly in the house.

So I shouldn't have been surprised to find Arwen waiting for me under my quilt.

She turned over in the bed and lifted the sheets for me. She was dressed in a blue nightie, her feet bare. "Can I stay with you?" she whispered, her face in shadow. "I can't stand the sound of them. And I'm so cold."

I hesitated. Was this a betrayal of Maura? But the chill

in the room had raised goose pimples on my arms, so I climbed in beside her, laying on my right side, my good side, the only way I could sleep without pain. In the queen-sized bed there was room enough for both of us to sleep without touching, but at first it was no warmer here. Waves of cold radiated from her skin. Arwen shivered as she turned over to face me. I was going to ask her where she'd been or why she hadn't answered when I knocked, but she spoke first. "Who's Maura?"

"What?"

"You talk in your sleep," she said. "Like there's someone in the room with you. It's kind of spooky actually."

"*I'm* spooky? Where were you all day?"

"Asleep," she said in a subdued voice. "I wasn't feeling well. So are you going to tell me who she is?"

"Someone I knew."

"Someone you lost." She propped herself up on one elbow, waiting for the story.

I told her all I knew and suspected, the abusive marriage, how Maura knew to take freshly counted bills that couldn't be traced, how she had a daughter I was convinced she wouldn't leave behind. I kept on, the whole story spilling out.

Arwen was quiet, but she scooted closer to me on the bed. "Unless you didn't really know her," she said.

I considered this. How much do we ever know about one person? Even someone we think we're close to. "All

I know is I got into a wreck after dropping her off at the hospital." I touched my skull, parting the hair to expose the mark along my temple where I'd cracked the windshield, forgetting the raw scar wouldn't be visible in this dark. "I haven't been right since."

"Who has?" Arwen touched the scar with one cool hand. "I knew you had a story."

I told her a little more, about the Christian Identity church and Mother Sophie's sermon on the End of the World. "I need to find out what happened."

"So that's why you went to church."

"The main reason, yeah."

Arwen settled into her own pillow, apparently satisfied. "She's gone, either way," she said in a sleepy voice. "Maybe let her be gone. These people sound dangerous from what you've told me. You don't fuck with fascists."

"I'm not afraid."

"That's because you have a death wish."

I bridled at this, though I knew it was partly true. Wasn't that my whole reason for staying here rather than going home to Chicago? Did some part of me long for apocalypse, for the whole world to come crashing down as mine had around me?

And what about you, Arwen, what's your story? In prying the mystery from me, I couldn't help noticing she'd avoided saying anything about herself. I turned to ask her, but her eyes were shut, her body softly breathing.

We lay together, not quite touching, our bodies warming under the blankets, and somehow even the not-touching felt oddly intimate, the small space between us charged with energy.

Maura, oh Maura. I don't know what to do anymore. I only know I can't stop until I find out what happened to you.

Of Mountains Moving

On Tuesday morning, I went looking for The Land. The address Roland had given me took me into the wilderness that bordered state forest land, along winding gravel roads crowded by towering red and white pines, needles gleaming silver in the freezing sleet. Roland had drawn me a map by hand, but I got turned around and ended up heading the wrong way for a good twenty minutes before I realized my mistake. The freezing rain clung to my windshield wipers until they scraped against the glass like claws. Half-blind before an iced-over window, I had to drive much slower than I wanted. Whatever study they had planned I would be at least an hour late.

Was this a sign that I should just turn around? Maura had told me that Elijah's aggravated assault conviction had been plea-bargained down from attempted murder, the victim attending the trial in a wheelchair. Yet, I kept going, picking my way over gravel roads, the wheels slurring for purchase, until I came around a bend.

I knew the place immediately when I saw it. From the road I could only make out the barest glint of the Airstream trailers and mobile homes pitched among jack pine and cedar on a slope of southern exposure. A torrent of snowmelt gushed down a channel near the driveway, ice bobbing in the dirty current. I didn't know if I could get the Continental up such a steep road, slick with running slush.

I gunned the engine hard, fighting with the steering wheel to keep from sliding off into the engorged creek that paralleled the driveway. At one point I passed a deer stand near the driveway, and I glimpsed a man in a rain poncho, a walkie-talkie held to his face. Higher up, I coasted to stop at a pullout where a motley assortment of vehicles parked: a rusting Ford station wagon and several trucks, including a tow truck with WINTER'S SALVAGE printed on the side. So, he really was here. To prepare a way, Mother Sophie had said, implying that he needed prayer because of some kind of breakdown. He was here with Sarah at The Land, a place where Maura had never wanted to return to. Here among a Family that was not a family of blood but belief, home in a hiding place armed against the end of the world. What the hell was I doing?

By the time I parked the Continental, reversing it in

so I would have an easier time picking my way down, Roland had come out to greet me, dressed in a slicker and a wide-brimmed hat, an umbrella hoisted over his head, the cherry of a cigarette burning in his mouth. He came to my side of the car and held up the umbrella to shield us both. "We thought you weren't going to come," he said when I opened my door and climbed out stiffly, my hip aching after the long drive.

"I got turned around," I said. "Did I miss it all?" Steam hissed out from under the hood of my car, the taxed engine smoldering after such a climb.

"We don't aim to be easy to find here." And wasn't that true? Seeing the place in person I wondered if Maura could be hiding here after all. How would you find a hidden person on such a sprawling property? Roland leaned over with the umbrella, taking one last drag off his cigarette before tossing it into the slush. "And no, you didn't miss it. We don't follow any official timeline. We were just getting ready to pray over Mother Sophie."

"What's wrong with her?"

"Nothing wrong with her, except her blindness. We're gonna try a faith healing. Come on, it's this way." He led me toward the lone standing building, an old log cabin buttressed by a stone foundation, the left side sprouting a tower and palisade like some ancient crumbling keep. I could see the outhouses set between the trailers, knew from Maura how men like Elijah had grown sick one summer from digging the sewer lines. Climbing the sloping path beside Roland in the falling sleet, I couldn't disguise my limp. "Are you hurt?" he asked, leaning in since he was a good four inches taller than me.

"It's nothing," I said. Meshach was the one who stood in the fire. Here I could not be a wounded young man, but instead someone strong and fierce. "Just pulled a muscle while out snowshoeing." Also, someone who apparently couldn't help telling lies. They couldn't know about the accident, which had been spectacular enough to get mentioned in the paper along with the robbery. They might be able to connect the two and ferret out who I was.

We trudged up the slope, Roland pausing when we were under the dripping eaves to fold his umbrella and study me with his measuring gaze. I thought for a moment he might pat me down or ask me if I was carrying a wire, but whatever flash of suspicion he was entertaining he shook away and opened the front door to usher me inside.

The cabin smelled sweetly of smoke, a homey place with a copper pot percolating on a woodstove, Mother Sophie nestled in a velvety green recliner, her slippered feet up on an ottoman. Pastor Elijah stood beside her, his shoulders squared, his cheeks ruddy in the heat of the close room. He'd shaved his mustache and sideburns, buzz-cut his hair in a military style, which made him look boyish rather than tough. Accompanied by a tall, blond woman, he didn't look like someone who'd just had a nervous breakdown. A young couple I didn't recognize at first stood beside Mother Sophie on the other side, neither one bothering to look my way. Roland and I stamped the slush from our boots in the entryway and hung our coats from pegs in the log wall.

Pastor Elijah crossed the room, clasped my hand in a firm handshake, and introduced himself as Eli. "You must be the Meshach I've been hearing about. A prophet, from what I'm told. Well. I'm pleased to finally shake your hand."

The woman hovering close behind Elijah stepped around him and introduced herself as Caroline, Roland's sister. She looked a little like her brother, bony-chinned and broad-shouldered for a woman. She wore a red-and-black-checkered dress that buttoned down the front, and her red lipstick smudged her front teeth. I remembered spotting her the first time I'd been to Rose of Sharon and heard Elijah speak. She had been the woman in the bright shawl who sat beside Sarah, Maura's daughter. I was disappointed that Sarah wasn't here. I wanted to see her again, a living memory of Maura.

Elijah squinted at me. "I almost feel I know you from somewhere."

I shook my head, my throat thick with worry. He wasn't talking about my first visit to Rose of Sharon. Could it be that one night after closing Elijah had seen us in the parking lot? I knew he had never been into the bank branch, but was it possible that a suspicious man like him might have staked out his own wife? How had Maura explained away her lateness coming home? I felt sure he had seen me before, even though Maura had never introduced me to him. The way his small, gray eyes puzzled over me, it was only a matter of time before he figured me out. "I don't think so," I said.

"Maybe it's just that God intended us to meet. Come on in and join us." He introduced me to the young couple, Brian and Lisa, though they hardly looked my way.

Regal as a queen, Mother Sophie sat back in a recliner, her white hair brushed so finely that it gleamed silver. Her recliner was situated near a woodstove and surrounded on two sides by floral sofas, a coffee table with scattered books and brochures between them. I looked around the room as I came closer. I noticed the homey touches at first glance—the Confederate flag tacked up on one wall and the musket above the mantel—but now I saw the guns leaning near the door, at least two shotguns and one ominous-looking assault rifle. The wall facing the driveway gleamed with metal sheeting hammered in for reinforcement. A folding ladder climbed into the eaves where there must be some kind of lookout. Along with the ticking of the woodstove, I heard the low chatter of a police scanner, grainy and crackling.

Mother Sophie beamed up at me from her chair. "I

knew you would come, Meshach." Her eyes fixed on a place near where I stood. Up close, her face was so deeply wrinkled it reminded me of the whorls in a tree trunk. "We've eaten all the cheddar biscuits, but there's tea if you want some."

"I'm fine," I said, though I was shivering from the rain and damp, my teeth clacking.

She peered in my direction. "You familiar with Matthew 17? It's what got this started."

"No, ma'am."

"The verse says that if you have the faith of a mustard seed you can move mountains. So Elijah, here, gets the idea that if all things are possible through prayer, they are going to heal me tonight. Make these old eyes see again. How does that sound to you?"

"It would be a miracle," I said.

"It would be that indeed," said Mother Sophie. "In the last days, we will see things that cannot be explained. I would like to see them, anyhow."

In a low voice, Elijah said to me, "If you don't feel comfortable being part of it you can just sit on that sofa and watch."

I scratched at my arm, suddenly nervous.

"I want Meshach to pray over me. You can do it, right?"

I nodded and then felt stupid, because she was blind and couldn't see the gesture. This is not what I had pictured when they invited me to a prayer and Bible study. "Sure," I said, though I felt far from it. "So long as a rookie can't botch this."

"You can't botch prayer," Mother Sophie assured me. "But there's some ways of doing it that are better than others."

There wasn't much space between the sofas. I crowded in on the side next to the other couple. Lisa had coal-black hair draped to her waist, her eyes large and dark above high cheekbones. I recognized the woman who had spoken in tongues at church last Sunday, one of the Ojibwe. The very one I translated for. I felt nervous standing beside her, worried she might be overcome by the Holy Spirit again and what kind of trouble that might mean for me. Brian—his blocky face blondly bearded, his eyes set too close together—must have been her husband. Pastor Elijah, Roland, and his sister Caroline took up the other side, Roland holding a bowl filled with some kind of white paste.

"What's that?" Brian asked.

"Crisco," Roland said. "We wanted to use olive oil from the Holy Land, but there's none in the cupboards."

"The kind of oil doesn't matter," Pastor Elijah cut in. "Jesus healed with mud and spit. Crisco'll do."

Pastor Elijah dipped his fingers into the paste and bid Mother Sophie to shut her eyes. He rubbed around her eyes with it before dabbing her eyelids, mumbling under his breath. Then Roland held the bowl around for all of us so that we could also dip our fingers in and lay hands on Mother Sophie's face. From my awkward position I ended up getting her bony chin, where the soft down of a few white whiskers had sprouted. Her wrinkled face glistened with grease by the time we had all laid hands on her.

"If this doesn't work, you can bake my head in the oven like a fat croissant," Mother Sophie cracked, licking her lips.

"Quiet, you," said Elijah. "Mood has to be right. Let's do this."

We all shut our eyes as Elijah read the verse from Matthew again. "Lord God, You promised in your Good Book that all things are possible if we believe. Wherever two or more gathered, You are there also. We welcome You into this place."

"Jesus," Caroline murmured, "Holy Lamb of God."

Pastor Elijah went on to pray, invoking the story of Saul of Tarsus, blinded on the road to Damascus and then healed when he agreed to stop tormenting Christians and follow God. He continued, a mixture of invocation and story, the others around me all calling upon Jesus and me mumbling along with them, my fingers slippery against the old woman's chin. Minutes must have passed while we prayed, Lisa vibrating with tension that made the floorboards creak beneath her. I was conscious of Roland's cigarette smell, the light rise and fall of Mother

Sophie's bosom, her warm breath as it passed over my fingers. "We trust in your healing powers, Lord," Pastor Elijah said. "Amen." At last we stepped away.

Mother Sophie sat up in the recliner, her face shining. She blinked her eyes open and looked around. That had been some prayer. I held my breath, wondering for a moment if it had really worked. Her gaze found me. Then she laughed, a great belly laugh that made her chair shake. "Get this crap off me, I'm still blind as a bat."

"Actually, bats aren't truly blind," I said, and then regretted saying anything.

"That so?" Mother Sophie shook her head.

"Maybe a different kind of oil," Roland offered as he brought over a towel. "That Holy Land oil would have been better."

Pastor Elijah settled on one of the floral sofas and sank down with a sigh. The rest of us joined him, finding places around a coffee table scattered with Bibles and colorful brochures. "We'll try again some other time, Mother," he said.

"No," she said, "this is how God intends me to be. I'll see again when he restores his Kingdom on Earth. I can wait till then. Then I will see Him, face-to-face."

Caroline smoothed down her long, checkered dress against the back of her thighs and sat beside Elijah, close enough that her leg brushed against his. Her mouth turned down when he inched farther away.

Without my asking, Roland brought over a steaming mug on a saucer and handed it to me. "You look like you could use it," he said. Roland took up a position standing near the door, his hand fidgeting in the pocket where he kept his lighter.

The tea went down the wrong pipe. A coughing fit commenced and my wounded ribs caused me to cry out. Tears sprang to my eyes. "Sorry," I apologized, when I quit coughing.

Elijah watched me with a look of concern. "You all right, Meshach?"

"I will be," I said. Don't mention the night of the accident, I told myself. *They can't know. They can't know you were with her. You, the last person to see her.*

"I understand you live in town?" Elijah asked me.

I shook my head and took another sip of tea, carefully swallowing. A bitter black tea with a dollop of citrus. "I'm tending a property for an elderly couple who have flown south for the winter."

He leaned closer, his hands clasped in his lap. "And you're a student?"

"At Northern. Still figuring out what to do with my life. Probably end up working with computers."

"Maybe he knows about the Sky-net," said Mother Sophie.

"Sky-net," Elijah said. "It's the Internet, Mother."

He and Roland were the only one who called her that,

Mother, but I knew they weren't kin. "All that won't matter soon," Mother Sophie said. "Whatever you want to call it."

"What do you think?" Elijah said to me. "About Y2K?"

I massaged the bridge of my nose. The heat in this cabin and the mustiness in the sofas made the room swim before me. "It's possible. I've read articles that lend credence to the idea, though many experts find it highly unlikely that we'll experience major problems."

"But what do *you* believe?" Mother Sophie said. "I don't truck with experts."

I could have told them then that I thought it was all bullshit, but in that moment I wasn't sure anymore. I'd seen things. I wanted to believe there was some meaning in all this. The birds killing each other. Maura's vanishing and my accident. I wanted to make sense of my pain. "I believe there's a great shadow that lies over the world. I never knew it was there until recently. I haven't thought much on these things yet, but I do believe something is about to happen."

"That's the situation, isn't it? Then you've come to the right place, Meshach. We can help each other," Elijah said, sitting back and cracking his knuckles, the sound sharp in the room.

One late-night shift when Maura and I closed together, I noticed that something was wrong. When she had bent to pick up a receipt, her face blanched, a quiet hiss between her teeth. Even the light had gone flat in her eyes, glassy and distant, fixed on some territory inside herself. Her movements were slow and deliberate, one arm cradled close to her side. Since everything had to be done under dual control for the sake of security, it wasn't long before we found ourselves back in the break room, counting twenties into stacks of five hundreds and banding them for the vault.

"You okay?" I said.

"What?" She wrinkled her face, one hand behind her neck. "Yeah. Must have just slept on my neck wrong."

"Seems like there's more bothering you than your neck."

Maura kept on counting twenties and snapping the bands in place. "Forget it."

"Maybe I can help."

Maura set down her stack and turned to face me, her jaw clenched. "I'm only going to say this once, okay. Married people fight. It's normal. Totally normal. So, as much as I appreciate your concern, I would like to be left alone today. Got it?"

He hurt you, didn't he? The words were on the tip of my tongue, but stayed there. In the two years I knew her this happened every couple of months. Maura would disappear inside herself for a week, grow cold and distant. But I never saw any bruises.

I was lost in my own thoughts when Brian said

something to Elijah about dynamite, the best place to set it on a bridge.

Elijah looked my way, assessing how I reacted. I remembered passing over the only bridge that led to this place as I drove here through the sleet. My stomach grumbled audibly. I hadn't eaten anything all morning.

Lisa rose up without saying a word and plucked the empty biscuit tray from the coffee table to carry it over to the sink. What was I getting myself into here? Only a few years ago Timothy McVeigh had blown up a federal building in Oklahoma City. These people had dynamite and they were planning to use it. *You don't fuck with fascists*, Arwen had warned me.

"We're here for a Bible study," Elijah said to Brian in a firm voice.

Shaking her head, Caroline stood up from her place beside Elijah. She stretched her arms behind her head and said something about going to check on Sarah. Should she make her something for lunch? Elijah nodded without looking at her. What was going on between them? Without bidding goodbye to anyone else, Caroline strode away, her black lace-up boots clacking on the wooden floor.

After washing the tray, Lisa rejoined us, sitting right beside me. "I hear we were partners on Sunday," she said. Her voice was mousier than I expected. She did not seem capable of the strange, throaty language she had spoken just a few days ago.

"I had the easy part," I said.

Pastor Elijah only shook his head. "No one could translate for her before."

Lisa smiled at me shyly. "So, how long have you known the Lord?"

She asked it so casually, as if God were a next-door neighbor who sometimes stopped in for a visit, bringing milk and cookies.

I thought of Arwen's sharp profile in the dark, her worry over my going to church. I thought of Maura, singing a hymn that seemed to contain all the brokenness of this world. "I'm only getting to know Him," I said. "It's why I'm here."

"This is a good place to begin," Elijah said. His voice was soft, almost eager. "Would you like to pray with us?"

Again, I felt that pull. If there was such a thing as God, I wanted to know Him. I wanted Mother Sophie to lay her hands on my skull, heal my pain, take away my darkness. I wanted to find out what happened to Maura. I wanted my world to make sense again. "Maybe not now."

It swept over me at once: the air in the room stagnant, the left side of my face numbing, my vision tunneling. When I looked at Elijah, a halo of light surrounded him. I looked away quickly, noting how the aura surrounded Mother Sophie as well. The aura was not a good sign, nor the numbness in my face. Such sudden sadness pouring into my head, soul-deep. I knew what this was. Prodrome, the doctors called it, a sign that a migraine was about to wallop me anytime. Dark wings beat at the edge of my vision. It might hit in ten minutes or the aura could last all day before the migraine had me in its talons. "I don't feel so hot just now. I've got to go." My words sounded slurred in my own head.

"Get him a Bible, Roland," Mother Sophie instructed. "You take it home with you, Meshach. But don't go reading it chronological. Start with the Gospels. The book of Mark. Then backtrack to the prophets, like Isaiah. You'll love Isaiah. Pray as you read. God will speak to you through the verses. You'll meet Him there."

"Please. I need some fresh air," I said.

"I'll walk him out," Elijah said. He didn't bother with any coat as he opened the door and walked beside me out on the porch after I got my shoes and coat on. "You sure you're okay to drive home?" Melting snow dripped from the eaves, but at least the rain had stopped. The aura lit up my whole world, like I walked among angels.

"I'll be fine," I said. I zipped up my parka, Bible in hand. The cold woke me. I could breathe again. I had an emergency baggie with sumatriptan and Percocet in the glove compartment of my car.

"I hope you weren't bothered by anything Brian said. He came home from basic training down in Hattiesburg with a little brain damage after a chopper he was riding in crashed. Everyone died but him. So he says the oddest things at times, but don't pay it any mind." Elijah gestured at the trailers. "This here is home for many of us. It's a good place. Mother Sophie named it The Land, because it's a safe place. Maybe the last safe place in the coming days. You know where we are now. You're welcome here anytime, Meshach."

"Your whole family lives here?" Here was my chance. I thought of what I needed to say, the real reason I had come here.

Elijah frowned. "My daughter is with some of the older children. I should join her for lunch." He rubbed his face with his hands and yawned. "Ever since her mother went away, she gets nervous if I'm gone too long." He spoke like Caroline hadn't even gone ahead of him to care for Sarah. Had he already replaced Maura with another woman and now he was embarrassed about it?

"Went away?"

"What you said in there about the shadow that lies over the world. That's true. And sometimes the shadow finds its way into people." He set a hand on my shoulder and we stepped out from under the eaves. "Can I ask you a favor? Pray for my family."

I swallowed. I needed to press this without sounding suspicious. "Where did your wife go? If you don't mind my asking."

"I don't know." He looked at me, his small eyes

glittering, his mouth clamping hard enough to grind his teeth before he breathed out again. "I really don't."

He looked off toward the Airstream where he must be living with his daughter. "What're you doing for Thanksgiving?"

When I looked at him blankly, he continued, "Turkey Day? Two days from now? If you haven't made other plans."

"Okay," I said, my voice barely audible.

"Okay," he said. "We eat at noon. You know the way."

A
Grave
in
the
Woods

Kaiser's bellowing bark boomed throughout the house when I came in through the front door. I called and called Arwen's name, not hearing any answer. Kaiser's barking alternated with low, ominous growling, beckoning me to the lower level. Halfway down the spiral staircase, I spotted the source of the old dog's distress through the bay windows: an ancient stag, his antlers like small trees, was gorging on the neat rose-hedge borders along the birches. He must have sensed me watching because he lifted his heavy head, his jaws slowly grinding, and peered myopically in my direction through eyes filmed over by cataracts. He was the largest whitetail buck I'd ever seen, another marvel in a winter of wonders. Had the stag come so close to the house because he was both storm-blind and starving?

Kaiser yapped as he clawed at the door of his kennel.

I let the dog out and tried to hush him as he went to the windows and climbed up on his back legs to bark at the stag. His barking grated on my frayed nerves, so I opened the door, meaning only to shout and chase the stag off before it destroyed the Krolls' rosebushes. Before I got a word out, Kaiser shot through the gap.

Kaiser bounded into the sleet and barreled up the icy path. With that immense rack, and weighing several hundred pounds, the stag could have stomped the German shepherd into hamburger, but you don't grow old in these woods unless you know when to fight and when to run. His black nostrils flared and he snorted once, a dismissive sound. Then he turned and vaulted over the hedges, vanishing into the woods. I shouted at Kaiser to come back, but he bolted after the deer.

I turned back to the house, the windows like dark eyes on this gray day, my senses flooded with foreboding. I thought I felt someone watching from within. Or had I seen a ghostly reflection of myself in the glass, urging me to turn back? Vertigo tilted my world on its axis. The last place I wanted to be if a migraine took hold of me was out here in the snow again, but I had to bring Kaiser home. I had been charged with keeping the old dog alive.

I hobbled after him up the well-trodden path, past the frozen-over koi pond, the ring of birches and rose hedges, and into a forest of white and red pine where I was at least partly shielded from sleet that had begun falling from a slate-colored sky. My hands in my coat pockets, my hip aching, I trudged after Kaiser down a worn deer trail. The stag was long gone. Amid the pines I sank in deeper pockets of snow and ended up leaning against one of the trees when nausea made my world spin. I inhaled the terpene scent the bark released, a vanilla fragrance that grounded me, and called after Kaiser.

His age caught up to him in the pines, the old hound floundering chest-deep in the drifts. Yet he refused to heed my voice and turn around, instead plunging on. This was farther than we'd ever been, to the very border of the eighty-acre property, where the Wind River carved out its deep-bellied gorge. I heard the song of it far below, angry and tumbling with snowmelt, ice, and boulders cracking like knuckles. Bone on bone. Kaiser halted here at the edge of the world. As I came closer, I saw why.

Low iron fencing surrounded a small cemetery on a knoll that overlooked the river, iron posts jutting like black spears from crusty snow, gray tombstones within furred with moss and lichen. Kaiser's breath came raggedly; ice clung to his belly and bearded his muzzle. Beyond the shelter of the pines, I felt the full force of the wind sweeping out of the North, a wind that smelled of snow. The old dog groaned softly as the gate swung open, rusty hinges whining in invitation. Kaiser knew this place.

He ambled beside me as we stepped past the

gates—black iron to keep out evil spirits—my breath torn from me in ribbons. I knew from the old man that the Krolls had bought this land a hundred years before, the original homesteaders, the only Germans in a valley settled by Finns. This had to be a family cemetery.

The tombstones had been sculpted by wind and seasons of hard frost into leaning, tortured shapes. We were moving through time as we walked deeper into it, the first graves the oldest, going back to 1879: Heinrich. Gretel. Hans. The names became increasingly anglicized as I went along. Arnold. Helen. Gregory. The Krolls did not appear to be a long-lived people: Arnold died in Ardennes, a hero of the Battle of Bulge according to his tombstone. Why had they buried him here instead of in a veteran's cemetery? His sister, Helen—if that's who she was—only lived into her fifties. No wonder the Krolls had been desperate to snowbird to the South Padre Island. I kept going, tracing the names with my bare hands, reading the story of a family in the mossy braille. It was not a happy story, but they had brought me here, the stag and Kaiser.

I stumbled at one point and dropped to my knees. The grave before me occupied the very edge of the cemetery. A stone angel crouched on a small tombstone, an androgynous form with wings, head bowed in sorrow. So close to the ravine whoever slept here would have a good view of the river. This grave was one of a few someone had tended recently, leaving an urn of plastic begonias before it. It was also the only tombstone with an angel on it, so I knew before I read the name that I was looking at a child's grave, though the dates were buried in a snowdrift.

Vertigo swept over me once more, and I stepped out of the shell of my body, rising on dark wings into the winter sky, until man and dog were mere specks on the ground, tiny things rooted before a chasm, so high up the wind brought flakes of snow mixed in with sleet, and then it felt like I was falling down and down into my own body, the shock of it knocking my breath from my lungs and bringing me to my knees.

A brief darkness.

Kaiser must have nuzzled me awake. I clung to his ruff, drawing warmth and strength from the watchdog. I didn't want to look at the angel anymore.

The name printed on the stone: Arwen Kroll.

"You knew this whole time," I said to the dog. "If she's buried here, then who is that back at the house? Who is playing the part of a dead girl?"

I don't remember the long journey home with the dog, nor taking off my boots, nor swallowing the pain pills that now fogged my thinking. I couldn't remember any of it and those gaps bothered me when I woke the next morning.

I WOKE TO ARWEN knocking on my door. "Lucien? There's

someone here to see you." With my skull throbbing in time to her fist, I could hardly process Arwen's voice, my mind still half-planted in a dream world.

When I pulled back the covers and sat up, I saw that I was wearing the jeans and sweater I'd worn out to The Land. A lingering residue of pain leftover from the migraine yet held me in thrall. I rubbed my face in my hands, trying to wake my brain from a narcotic fog, as I struggled to remember.

"Lucien?" Arwen knocked again.

"Just a minute," I called in a hoarse voice. I took a couple of long breaths to calm myself, inhaling through my nose and breathing out through my mouth. "I need a few minutes."

After Arwen went away, I tried to get my bearings. I didn't want to see whoever was here. I needed to figure out what the hell was happening. If that was Arwen's grave, then who was this stranger who had invaded the house and my life? My mouth felt as if it had been stuffed with cotton. I needed water. I needed grub. When had I last eaten? I needed peace. What I didn't need was another visitor at the house or any more mysteries. For a moment, I wondered if Roland had followed me home, or if my mother had flown up from Chicago because she was worried about me. Whoever they were I just wanted them to go away. Still, I stood and opened the door.

From the hallway I heard Arwen's sharp laughter and a male voice so low it was more growl than speech. I knew that voice. Noah Larsen, one of a few friends I had since I was an introvert on a college campus where everyone fled for the Cities on weekends, a reverse migration. With his darker skin, he should have been a misfit on a largely white campus, the only black hockey player I'd ever met, but Noah had an easy way with people. He sported mutton-chop sideburns and drove a rebuilt 1982 Pontiac Firebird Trans Am, a genuine hardback T-top just like the one on *Knight Rider*, which Noah could tell you all about in his best imitation of the Hoff. Shit. How had he tracked me down here?

I shuffled down the hallway, the pain sharp in my hip. It sure as hell felt like I'd been on a long journey.

Arwen perched on one of the counters, her shapely legs swinging out. She was dressed in a faded black Ramones t-shirt and a denim skirt that drew my eyes to her bare legs and feet. Whatever Noah had said to make her laugh caused her to tilt her head back and expose her pale throat. Noah sported a tight turtleneck with a thick gold chain around his neck, acid-washed jeans, and his trademark Doc Martens as he leaned casually against the kitchen table, wrapping up his story. I felt a flash of jealousy that I didn't fully understand. Maybe it was how natural they looked together. Maybe it was that I'd always envied Noah. Back then I only saw how being black made him special. There was so much I didn't know.

NOAH GRUNTED "HEY," WHEN he spotted me and gestured at the six-pack of Dr Peppers he'd brought along—my favorite drink, which I imbibed at parties while everyone else got soused on beer and tequila—slipping one from the plastic ring and tossing it my way. I caught it by the fingertips and cracked it open while Noah glanced sidelong at Arwen and then back at me, crooking his left eyebrow as if to say, nice job. He didn't know the half of it. Noah had not been a fan of my involvement with Maura.

I took a long drink and tried to smile. His being here complicated things. I could no longer imagine Arwen as a ghostly seductress, my winter priestess. His being here made her real, a flesh-and-blood problem. I felt disoriented, my mind mixed up between dream and memory. "How'd you know where to find me?" I said. No one was supposed to know where I was.

He frowned at the unfriendliness of the question. "I called your mom."

I nodded—Noah had come home with me to visit Mount Greenwood and Chicago one winter break, so he had the number. I took another long sip, hoping the sugar and caffeine would cut through the muddle of my thinking.

Arwen watched me curiously, no longer smiling. "So . . . you guys met in chem?" She looked between us as if she couldn't figure out our friendship. It was a mystery to me as well.

"I was going pre-med," I said, pulling up a seat at the kitchen table because I needed to sit down. "But it didn't work out." Part of what I'd learned in college is that I wasn't as smart as I thought I was.

"Lucien's a computer geek," Noah said. "Pre-med just wasn't his path."

"Don't sell yourself short, anyhow," Arwen said, somehow detecting the undercurrent of self-pity in my statement.

Whatever happened the night before, the warmth between us seemed to have dissipated. Or was I losing my hold on reality? The ancient stag, the journey through the woods, the cemetery at the edge of a chasm? My mind wandering in and out of the black-and-white movie of my life, dark wings at the edge of my vision. All a dream?

"I don't picture you as a doctor or scientist," Arwen continued, hopping down from the counter to help herself to one of the Dr Peppers. "A priest or poet, maybe."

"You're traveling further and further down the pay grade," I muttered. "Next you'll have me playing violin on the street corner for pennies."

Noah chuckled but not Arwen. "It's not that you're

not smart enough. That's not it. You just don't have the hardness that science requires." She paused, her cheeks coloring. "That cool detachment. You're one of those people who feel things too much."

"You've only known me for a week."

"Our Lou is a gifted programmer," Noah cut in, calling me by the nickname he'd given me shortly after we first met. "He tell you about the game he's designing?"

"She's seen it," I said. "What'd she tell you about herself?" I nodded toward Arwen, hoping to change the subject.

"Just that she came here from Bellingham. And that her parents own this place."

I looked at Arwen and tried to put a fix on what I'd seen out in the woods. A grave. A grave with her name on it. "Your parents will be surprised to hear about your return."

Arwen's brow furrowed, but she didn't try to defend herself.

"I mean, some places are harder to come back from than others."

"Okay," Noah interrupted, not liking my tone. He rapped his fist on the table. "So, I need to get going here. I just wanted to check in with you, my man, because I've been thinking of you. I also wanted to see what you're doing for Thanksgiving. My mom says you're more than welcome to join us down in Duluth." He glanced over at

Arwen. "And you, too. We always keep one empty chair at the table for an unexpected guest."

An unexpected guest. That certainly described Arwen. And I wasn't surprised he was leaving so soon, since Noah couldn't stand tension or conflict. Everyone got along in his copacetic world and that was how it should be.

"Thank your mom for me, but I've made other plans." The way Noah studied me I knew I had to say more. "I'm eating with some people from church."

"You go to church?" Noah couldn't keep the suspicion out of his voice.

"Place called Rose of Sharon," I said.

"It's one of those Christian Identity churches," Arwen added, not so helpfully because Noah still looked puzzled. "A church for white people."

She half made it sound like I approved of such notions. Truthfully, they had only made passing mentions of race in my presence so far. "There are some Indians there, too," I said. "Ojibwe from the reservation, I think. Anyhow, you know I'm not a racist. You know why I'm going to this church."

"Oh," Noah said, but as understanding sunk in he looked no less troubled. He knew that Maura's husband had been a pastor, knew about the man's violent past and white supremacist connections. "Oh, shit."

I rose from my spot on the table when he got ready to leave. I wanted to walk him out, make sure we parted on a decent note. It should have been a happy reunion, but with an assist from Arwen, I'd soured the mood. "Thank you for coming here. For finding me."

In the foyer, Noah plucked a black leather coat from the rack and shrugged it on. "You should call your mom," he said in a flat voice. "She's worried about you, Lou."

"I will."

Noah set a hand on my shoulder. "I don't think you should be hanging around those people. It's a shit idea. You have to let some things go."

I didn't say anything because he was right. He squeezed my shoulder — the uninjured side — and stepped out into the cold, where sleet had changed over to a sugary snow that powdered his Trans Am.

Arwen hadn't waited around in the kitchen, so I boiled water for Top Ramen, cracking an egg on top of the noodle-brick. Downstairs I heard the grainy crackling of the projector starting up.

I felt guilty for how I'd behaved when Noah visited, so I took two Dr Peppers and wandered into the den. The cans were growing lukewarm, but I passed her one as a peace offering and sank into the opposite La-Z-Boy beside her. On the white screen, Orson Welles played Harry Lime, a baby-faced raconteur in a black suit and rakish black hat, pacing inside a Ferris wheel gondola rotating high above a divided post-war Vienna. His friend Holly tries to confront him with the evil he has learned about and to remind him that he once believed in God.

"*The Third Man*," I said. I had watched it before on the old man's Betamax collection. "This—"

"Sh!" Arwen hushed me and rightly so. The scene was iconic in cinema.

In a fogged window, Harry Lime wrote out Anna's name. The people below, tiny from such a distance, were "dots," mere abstractions. Their deaths meant nothing to him. As the gondola coasted to a stop and the two men stepped out, he delivered his last appeal, a speech that tried to justify evil by pointing out that during the violent reign of the Borgias great minds like Leonardo da Vinci and Michelangelo thrived, while the five centuries of blissful peace the Swiss enjoyed produced nothing more than the ordinary invention of the cuckoo clock.

I leaned over. "The villain always gets the best lines."

She hushed me again, the movie drawing close to the climactic final scenes.

Why this movie, Arwen? Post-war noir. A movie about the ambiguity of evil, the villain with his perfectly banal name. It's possible for ordinary people to justify any diabolical action. I always felt terrible for Holly, the drunkard as moral compass.

We sat in darkness as the credits rolled. "He's wrong," I said as the orchestra music faded. "Harry Lime's famous soliloquy on the merits of evil."

"Of course he's wrong," Arwen said, her face in-shadow. "He's a sociopath who profited from the deaths of children."

"No, I mean about the cuckoo clock. It was invented in Germany, not Switzerland."

Arwen laughed. "Are you going to deny the Swiss yodeling and Ricola cough drops as well?"

"No, five hundred years of peace and democracy ought to count for something. I grant them yodeling and all-natural cough drops made from thirteen healing herbs."

Arwen held out her half-empty Dr Pepper for a toast and we clinked our cans to that. The words were there on the tip of my tongue. What I had seen earlier in the woods. I needed to be straight with her. But what had I seen? "Arwen?" I started to say something and stopped. I was thinking of Harry Lime writing Anna's name in the fogged window, how easily this world erases us. The more I thought about it the journey seemed more dream than real. I had to make sure first.

The screen before us had long gone blank as the reel reached the end, the film slap-slapping as it revolved. Arwen stood up to take care of it. I snapped my recliner shut and stood beside her. In the dark, with the projector shut down I couldn't read her eyes anymore. "Never mind," I said.

She held the reel against her chest, not quite looking at me. She looked lost in thoughts of her own. With her short haircut and feral features, her dark eyes hinting at secrets, she could pass for one of the fae who held a key to the underworld. Ghost or not, I was starting to realize that I needed her. "Okay," she said, dipping her chin and walking away.

The hour was already late after the movie finished, so I spent the rest of the evening going between my bedroom and the office downstairs where I'd rigged two computers to work on programming *The Land*, standing and walking around when my hip stiffened. The pain in my body reminded me of my accident, the chassis crushing around me, heat from the burning fuel line licking closer, the desperate screech of metal as the paramedics worked to cut me free. My death and rebirth. It hit me then. The answer was right here in my own body, in my memory, in the lingering pain. I didn't have to save the fool in the woods. *Let him die, so that he can be reborn.* I worked feverishly, sketching the scene by hand before digitizing it: a new cutscene with the fool's body in the woods as an unkindness of ravens descended. Instead of feeding on him, they lift him into the sky and carry him deeper into the woods before setting him down in a graveyard and flying off again. The corpse stirring in the grasses, waking, not dead after all. The screen flickering with shadows beyond the edges of the grave where it looked like something was walking toward him, either the queen or Death himself, a figure from *The Seventh Seal*.

When I watched it play out, I realized I couldn't remember creating that part of the scene. My fool might have escaped death, but whatever was coming toward him spooked me.

If the world ended a month from now, billions of tiny microcomputers embedded in everything from toasters to jet airplanes dying at the turn of the clock, a programming error that went back to the invention of computers themselves, then my minor programming victory didn't matter. Yet it felt like something I had to do.

Later that night Arwen visited my bed in her nightgown, slipping under the covers without a word and lying down with her back to me. Were these nocturnal visits going to be a regular occurrence? We hadn't touched the night before, the small space between us humming with energy. Outside, the wolves returned to the birch grove, scrounging for scraps of raven revealed by melting snow. One howled as if in greeting and I thought of that amber-eyed female I'd seen when they first came and how she hadn't seemed afraid. The others joined her, an eerie night chorus. Arwen tensed beside me in the bed, her body going rigid. It sounded like they were right outside the window. How small that sound made us feel, how large the night. A long shiver passed through Arwen, and she turned over and took my left hand in hers and pulled me closer. She drew my hand to her stomach, against the soft nylon of her nightgown, squeezed and held on. I inhaled the faint scent of cloves in her hair, felt how our bodies curved together without quite joining at the hip. In this way we held each other until the wolves wandered off. Arwen relaxed, let go of my hand. Her breathing steadied and then deepened as my hand fell away. She appeared to be one of those people who just hit a switch and went to sleep in a second, but I couldn't and I lay awake for a long time after. Here, without my asking, was another mystery. "Who are you?" I whispered to her sleeping form.

Place of Safety

While Arwen slept in that morning I plugged the phone cord back into the wall—when had Arwen yanked it out and why?—and called my mom.

"Oh Lucien," she said. "I was so worried about you."

"I'm okay, Mom," I assured her. "Better than okay." I told her about Rose of Sharon and the new friends I had made at church, but there was so much I couldn't say. I didn't mention their apocalyptic beliefs, or Y2K, or the currents of white supremacy in their sermons, or the cabin barricaded against the end of the world, assault rifles leaning against a wall hammered in with sheet metal. I didn't tell her about Arwen or the grave in the woods. I didn't tell her about my devil dreams or the storms of ravens, harbingers of the apocalypse, or my uncertain hold on reality. I didn't tell her I was risking my own life to find out what had happened to my lover, a married woman I'd been having an affair with.

"You sound better," she said, and it was true. There were weeks after the accident when I had wanted to die. I had been wrecked both physically and spiritually, a drained monotone on the other end of the phone. I felt more alive than I had in a long time.

I heard a toilet flush down the hallway and then the sink running. Arwen didn't intrude, but I sensed her, listening. I remembered my mother warning me as a teenager that every person you slept with, you would carry with you the rest of your life, even if it was just a passing encounter, and that these were sacred matters my hormones shouldn't rush me into.

"I'm sorry I didn't call. I've been busy."

My mom sighed. "I'm glad you met people, Lucien. When I think of you alone in that old house, it hurts my heart."

Alone? That had been the winter I thought I wanted, but the world made other plans. "What about you? What are you doing on Turkey Day?"

"Oh, you're not the only one who's been going to church. There's these ladies—they put on a supper for the homeless in the area. I'll be helping this year."

My heart gladdened hearing this. I didn't want my mom to be alone on Thanksgiving either. I worried she would start drinking again, the holidays a hard time with both her parents dead, her brother working odd jobs up in Anchorage, and five hundred miles of icy highway driving between her and her only child. We chatted awhile longer and I thanked her for giving Noah the address. She asked me when I would be coming home again. I was coming home for Christmas, right?

"I don't know, Mom."

"Just for a few days, Lucien. I've missed you so much. You can fly into O'Hare." She paused, gathering in a breath, her voice straining for lightness. "I don't want you to try the drive in that ridiculous gas-guzzling boat your father made you buy. I'll pay your airfare. That old house and dog will be just fine. You can get Noah to care for them."

I hesitated. I couldn't put her off forever. If Y2K happened there would likely be no climbing into the stratosphere at six hundred miles per hour in a jumbo jetliner. Even our cars would die, all that horsepower fizzled by a lousy computer, along with billions of microprocessors. Were computers the rot at the center of all that was wrong with modern society? Despite my programming ambitions, a part of me wanted it to happen. Maybe it was time for humanity to start over. But if it did, it might be a long time before I saw my mother again, if ever. I didn't want that. "Yeah, Noah might do that for me," I said, though I knew I would just ask Arwen. Mentally, I tallied all the things I had to do before the world ended. If. "I still have things to take care of first."

"Lucien," she said in a shaky voice. She was doing her best.

"Okay, Mom. Let's do Christmas. I'll talk to Noah and then come out for a few days."

"It's going to be so nice. You just made your mother very happy."

AT THE BASE OF the driveway leading up to The Land, several Chevy trucks were parked just off the gravel road, half in the snow-laden ditch. I parked behind a rusted-out Pontiac Grand Am and hiked up the hill, walking where tire treads had compacted the snow, trying not to think about the man in the watchtower, likely glassing me through his scope. Back at the Kroll house, Arwen was making do with chicken nuggets and some canned yams scavenged from the pantry for her Thanksgiving.

The scene up top looked festive. They had stretched canvas sheets among the pines between the old log cabin and trailers squatting on log foundations. I felt like I was stepping into a scene from a previous century. Cook fires burned at the outer edges of the billowing canvas shelters, women in dresses and scarves bending to tend to Dutch oven pots tucked in the embers. Before a hollowed-out firepit one man turned a huge metal spit with two turkeys basting on it, juice dripping into the flames. Children chased mongrel dogs between the fires while a boy with a shaved skull perched up on one of the tables strumming his guitar, teenage girls below him locking heads as they whispered.

Mother Sophie must have known I was coming because she stood at the edge nearest the driveway. "Welcome, Meshach," she said as her misty eyes found mine. And even though my body ached from the long climb, lungs pushing up against ribs still on the mend, I felt welcome.

"How'd you know it was me?" Had her hearing sharpened to make up for her loss of eyesight, so that she could detect who was coming by the mere sound of footsteps in snow?

From one pocket in her dress, Mother Sophie pulled out a walkie-talkie. It squawked in her hands. "He's here," she said into it, smiling in my direction. "Over and out."

From out of the corner of my eye, I spotted Roland's sister, Caroline, dragging a little girl behind her. The girl's blond hair looped in pigtails, her small body stuffed in a pink puffy snowsuit too large for her. Tears slipped down her cheeks, her huge hazel eyes brimming. I recognized Maura's changeable eyes, flickering green in bright light or dark as the clouds overhead. Here was Sarah, Maura's daughter, who I'd been longing to see. I felt a catch in my throat, remembering the girl's mother, Maura, who I'd come here for.

Caroline's bony chin jutted out as she let go of Sarah's

hand and gave her a tiny shove in Mother Sophie's direction. Caroline didn't even look my way. She brushed a loose strand of straw-colored hair from her eyes, tucking it back into her scarf and puffed. "Will you take her, Mother? She doesn't want to play with the others. She won't listen."

"You're not my mom," Sarah wailed as she ducked behind Mother Sophie's voluminous skirts.

Mother Sophie thanked Caroline and sent her away. She rested a hand on the top of Sarah's head. "This is Sarah," she told me. "She lives with us now."

I glanced toward Caroline stomping off to rejoin a circle of men under the canopy and tried to sound nonchalant as I asked, "Her mom's not around?"

Ducking behind Mother Sophie, Sarah gave another muffled cry.

"Her mother's not in the picture," she said. Her eyes fixed on some point beyond me, her mouth crimping.

I decided to press matters, not knowing when I might get another chance. "What happened to her?"

Mother Sophie's frown deepened. She turned away from me and knelt so she was close to eye level with Sarah. "Can you do something for me, sweetie? Fetch Jack and the other boys and tell them it's almost time to eat."

"I don't wanna . . ." Sarah started, but Mother Sophie shushed her and brushed away the tears that had continued to spill from her liquid eyes.

"You remember what we talked about? I need you to be my eyes in this world. You fetch those boys and then you can sit with me at the meal. How's that sound?"

Sarah gave a grunting assent and skipped off, pigtails bouncing.

When she was out of earshot, Mother Sophie turned back to me. "What happened to her mother is a sad story. Stole money and run off. And I will tell you this honestly, Meshach. I'm glad she's gone. That one was trouble. Too much of the world inside her. She caused Elijah so much pain. Wherever she went, she isn't coming back." Mother Sophie's eyes narrowed above the hooked beak of her nose. It was clear she had not liked Maura, not one bit. Her malice surprised me. "Why do you ask?" she said, cocking her head. Her suspicion didn't feel natural to me.

Why did I keep coming here at a risk to my health? There are some things you don't want answers for, things you aren't meant to know. I didn't know, but this felt like where I needed to be. I breathed in the sweet smell of wood smoke and basting turkey. "I just don't understand why anyone would leave such a place," I said. I searched for the right words. "A safe place." The phrase rang false in my mind—this place felt like anything but safe, and I supposed it hadn't been for Maura—but I hoped I sounded sincere.

"A safe place?" Mother Sophie repeated my words. "You know The Land is our Place of Safety. That term comes from our faith tradition. It's what we've been building to escape the coming Tribulation." Her brief smile let me know I had been restored to her good graces. "Come along, now. I suppose you'll want to see what the men are up to."

She led me into the encampment, where eight picnic tables occupied even lines under the billowing canvas, kerosene lanterns swaying from ropes strung above. The swinging light and wind-whipped canvas gave me a sense of being on board a pirate ship heading into uncharted waters. Mother Sophie threaded her way between the tables until she came to one where a group of men huddled around something. Roland spotted us coming and flicked away his cigarette, smoke streaming from his nostrils as he tapped Elijah's shoulder. Elijah pushed away from the picnic table and came over to greet me like an old friend. I tried not to wince when he clapped my shoulder. Her delivery completed, Mother Sophie turned away, the walkie-talkie squawking once more in her dress pocket as she ambled away to give orders elsewhere.

"What do you think of our setup?" Elijah wanted to know right off.

Mud and slush clumped my boots and soaked into the hem of my jeans, and my clothing already reeked of a smoky, campfire smell. I liked it. A lot. "This is great."

Elijah nodded toward Roland. "He's the genius who came up with it."

Roland's brief grin revealed long incisors. Wolf teeth. "If this is the last Thanksgiving of the old millennium, we might as well go out in style," he drawled in his gruff voice.

"And it's the only way we could fit so many people from the church together in one place," Elijah said. "With more of us coming home to The Land, people from all over." He pushed his way into the circle of men and introduced me around. Brian, with his stringy blond beard and close-set eyes, was there, along with a gaunt dude with a skeletal face named Bjorn. I'd never met him before, but I felt an immediate visceral reaction, a cold ball of dislike in my gut. Bjorn didn't look like a member of the church, his head shaved down to stubble, a crooked nose broken in several places. A tattoo of a black iron cross crawled up out of his collar and spread like a stain on his neck. Why did I dislike him right off, aside from his appearance and unfriendliness? I knew why: because he was exactly the kind of neo-Nazi I'd been expecting when I first started visiting these people. "This must be the Birdman," Bjorn said. His eyes were cold and empty, and he didn't offer to shake my hand.

I turned away from him without acknowledging the nickname. Birdman? I wondered how the story of the ravens changed as it was passed around.

As I came closer, I saw that the men were gathered around a chessboard of all things. Elijah gestured at the board. "You play?" Even in a Carhartt jacket and orange hunter's cap, he still reminded me more of a college professor than an ex-con, his face clean-shaven, his eyes bright with intelligence. I couldn't figure him yet.

"A little," I said, with an uncertain shrug. In high school I had been second board on the team. Our chess coach, the computer science teacher who inspired me to learn programming, had been heartbroken when I quit my sophomore year. At the time I didn't have the courage to tell him I feared that if I stayed on the team I would end up going through high school never having been on a date, chess nerdery a surefire path to extended virginity.

"You heard of Bobby Fischer?" Bjorn asked. He drizzled tobacco juice into an empty Budweiser can in front of him. He played chess, too?

"I read some of his articles. From his column in *Boy's Life*." My coach had dutifully photocopied the articles on an old mimeograph machine so that when you read them ink came off on your hands, a blueberry stain that didn't wash off right away. I read so many I dreamed in blue, my mind puzzling over problems when I lay in bed at night. I had been so lonely then. Seeing this board now I realized how much I'd missed the game.

"His books got me through prison," Elijah said. "For a high school dropout to rise in the ranks the way Fischer did. That flash of brilliance. I wanted to understand it. I read his books and studied his blitzkrieg style. I wanted to take what he did in the chess world and apply it in real life. To business or leadership."

Brian wandered off, apparently uninterested in the game of kings. Bjorn leaned forward, speaking out of the side of his mouth as he drizzled more spit into the can. "He was one of us, you know. Belonged to the Christian Identity church before Jewish cockroaches drove him into hiding." He glared my way as he said this, as if he thought I was one of those Jews. Bjorn had the look of someone who wasn't happy unless he was torturing small, innocent creatures: puppies, hamsters, confused undergraduates who had wandered into a place where they didn't belong. Did you know this part about Bobby Fischer, Coach? This legend you taught us to idolize, the man who put chess on the map in America?

"The board here shows his third match with Boris Spassky in 1972," Elijah said, ignoring Bjorn's ugly comment. "From the World Championship in Reykjavík. Fischer went into it already down 2–0. It's the moment when everything changed in the chess world."

"He opened with Benoni," I said. I remembered this from one of the articles. "It cast everything into uncertainty. Spassky thought he was winning."

"Huh," Elijah said, sitting beside Bjorn at the picnic table. "Benoni means 'Son of Sorrow' in Hebrew. You know that too?"

"You think I'm a Jew or something?"

Elijah laughed, but Bjorn only stared. "No," Elijah said. "You wouldn't be here if I did. But it does strike me that you know more about this game than you let on."

I sat on the opposite side of the table. "You want to play it out with me?" Both comments were spontaneous, the words leaving my mouth before I thought about it.

Elijah set his elbows on the table, his hands under his chin, his pebbly eyes shining. He revolved the board around, careful not to disrupt the pieces, so his black pieces would face my white. "I get to be Bobby Fischer," he said. "You're Spassky."

Fischer had played black in game three. I studied the board and tried to ignore Bjorn as he went on a tangent about blacks having all the advantages in life as well as in this game, an entire welfare support system bought and paid for by taxes on whites. Elijah chewed on his lower lip, and I wondered if Bjorn made him nervous as well.

My pieces on the board occupied an impossible position. Elijah's black pieces were fighting for control of the light squares, a battle he was winning because of the advanced positions of his two pawns. He was the shadow, marching forward as Fischer had in Reykjavík. Spassky had lost the game long before this. I took off my gloves to maneuver my pieces. "We had a hard time with our chess club in prison," Elijah told me. Bjorn nodded along as Elijah moved his King to H7, exactly duplicating what Fischer had done in the real game. My death would come about by slow dismembering of my defenses. "People would burn the black pieces to use for inking tattoos."

"Dice and shit were banned," Bjorn added. "Can't have niggers gambling. No games on which someone can make a bet." His lips twisted. "You're fucked, by the way."

I kept my eyes on the board, hoping to see Elijah make a mistake. The cold nipped at my fingers. This was the first time I'd heard Elijah talk about prison, where I gathered he'd met Bjorn. "How'd you play then?" I asked.

"I made my pieces from origami," Elijah said. "I had a lot of time on my hands back then."

We'd reached the part of the game where Fischer offered up his queen. She floated out there in the open, vulnerable and exposed. The pieces were carved from soapstone, the queen elegant in her black gown. A lady of the evening, an invitation. I blew on my fingers to warm them. I knew the move for what it was: a trap. I took her all the same. I took her as Spassky had taken her. I took her because I had no choice.

"Strange, isn't it?" Elijah said, studying my face. "How chess demands sacrifice. You can't win unless you're willing to sacrifice everything. Even your queen." I met his gaze evenly, searching his eyes for any kind of remorse. I felt a fresh ache in the scar tissue along my collarbone as I thought of Maura and wondered if he considered her such a sacrifice, and then his bishop swept in like a righteous figure of judgment to remove my queen from the board. "Fischer understood that."

I wouldn't last much longer. The book here had already been written. Elijah continued his relentless march, sacrificing a pawn so his bishop could roam free and harass my king from hiding. We were two moves away from checkmate when behind us, Mother Sophie rang the dinner bell, the sound summoning children from the snowy woods, the bedlam of their cries putting an end to any chance for us to finish. "You lucked out," I told Elijah. "I was just preparing my surprise comeback."

He didn't laugh. All the men had turned to Mother Sophie who stood in the center of the dwelling now, her voice raised to be heard above the children. She rang the bell again for quiet. "This bounty," she began, "must remind us of the One who provides. Every delicious morsel of this feast has been cooked by the old ways. Roasted over open flames or cooked in embers. Cooked the old ways because what was once old will be new at the turn of the year. We know what's coming, even if the rest of the world doesn't. God's judgment."

Someone shouted an amen. Freshly spared my doom in chess, I didn't imagine judgment as something to look forward to.

Mother Sophie's prayer went on: "'When I snuff you

out,' he writes in Ezekiel, 'I will cover the heavens and darken the stars.' So it shall be for the great cities of the earth. All the world going dark. Absolute night. And where will we be when this happens? Here on The Land. Here in our Place of Safety. Here, where we will keep the light of our faith burning by the old ways. By the Refiner's Fire. For it is written in the Book of Revelation that salvation and glory and power belong to our God, for his judgments are true and just."

After a chorus of amens, we formed a line ringing the shelter, picking up plates and silverware at one table and making our way from fire to fire as the women served the children first, then the men, and then each other. There is something about eating outdoors in the cold that makes you crave the food even more. Whole potatoes wrapped in tinfoil opened up, blossoming with steam, the nuggets melting butter into greasy rivers on the plates. The stuffing puffed fragrant clouds of sage and herbs, the turkey, piping hot from the flames, dripped with grease, a feast worthy of a pirate king, especially if you ended up with one of the fat turkey legs like me. For a time the conversation ebbed away while we savored our meal in the frigid air, eating quickly before the cold could claim it, our faces close to the plate.

I sat near Elijah and Bjorn, the board pushed aside with the soapstone pieces tucked away in velvet bags, like precious treasure. Mother Sophie sat at a neighboring table, Roland hovering at her elbow and pointing out where her food was located by positions of the clock. Sarah sat beside her instead of her father, Roland's sister Caroline on the other side. Caroline's eyes bored into mine as though she were jealous of my spot. This was the fourth time I'd run into her and each time I had the distinct impression she didn't like me. Caroline looked away from me, staring a long moment at Elijah, willing him to notice her. I wondered again what might be going on between them. He didn't return her gaze.

Something about Mother Sophie's prayer still bothered me. "So if Y2K happens," I said, "what's the next step?"

"You mean when," Elijah corrected, impaling a prong of dark meat on his fork, "and we don't really know."

"What if nothing happens?"

Elijah sliced open a buttermilk biscuit, releasing moist steam. He gobbled it in two bites and chased it with a gulp of milk. "Then we go on as we have before," he said, wiping his mouth on his Carhartt sleeve. "We trust in God's plan. Maybe it won't happen right at midnight. God has his own time."

That sounded to me like a person hedging his bets. What did Elijah really think was going to happen? What about the dynamite Brian had mentioned? And why had Bjorn joined them? I decided to keep pressing: "What I mean is what if the computers go haywire and there are blackouts and all that bad stuff Mother Sophie talked about. The worst. The star of Wormwood poisoning the waters of the earth and so on. What if all that happens and instead of chaos, people help one another?" I was about to add a bit about neighbors helping neighbors, to call attention to this gathering here that had brought so many different people together, ex-convicts and pastors and children.

I didn't get the chance because Bjorn barked with laughter. It was a shrill sound, half-hyena. He talked with his mouth open. Yellow biscuits crumbling between yellowing teeth. "He's never seen niggers riot, has he? Burning their own hoods. Even dogs know better than to piss in their own water bowls."

Elijah set his fork down and rested one hand on my shoulder. My bad shoulder again. I tried not to wince. "My God, do we have an actual optimist in our midst?" His voice was faintly derisive. "Meshach, I believe you have a misplaced faith in humanity."

"He doesn't know," Bjorn said, shaking his head. "There's a war coming. A war between the races. We're getting ready for war here, boy."

After that I stuck to my food, braving even Caroline's green bean casserole, though the beans had gummed into a cold, gluey paste on my plate. I listened in from time to time, my attention wandering, and I learned that Bjorn had just been released from Stillwater, and that there were other "bruisers" who would be out before the turn of the year, men from "The Order" who would be good to have around when things turned ugly. Elijah got up and left the table and I trailed after, not sure who to latch onto, as he talked with a group of rough-looking skinheads who'd shown up late. I fetched some pecan pie and readied to leave. I wouldn't find out any more today. Not with so many people around. After mixing with the skinheads, Elijah went over by Caroline where he must have told some joke that set her laughing, Caroline's face aglow when he slipped his arm around her shoulder.

"I got something for you to do," Roland said as he came up behind me, appearing out of nowhere. He hadn't been talking to me much lately, and I had the feeling he suspected me for a liar. He leaned forward, his fists on the table. "You like coming here, right? You know by now this isn't camp and we aren't playing. Everyone here serves some purpose."

I nodded, wondering what I was in for.

"So, I have some ideas about how to harness your particular skill set." He didn't say any more than that, watching my face for how I responded. "We need help getting the word out."

Here, I had a chance to walk away. They didn't know who I was yet or why I was here. I no longer had a death wish. I had my game at home. I had this strangely intimate relationship with Arwen that I didn't understand.

I had friends, a mother and father who loved me. Why chase after a woman who was gone or worse? Why, when the more I learned about these people, the more scared I should have become? "What do you need me to do?" I said.

A Sort
of Indoctrination

A few nights later Kaiser and I took a different path past the birches, cutting south where we found a small clearing. A light wind swirled powdery snow in serpentine patterns before us. Overhead the bell of heaven stretched over the open field, infinite stars ablaze above. Winter brought the stars so close to earth I imagined I could touch them like leaves. We strode among constellations. Orion. Taurus. Eridanus, the Celestial River. No wonder the Greeks thought the gods sojourned in such a territory, a limitless night sky of transformations. Who was I becoming? Which story was mine? I wanted to be Perseus, who must rescue Andromeda from the whale before he marries her. Perseus, who trails Cassiopeia across a winter sky without ever catching her, for all eternity.

Did you get away, Maura? You were so afraid. Why didn't you tell me about the money? Why didn't you tell me what you were really trying to do?

Looking up at the winter sky, in the cold, crystalline air, I swore I heard a celestial music, a distant ringing like a struck bell. I felt the rotation of the earth under my boots. All this brimming starlight made me fear the aura that precedes a migraine had distorted my vision. No mortal is meant to walk among the stars. Something unnameable bloomed within me:

A voice says, "Cry out."
And I said, "What shall I cry?"
All people are like grass,
and their faithfulness is like the flowers of the field.
The grass withers and the flowers fall,
because the breath of the Lord blows upon them.
Surely the people are grass.
The grass withers and the flowers fall,
but the word of our God endures forever.
You who bring good news to Zion,
go up on a high mountain.
You who bring good news to Jerusalem,
lift up your voice with a shout,
lift it up, do not be afraid;
say to the towns of Judah,
"Here is your God!"

That's from Isaiah, a passage I had committed to memory earlier in my room, hoping to impress Mother Sophie the next time I visited, a passage I had read again and again because I was drawn to it. As I walked under a canopy of winter stars, I wondered what it would be like to be the voice crying out in the wilderness, a voice to warn this world, to call others so they repented and saved themselves before the end. The church had offered me something I had never had before, a purpose and a strange sense of belonging, if I wanted it. Prophet they had called me, though really I was a fraud. This made me want something from this moment to be real even more, to carry with me if I made it through this winter. If the end of the year was not also the end of the world.

I moved through each day like a man in a feverish delirium. The belief system of the people of Rose of Sharon, their paranoia and fears, had infected my subconscious. In one opiate-induced dream I wandered a smoldering cityscape, Kaiser beside me, not knowing if I was the last person on earth. Above us the stars flashed and fell, and the ground below groaned and shook. Such thoughts and dreams worried me, a distraction from my true quest, to find out what had happened to Maura. Yet even as I gathered information I planned to use against them, I didn't want to see any of them get hurt. When the Feds raided the Weaver compound the guilty and innocent had been punished alike. Maybe I had been sent not as a prophet, but instead to talk some sense into them.

When I wasn't working on my game, I read the Bible Mother Sophie had given me up in my bedroom, certain that Arwen would mock me if she caught me paging through it. I didn't want to hear any of her objections. I wanted this reading all to myself, so I sank into the story, flipping through Mark and Matthew until my attention was fully arrested by the Book of John, the most poetic of the Gospels, God dwelling as a Word in the beginning before coming back to earth, a chapter packed with cinematic scenes: Christ at the well facing down the men who have come to stone a woman to death—"Let he among you who is without sin cast the first stone"—I imagined in a deep Charlton Heston voice-over, the high, whistling soundtrack of a spaghetti Western playing in the background, tumbleweeds blowing past as the elders drop their deadly projectiles. And you know what? It's a good story. I mean, it has to be if it's stuck around for two thousand years. I'd never taken the time to imagine it all before, Christ born in a stable, God entering the muck and mire of human existence in such a vulnerable form, hunted by Herod, a child-killer. The journey of the shepherds and the magi. The way the world should never have been the same. But the world was the same, all these millennia later. If it was true, then God had walked among us in human form and in our blindness and selfishness we nailed our Creator to the cross. I could believe in a story like that. I knew all there was about blindness and regret. What I didn't understand is why anyone thought this world was worth saving at all. Maybe it wasn't. Maybe two thousand years later it was time for the world to die.

I told myself I was just reading the Bible so I would have things to say to Mother Sophie and the rest, time to investigate my mystery. I read it expecting boredom, the tedious drone of a hundred lost mornings in Sunday school. I hadn't expected poetry, or to be moved by the stories I found within. I didn't know what was happening inside me.

ELIJAH'S VINTAGE AIRSTREAM WAS one of the largest trailers in the encampment, a glittering silvery oblong shape clenched between huge granite boulders like a bullet between teeth. Elijah was just stepping out of it as I made my way up to Mother Sophie's cabin after parking the Continental. He was dressed in quilted flannel and jeans, a coffee mug in one hand as he hailed me and called me over. "Just the man I was looking for," he said. "You want to join me for some coffee?"

I nodded and walked over. Mother Sophie hadn't set any direct time for our talks. I'd been coming nearly every day since Thanksgiving, and we sat down in her cabin whenever I showed up. She wouldn't mind. With Elijah gone so often on calls for his towing company, this was a rare opportunity.

Elijah ushered me into his trailer after apologizing for the mess. The table across the stove was covered in pamphlets and flyers along with a scattering of peanut shells that he brushed aside, not minding that some of the shells ended up on the linoleum floor, where caked boot prints marked out a path to a back bedroom. Elijah plucked up a rumpled sweatshirt from one padded seat at the table and bid me to sit down. He asked me if I objected to Sanka, since he was weaning himself from caffeine. A sharp, singed odor hung in the air; in the small sink I could see a pan of dried egg yolk soaking in suds. I set the Bible I'd carried in for my talk with Mother Sophie on the table and told him to add in plenty of sugar and cream.

The flyers before me had the words IT'S OKAY TO BE WHITE on one sheet and SAVE YOURSELF FROM CULTURAL MARXISM printed on another, along with the address for Rose of Sharon. I had a bad feeling that these flyers were part of Roland's plan for me, so I ignored them for now.

While he set a kettle of water on a tiny woodstove, crackling with heat, Elijah chatted on about his daughter, Sarah, off at a home school Caroline was running in one of the nearby trailers. I kept my face impassive, knowing that Maura would have ended up a co-teacher at the school, a fate she dreaded. She loved her daughter, but not other people's children so much.

There were reminders of her everywhere in this place. Alongside crayon drawings by Sarah, a photo of Maura and Elijah holding hands up in the mountains decorated the icebox, an endless desert plain stretching behind them, Elijah squinting into the sun. Maura looked young, deeply tanned, and—as much as it pained me to admit it—happy. I also spotted Maura's black guitar case—plastered with stickers from coffee shop folk artists such as Ani DiFranco, Emmylou Harris, and the Indigo Girls—propped against a wall by the bathroom door. Looking at it, I remembered her own lullaby, how it had been supposed to call the fox away. I could hear her voice, faintly smoky, if I shut my eyes.

Now here I am in the fox's den, but where are you, Maura? Would you have really abandoned your music as well as your daughter?

I knew that had been one of her daydreams, to get back to the desert, a place where she would never be cold or deal with snow again, because "you don't have to shovel sunshine," she'd said. A place where she could work on her music, maybe even record an album one day. A place where she would be free of him. She would tell me this and then with a toss of her hair dismiss it all again.

Maura's presence was everywhere in this room. The ghost of her sandalwood perfume, like she had just been here and gone, drifted in the undercurrent of more pungent odors, the wood burning in the stove, scorched eggs in the sink, and the musk and souring hopes of a man who had some kind of nervous breakdown, if what Mother Sophie had said was true.

A few months before she left, Maura had cut her hair pixie style. The first time I walked in the back break room and saw her, I'd done a double take. "Whoa," I said.

"You don't like it?" Maura had watched my face, her eyebrows arched, her cheeks brightened with a splash of rouge. The short haircut accentuated her bright, hazel eyes.

"I do," I said, stepping closer. "It brings out your eyes. You look like Dorothy Parker."

"I was going for a young Joan Baez."

"Who?"

Maura smiled tentatively. "I'm guessing neither of us knows who the other is talking about. Fair's fair."

I stepped closer. "Dorothy Parker wrote this poem called 'Flappers' during the Jazz Age." I searched my mind, trying to recall how it went. "Her golden rule is plain enough / Just get them young / and treat them rough."

Maura didn't laugh and despite her brave new haircut, her transformation, she appeared nervous and uncertain. "I think she and Joan Baez would have gotten along just fine." She ran her hands through her hair, revealing one elfish ear. "And, I do feel like a new person. Like anything is possible. Elijah hates it. He's so pissed he won't even speak to me."

"Forget him," I said, thinking he must be the source of her distress. I looked up at the lobby cameras to make sure the other two tellers, Dorothy and an older woman named Monica, were engaged in transactions. "I think you're even more beautiful now."

I leaned in for a kiss, but Maura put a restraining hand on my chest. "Not now. I'm wearing lipstick. And if I don't get back out there soon, they'll get suspicious." She sighed. There was no sparkle of flirtation in her eyes, her voice drained of emotion. "Listen, Lucien. I need a friend more than anything right now. For so long, I've been trapped. Like there's no way out, but I think I know what I need to do now. I'm going to make my break."

My heartbeat quickened. Was she talking about divorce? Would this make it possible for us to start a relationship? I wanted so badly to hold her again.

"And when I do," she continued in a soft voice. "We won't be able to be together."

"What?" This jolted me.

"If it comes out that we were together, Elijah will use it against me in court." She spoke a low rush, her words hurried. "He will take Sarah away from me. I won't let that happen." She glanced away from me at the cameras and chewed on her lower lip. Her hands remained on my chest, near my beating heart. "You have so much life ahead of you. There are things you can only experience once for the first time. Like having a child. It's the most powerful, life-changing moment I can imagine. You need to be with someone who hasn't felt all that before, so you can experience it together. You only get one chance to be new. It's a gift."

Even as she held a hand against my heart, I pressed against her at hip level. She didn't pull away. "I don't care about any of that," I said. "I want you."

"You don't get it," she said, but her eyes were luminous. She pressed her face against my chest, sighing, her body relaxing against mine. She loved me, too. I felt it in the sweetness of her touch. "What am I to do with you?" I felt her quiet laughter against my chest. "I have to go. You, however, might need to stay here a few minutes. Just until that tent in your slacks lowers."

Elijah set the mugs down and then got out a wooden chessboard from another cabinet, the elegant soapstone pieces nestled in their black velvet bags. "You got time for a game?"

"Sure," I said, pleasantly surprised that he'd remembered. "But I get to be black this time."

Elijah handed me one of the bags and shook out his pieces. "We'll start from the beginning. We never did get a chance to finish our other game. I've been thinking about it since."

We arranged the pieces and when he opened with his white pawns to C3 and D4, I responded with Benoni, the Son of Sorrow, just like Bobby Fischer, one pawn to C5, my knight challenging, and going fianchetto with my bishop on the kingside.

Elijah wagged a finger. "This is why I like having you around," he said. He took a long time deliberating his next move. He would need to establish outposts on the C6 and E6 squares. My job was to get those lanes open for my bishops and to avoid trading them early. He didn't play with any chess clock, so this meant each of us had as much time as we wanted for moves, and Elijah proved to be a slow, methodical player, cracking open more peanut shells between moves.

My attention wandered, usually my fatal weakness in matches. The best chess players can envision the entire board three moves ahead, all the various possibilities spanning out in their brains. On my high school team, our top board had been a guy with Asperger's, and he could bring his full mind onto the board, shutting out everything else around him with a concentration so complete he nearly stopped breathing. I moved in the moment, by comparison, hoping for my opponent to make a mistake.

The shelf across from us was stacked with paperback Westerns, most of them by Louis L'Amour or Zane Grey. While Elijah deliberated I picked up a copy of *The Lonesome Gods* and flipped through it until I came across a heavily creased page with an underlined passage about how intuition is a higher form of knowledge, one that connects us to lost gods and the ancients who walked these lands before us. Touching the scored words, I knew Elijah was a mystic. "This is good stuff," I said, thinking of my nightly sojourn under the stars with Kaiser. How I imagined being the voice in the wilderness.

"It's one of my all-time favorite books," Elijah said, when I looked up from the page. "It's the one that gave me the strength to break away from home and family and set out on my own path. I thought I was being led by intuition, like Vernon in the novel. My parents had lost their way, forgotten the strength and purity of our Anglo-Saxon heritage." As he said this he moved his knight to put pressure on the D5 square, a move I was anticipating.

"Your parents didn't agree?"

"Oh no," Elijah said. "My dad taught math at the local junior high. They didn't know what to do with me. In those days, I thought my anger was my strength." He studied the board, his hands under his chin. "What's your last name, Meshach?"

"Swenson," I said automatically. I didn't see any reason to lie about this.

Outside, we heard heavy footsteps, boots crunching through snow. I wondered who was coming this way, but Elijah didn't even look up from the board.

"Swenson makes you Scandinavian, a descendant of Vikings. A conqueror like Bjorn. Roland will be pleased to hear it." I found it curious he didn't say whether or not it mattered to him. A knock came at the door a moment later. "I don't think we'll get a chance to finish this game, either," he said. "Roland's going to want to talk to you about these here flyers."

I felt a sinking disappointment. Here I was playing chess with a violent ex-convict, a known neo-Nazi, a man I had cuckolded, and I was enjoying his company. *He's the enemy*, I reminded myself, *you're not supposed to like him*. The flyers had been shoved aside for the chessboard and I'd been doing my best to ignore them. "I thought my anger was my strength," Elijah said, his eyes studying the board as if memorizing it so we could continue the game later. "But I was wrong." The knock came again and Elijah looked up and met my eyes. "He's going to ask something of you. But you don't have to do it. Understand?"

I was too surprised to say anything before Elijah got up from the table to let Roland inside. Roland stopped to warm his hands over Elijah's woodstove before neatly folding his coat over a chair nearby. Waves of cold still radiated off him when he squeezed in beside me at the small table. While Elijah put away the chess pieces, Roland traded the copy of *The Lonesome Gods* I had been paging through for a book of his own, laying it before me. With a cover the dull red of drying blood, his paperback copy of *The Turner Diaries* didn't look like much at first glance.

"This book will tell you what we're all about here."

I gestured at the Bible I'd brought along. "I'm already meeting with Mother Sophie to talk about the book of Isaiah."

"That's good," Roland said, "but this here is another kind of instructional book. Mother Sophie tells me you're between jobs."

"You could put it that way," I said. I opened his book and saw where someone had printed the words *We must secure the existence of our people and a future for white children* in block letters on the inner leaf. Fourteen words in all. I would soon learn that these were *the fourteen words* around which they based their mission here on The Land. I shut it for now and studied the front and back cover.

On the back the slogan *What Will You Do When They Come to Take Your Guns?* was printed in bold black letters. On the front cover a young man and woman crouched behind a fence. She clutched an assault rifle while he squatted with the twelve-gauge up against his shoulder. On the other side of the fence an oblivious cop approached while behind him a squad car with the words EQUALITY POLICE was just pulling into an alley.

The book looked tawdry and self-published, but looking at it also filled me with foreboding. I was about to go in deeper with these people. Is that what Elijah had tried to warn me about before Roland came in? Why?

Elijah tapped the front cover. "That was me and her, right there. My Maura. We were going to upend the system."

"Maura?" I said. I didn't ever think she had shared his sympathies. Those few people of color we had for customers she had treated with a cold equanimity, "Your wife?" In the few times I'd been around him he rarely mentioned her. This was another strange thing to me, how Elijah could be so completely different around different people. Around me, he turned contemplative, but Roland or Bjorn brought out his aggressive side.

"She was, yeah."

Was? Holy shit. "What happened to her?"

Elijah sipped from his Sanka, which must have gone cold by now. "She stopped believing," he said.

"You take that book home with you. I want to know what you think." Roland interrupted my train of thought. He reached around me and picked up the flyers. "If you're between jobs, then maybe you can help us get the word out. You think you can hang these up on campus?"

I accepted the flyers, glancing once more at the words. I didn't see anything offensive in it. It was true, right? There wasn't anything wrong with *being* white. As for the other one, I had only vague notions of what they meant by cultural Marxism. Weren't these ordinary thoughts most Americans held to be true? My upbringing had certainly raised me to hate "pinko commies," as my uncle Nolan called them.

Elijah studied me across the table. "They find out you're the one spreading those and it's all over for you at school."

"Don't scare the kid," Roland said, shaking his head.

"He needs to know how the world treats people like us. There's always a price for things. He needs to know that there will be a price."

"I do know," I said, making up my mind. I knew better the price than he realized. They were testing me here and I had to prove myself. If I could prove myself, I could keep coming to The Land. Then I might get the answers I longed for. For those answers I would pay anything. Distributing these flyers didn't seem like too much to ask. "I'll put these up if you think it will do some good."

"Getting the word out always does good," Roland said. "These pamphlets might look like a joke to some people. But they will rile up discussion. The kind of discussion your politically correct professors won't care for. The kind that might bring the right kind of people our way."

"Just don't push things too far," Elijah said.

Roland put his arm around me and scowled across at Elijah. I also didn't understand his concern. Did Elijah doubt me, or was he trying to protect me? I didn't know, but I vowed that if he had something to do with

Maura's going missing, I would make sure he paid a price as well.

"I hate censorship," I said. "I can't stand it. A university should be a place where people debate ideas freely." I held the flyers to me, met Elijah's hard gaze. I had halfway convinced myself what I was saying was true. "Maybe they need to hear this message."

ON THE WAY TO campus I passed the looming facade of the Aurora Bay State Hospital, which looked like an old mansion from the front, all red brick neo-Georgian revival, the modern facilities spanning out behind, concrete and gray and lacking any character. I wheeled my Continental around at the next intersection. I may have been given a task, but I had another mission. If you lose something, one of the best things you can do is return to where you lost it. This was where I had lost a person, the sight of her vanishing.

I pulled around back, the circular drive where the ambulances roll patients into the emergency room by gurney. I parked against the curb, across the street, where Maura had asked me to drop her off that night. My engine rumbling, I sat in the car and shut my eyes, remembering. The rain drumming on the roof, the low murmur of the radio, and Maura's tremulous voice. "I can make it on my own. You can't go in with me. You can't." Her face ashen — tight with pain — as she urged me to leave her. The last glimpse I had of her, standing under a streetlamp, her handbag clutched against her belly.

And I had driven away and not a mile from here my Civic hydroplaned right through a stop sign and a kid in a pickup plowed into me. Ten days later, when I could walk again, I had made a habit of going downstairs to quiz the night shift staff if anyone had seen Maura enter the hospital, but none remembered a woman matching my dazed description.

I thought I knew why she didn't go in, not with five thousand in stolen bills burning a hole in her handbag. But where else could she go for help if she had miscarried? And why had she been so afraid?

I stood where she had stood, watching a past version of myself drive off into the rain. Below me, the steeply sloping street dropped away toward Aurora Bay. Wind hurried high clouds across the water, and the sun speared through in silver shafts and the bay burned like molten gold where light touched water. Beyond, the vastness of Lake Superior brewed with squalls of snow, a darkness shimmying this way in skirts. I imagined this inland sea, the burying ground for many shipwrecks, as a great, breathing thing. The swirling clouds snuffed the last of the sun as the first fat flakes flew past. Maura had not gone this way.

In the other direction, I walked where she must have walked that night, and when I saw it on a shelf of land above me I stopped in my tracks. A square, homely structure with a glass windbreak. A bus stop. It gleamed there, a beacon of safety. Of course. Maura was so smart, so resourceful. She might have been driven by desperation to steal, but she was a planner.

The wind whipped more flakes past me, a thickening snow flying horizontal. I wanted to keep going, to climb the hill and sit on that bench in the shelter, as surely Maura must have sat, waiting for the warm bus to fan open its doors like great gills, a behemoth that swallowed her whole, like Jonah, and carried her elsewhere.

Surely it must be so. It had to be. Behind me the bay frothed and the hospital that had been my prison glowered, a facade of concrete and blank-eyed windows.

Tell me you got away from all of this, Maura. Tell me you made it. I know you did.

I couldn't go any farther. Before the storm intensified, I had a job to do. If Maura had gotten away, she might come back. I needed to stick with these people. I needed to know more. I knew that Roland would find some way to check up on me. I limped back to my car and drove away. I needed to make it to campus at a time when classes would be in session, to make sure no one saw me. I needed to go now.

Stranger in
a Strange Land

I continued on to campus, my first time returning since my shaming in front of my biology class. Roland had copied two dozen of each flyer. Before I left he gave me a circle of Scotch tape and a small box of thumbtacks, which rattled on the passenger seat beside me now. I felt my vision narrowing, casting the falling snow in a blue light. My aura had returned. Sometimes these auras could last for a day before the migraine struck, and when it did it would be a doozy. I didn't know why the migraines were coming more frequently. I was supposed to be healing, but the dark wings of a migraine, ever present, beat at the edges of my sight.

By the time I made it to NMSU the clock radio read 2:45, which meant classes would let out soon. I considered if it would be better to hang up the flyers among the milling masses hustling between classes, their shoulders burdened by backpacks heavy with textbooks, or to wait until 3:00 when everyone was safely in their classrooms. I decided on the latter. I was doing this so I would continue being accepted by the people of Rose of Sharon, a new recruit, but I sure as hell didn't want to get caught. Elijah was right about that. My time at Northern might already be done, but any further black marks on my academic record might quash any hope of ever finishing my degree.

So I was tempted to open my window and just toss the papers right out here in the parking lot, or drop them into the dumpster where they belonged, but I felt certain Roland had assigned me this task because he was testing me. If I succeeded, we might make the news. Stirring up the hornets' nest was part of the goal, he told me. That way we might draw others with our "sensibilities" from out of the shadows to join us. I just didn't want my name linked with these stories, didn't ever want to have to try explaining this to my mother, or anyone else I loved. Yet, were the messages really so wrong? Why shouldn't white people take pride in their heritage?

A few minutes before 3:00 I left my vehicle and crossed the icy parking lot, trying not to slip, the flyers bundled inside in my coat. My eyes watered, the world around me soaked in aquamarine light, and I knew this wasn't from the cold. The most intense migraines were like being dunked deep underwater, intensifying pressure that made it feel like my frontal lobe was going to explode, all while being held under by an unforgiving hand. It was coming.

I penguin-walked my way across icy patches in the parking lot where the wind-whipped snow gathered, and ducked inside the first brick building, which happened to be the largest and oldest on campus, Zebulon Hall, where even now someone in admin was likely processing academic suspensions, the dim green monitor spelling out fates for students like me. At this drowsy hour in the middle of the afternoon there were few people about, so I managed to pin the flyers to bulletin boards on the lower levels, passing only a couple of maintenance guys in the hall. From Zebulon, I made my way to Jackson and Patterson Hall and then to the science building and the MLK Library. Whenever I passed newspaper stands for the campus paper, *The Voyageur*, I slipped flyers on top of copies, aware of the irony that this very paper might be carrying a news story about us in the coming days.

I knew I only had about ten minutes before classes let out. I was down to a handful of the flyers and should have cut my losses, but I am nothing if not dedicated. So I kept going within the MLK Library, pinning two to a bulletin board right outside the front entrance. A librarian with a frizzy brown perm, a woman so short only her head peeped above the counter, watched me curiously.

I doubted she could read the words from her distance, about twenty feet away, but there must have been something suspicious about my presence, my boots squeaking on the marble floor. "Young man," she said, without approaching. "You need to get those stamped by Student Life before you hang them up. Otherwise, they'll get taken right down."

"Sure thing," I called out. "I'll do that." I bundled the rest against my coat, my hands shaking, and hurried away, hoping she didn't notice I'd left them up. My head down, my hands tucked in my coat along with the remaining flyers, I was so intent on getting out of there, I didn't see him until I nearly ran right into him.

Noah loomed before me, alone in the halls. Rarely was this man ever alone—Noah one of those extroverts who couldn't stand to be by himself for more than a few minutes. I stopped so suddenly that I lost my grip on a few of the flyers, and to my horror they fluttered out before me, landing at his feet.

Noah's face broke into a wide grin. "Are you going to throw confetti at me every time I run into you?" He bent to pick up the pages. I watched his face, watched as his smile vanished as if he'd just swallowed something bitter. Wormwood on the tongue. "Lucien? What's this?"

"Hey, Noah." My face flushed with heat. I felt like a kid caught looking at porn by his mother. That sense of wrongness was quickly followed by a contradictory sense of outrage, at myself and at Noah for intruding into my life once again. "It doesn't mean anything."

He looked back down at the pages he held, his lips moving as if puzzling over the words.

"Just give those back," I said, my face coloring. I could have told him that it was all an act and I was only pretending, so I could investigate the people of Rose of Sharon. Noah knew some of my situation. But I was tired of explaining myself, weary of justifications. "There's nothing wrong with either of those messages."

"This is like . . . it's like some kind of white supremacist shit," he said. As he spoke the aura surrounded Noah, haloing him like a dark angel. His low voice rumbled out. "I mean, what the actual fuck? Are you one of them now?"

"So what if I am?" I shuffled my feet, looked away. "I mean, you're half white, too. Why not be proud of who you are?"

Noah looked at me the way he would at something unpleasant caught between the treads of his shoes. Classes had let out so a crowd of students were coming our way. Noah, with his feet planted firmly in the middle of the hall, practically barred the way. His lips peeled back to show his teeth. "You think you can say that because my mother is white? Because of some fucking percentage? People aren't percentages. I'm black. You have black skin, that makes you black. Christ, Lucien."

"There's nothing wrong with having pride in your heritage," I said, parroting one of Roland's lines. The words sounded hollow. The students began to stream around Noah and me in the hallway, edging around us cautiously.

I'd never seen him angry before, his nostrils flaring, and I thought for a moment he might hit me. I could feel others in that hallway turning toward me—obviously wondering if there was going to be a fight—and I dropped my eyes, my defiance leaking out. I wanted him to run into me, to shove me against the wall, let him show his anger. But when I looked up again, tears slid down his cheeks. His tears shocked me worse than any blow. He let the flyers he held drift to the ground. "You're not worth it," he said. "I can't believe I ever thought you were."

I felt rather than saw Noah move past me, and as he walked past without touching me, his indifference hurt worse than any violence. Maybe violence was what I craved. I wanted someone to hurt me. I wanted enough pain to fill up the great hollow space inside me I had felt ever since Maura vanished.

No one stopped to pick up any of the pages. I left them where they fell.

After the long, cold walk to my car, I sat behind the wheel with the heater on full blast. Already my vision was pinching down to a dark and narrow eventuality.

The migraine was going to hit soon, like a storm grinding out from the furthest corner of my mind. Solar flares and dark wings. I fished in my glove box for the spare sumatriptan I kept there and came up empty. I started the car, gunned the engine, and left Northern for what I hoped was the last time. The cassette player hummed with Morrissey's "Everyday Is Like Sunday," ordinarily suitable for my dreary mood.

I didn't realize until halfway into the drive that I wasn't heading home — not to the place where I lived with a mysterious girl and a geriatric German shepherd — but toward The Land, toward the people who had just alienated me from one of my few remaining friends, toward a place where I didn't have any medicine or bulwark against the coming pain. Morrissey crooned from the speakers. I shut him off before the music made things worse. The first boiling dark wave was coming and I didn't know if I could make it the whole way.

By THE TIME I made it inside Mother Sophie's cabin, I'd already vomited once, so intense was the pain in my skull, emanating to every part of my body. Elijah had just been backing out his tow truck when he saw me pull into the rough lot, parking sideways. I don't remember the drive there, but I remember how he took me by the arm and helped me up the hill to Mother Sophie's cabin.

Half-blinded by pain, I only saw the silhouettes of

people hovering around me. Elijah set me on the couch and then Mother Sophie floated over me, the white nimbus of her hair like a cloud. Some of my vomit had dribbled and dried on my shirt collar. I smelled it against my skin. When another wave of pain wracked me, spikes driving into my forehead, I twisted there on the couch. I may have even cried out. I don't know.

What I know is that I felt her hands, sure and steady, part the hair on my crown. She pressed down with her thumbs, hard as if trying to drive the pain from my head, and then I heard a distant murmur as she began to pray in an unearthly tongue I have never heard again since.

The pain was like an explosion behind my eyeballs, a blizzard of snow and shadows. My throat burned. It felt like the only thing holding together my skull was the pressure of Mother Sophie's hands. She went on speaking in tongues, sometimes using English to call on the Holy Spirit and the healing hand of God. My mind was full of dark beating wings. I had a vision of that day in the woods with the ravens, driven mad by the voice of the Enemy, but this time Mother Sophie stood beside me. The birds whirled all around us, a maelstrom of death, but she was there, too, and I clung to her as the Enemy called out for me, and the birds, their beaks like blades, could not touch us.

I don't know how long she prayed for me, but I heard a crack in my brain, an audible snapping sound, a void opening that I might fall into if a hand did not hold my own, and in my mind's eye the storm passed and the last survivors of the raven massacre were climbing those ladders of clouds into heaven and she was there with me, untouched in the carnage, and then I could see again, and I could breathe again, and the pain was gone. Not just gone, but wiped clean. I felt a freedom from pain so pure and total that I wanted to weep. I gasped.

"Mother Sophie," I said, because her hands were still pressed against the crown of my head, "it's okay. I'm fine now."

She stepped away from me. When my eyes focused, I saw Elijah was still there in the room. "I'll get you some water," he said and he went over to the tap.

"I get migraines, sometimes," I said. "Pain so bad I black out." I swallowed dryly. I was afraid of talking about the migraines too much, afraid their mere mention would cause the pain to come back.

"I felt something else inside you, child," Mother Sophie. "A darkness that needed tending."

I remembered that sense of evil I'd felt watching the birds kill each other. A supernatural darkness that reached for my mind. I had been haunted by a demon and now that demon was gone? Impossible. But how could I explain that I was sitting up on the couch, clear-eyed and free of pain? When my migraines hit, they could last for days. They didn't just suddenly vanish, and the most powerful of my medicines sometimes only blunted the edges of pain. She had healed me. She had called upon God and made me whole.

"I can't feel any pain," I said. "It's gone. Is this a miracle?"

Mother Sophie rubbed her hands together and spread them out, palms up, her smile beatific. Elijah, still dressed in his work coveralls, who surely must have ignored the call to watch over me, sat down beside me and handed me the glass of water. "Do you want to keep praying?"

I drank thirstily. "About what? I feel fine. Better than fine."

He leaned forward and there was an eagerness in his expression that looked nearly like hunger or thirst. In time I would understand. A new believer is like wine poured into a golden chalice. They carry with them the flush and fire of pure faith, undiluted by doubt. It's a little like falling in love for the first time. Old believers, those more mature or wise in the faith, only get rare glimpses, an occasional reminder during an inspired moment of worship, but with new believers they can drink again from the chalice and remember afresh what it means to be reborn.

"Your body and mind are fine," he said. "It's your soul I'm talking about. Your relationship with God. I'm asking if you want to be saved."

There were tears in my eyes, so relieved I was to be

free from the migraines. Please God, let this be real. How could I possibly say no to the chance of being reborn? Who hasn't wanted to be carried, whole and unbruised, from the wreckage of their lives?

I DIDN'T RETURN TO the house until early afternoon the next day. After praying with Elijah and Mother Sophie, I ate dinner with them and ended up sleeping on one of the floral sofas in Mother Sophie's cabin. We had talked a lot about my newfound faith and the Bible, and from Mother Sophie I learned some of the more bizarre tenets of their particular sect, such as how they considered themselves the "true Jews," while the Zionists who controlled our media and our government were the spawn of Satan and had been oppressing us for centuries.

I didn't want to hear any of this from her. I wanted the poetry I had discovered in Isaiah, the healing of my mind. The more she talked the more I doubted the miracle of my own healing. When I prayed with her and Elijah for my personal salvation I had longed to feel something. God's presence like light at the base of my spine. An assurance that I was not alone in the universe. But what I felt was nothing. Nothing at all. Zero. Zilch. Nada. And that sense of nothingness was incredibly frustrating because in that moment I wanted to know God, the Maker who had taken away my pain.

In the kitchen with Arwen later that afternoon I tried to make sense of it while she busied herself making a peanut-butter-banana-mayonnaise-raisin sandwich on toasted oat bread. Arwen hadn't slept well the night before, up worrying about my absence, and she listened quietly while I spoke.

"So you think it was some kind of miracle?" she said with her back to me while she whisked the mayonnaise and peanut butter in a separate bowl.

"How else would you explain it?"

Arwen gave a small shrug, not bothering to turn around. I told her about my salvation and waited for her to mock me. She didn't. She didn't say anything at all. She carried over two plates with thick sandwiches cut into triangle slices, banana chunks spilling out. I got up to pour us each a cold glass of milk and then rejoined her at the table.

Neither of us ate right away. "You don't have anything to say?" I asked.

Arwen gave another small shrug. "Why does it matter whether you felt anything? Feelings come and go. They don't make a thing real or not."

I scratched at the two-day-old stubble on my chin. "I have this sense that faith is a matter of intuition and not intellect. So the feelings matter."

Again, she didn't say anything. I hadn't told her about my public humiliation at Northern. I had already lost one friend. I didn't want to lose another.

"I find myself in a curious state of doubt," I said.

"That would describe most of us," Arwen said, "except those people at your church."

It even described some of them, I thought, thinking of Elijah and how he'd remained silent while Mother Sophie talked about Jews belonging to the devil. "No, I mean about this sandwich you've fixed me here. I'm having trouble understanding the dubious decision to add mayonnaise. It feels like a mistake, the way you can ruin pizza by adding anchovies . . . or the 1988 movie *Cocktail*, starring Tom Cruise . . . or Hitler's decision to invade the Soviet Union in World War II."

Arwen raised one eyebrow. "Try it," she said.

I hadn't eaten breakfast, so despite my doubts I raised the toasted bread to my lips, inhaling the scent of banana. I held the sandwich poised there and looked at Arwen over the top of it. Was this a trick? Mayonnaise and peanut butter were an unholy union. I nibbled cautiously. The taste did not immediately repel. I took a larger bite and chewed. "Huh," I said, after swallowing.

"I know," she said.

"I didn't say it was good. The textures are . . . interesting." I kept eating.

"The mayonnaise, right?" Arwen said, between bites of her own. "It's like the secret sauce at Jack in the Box."

"It *is* like that. Exactly."

"It adds just a touch of sourness," she went on, covering

her mouth with one hand. "A hint of it at the back of your tongue to balance the sweetness. Plus, it makes the peanut butter creamier."

"How have I gone through this life without fully understanding the wonders of mayonnaise?"

Arwen smiled and took a drink of her milk. "You don't have to eat the rest," she said.

"Here's the thing," I said. "I do like it. Before the world ends, more people need to know about the invention of this sandwich."

We continued to eat in companionable quiet. I drew in a heavy breath. I could have told her about Noah, but there was something pressing on me even more. If Arwen was my sole remaining friend, I needed to be straight with her. So instead I told her what I'd seen a few days before, the stag and Kaiser giving chase and the cemetery at the edge of the world. "There was a grave there," I finished, pausing before the words tumbled out. "With your name on it."

"Ah," she said, dabbing at her lips with a napkin. "That explains your strange comments when your friend visited. So, that would make me what, a ghost or a liar?"

"Not a ghost," I said.

"So you read the name, but what about the dates on the stone?"

I thought back, trying to remember. "It was half buried in a snowdrift. I don't think I could read the date."

Arwen folded her napkin and dropped it on top of her last remaining triangle, her appetite apparently gone. "Albert had a little sister named Arwen. He cherished her. She was only four years old when she followed him down to the river. He turned away for just a moment, looking for the perfect skipping stone. When he turned back she was out in the river, balancing on a boulder. One slip and that was it. The current took her away. They didn't find her body until the next day."

"Shit. I'm sorry."

Arwen stood and picked up her plate and glass, her eyes distant as she looked out the window, where it had begun to snow again. "It's okay. I do feel like a ghost some of the time. Or someone haunted by one. I imagine her out there in the night, this drowned little girl. Water drips from her hair and fingernails. Her skin is wrinkled and gray, the way it gets if you spend too long in the tub. She calls my name. Our name. She's so lonely and cold. And sometimes, I feel like she's inside me, like she's found her way into me. A voice whispering that's not my own." Arwen forced a laugh, either trying to make light of her spooky story or to recover some of the lost mirth between us. "That doesn't make any sense, does it? But now you know why my dad is so incredibly disappointed to see the woman his Arwen grew up to become."

She turned and headed downstairs. When I finished my sandwich, I followed her.

In the den Arwen sat with her legs crossed reading from the *Gemäldegalerie Linz*. A scrap of yellowed paper had slipped from the book. I picked it up and held it in my palm, the thin paper fragile as a leaf, the words *Berghof, May 4, 1945* written in a smear of lead pencil. Arwen had the book open in her lap, the page showing an expressionist painting of a nude couple sprawled together in the woods, their intertwined limbs green-tinted and blending with the vines and branches around them. Arwen was watching my face.

"Berghof," I said. "This came from the war."

She nodded and returned her attention to the artwork. "You're putting it together."

Linz, she had told me. For a museum that *was to be built*. "Hitler was from Austria."

"Most of the artwork in this book was stolen by the Nazis for a museum Hitler planned to build in his hometown. The ones they deemed 'degenerate' they burned. Some of the art they stole has never been recovered." Arwen told the story in a somber, measured tone, tracing the voluptuous lines of the lovers on the page rather than looking at me. "My great uncle brought this back from the war. They had already lost one brother, in Ardennes. So he stole it really, from Berghof, one of Hitler's residences the Allies captured after the fighting was done. Before he died he passed it along to my father, a souvenir from the war."

"It must be worth a lot—"

"Priceless," Arwen said, glancing my way. "This is Albert Kroll's most cherished possession. He takes it out to look at every night. Holds it like a child. But it doesn't belong here. As I don't belong here."

She went back to paging through the book, her shoulders hunched, so I left her alone. In my room, I read from *The Turner Diaries*, the book Roland had given me. Between my reading and the revelations about the stolen art in the album, I grew anxious. *She stopped believing*, Elijah had said about Maura. *Was* my wife.

If you read *The Turner Diaries* you know what happens to those who stop believing. Early on in the novel a young woman is executed for sleeping with a black man, a placard with the words RACE TRAITOR hung around her neck. This is just one of many violent, disturbing incidents in a novel that ends with a group of white rebels gaining power over the planet, but only with the help of nuclear weapons used to annihilate other races. I felt a burning in my chest while reading it and remembering my conflict with Noah in the halls, a pressure building behind my eyes. *The Turner Diaries* was poorly written, the prose amateurish, but the story infected me with a sense of paranoia that seeped from the pages into my fingertips and into my sleep and dreams. It wasn't just that there was a race war coming. The novel showed me that the races were already at war and I'd been on the losing side all this time. And things were about to get much worse, the book insisted, a sibilant whisper vibrating inside my head. Which side will you choose when the time comes? I let that whisper linger, resisted stamping it out.

LATER THAT NIGHT I woke when I felt a cool breeze, a floating of the sheet as Arwen slipped beside me in the bed, bringing with her the aroma of crushed leaves and cloves, earth and pinesap and rain. "Do you mind sharing your bed with a ghost?" she said.

"Not at all," I said in a sleepy voice. I was still half-awake anyway. "Most of my previous companions have been of . . . a phantasmagorical nature."

"I'll bet," she said. She lay down in her dark nightie, so that only a few inches and the barest covering of nylon and cotton separated us.

"I don't know anything about you," I said, after she'd settled in against her pillow, in case she was tempted to turn over and go right to sleep again. "Tell me a story."

"Once upon a time," she began, "there was this guy who asked too many questions. It got him into all kinds of trouble."

"I don't like this story," I said. "The protagonist sounds like a jackass. I want a story about you."

Arwen sighed.

"Something real."

She made a soft, irritated *pfft!* sound as if there was

any other kind of story she might tell. She turned over so she faced me, her eyes unreadable in the dark. "Okay," she said. "When I was a little girl I thought I could heal with a touch. Plants, animals, even other people. I think I got the idea from gardening with my mom. She must have said something about me having a green thumb and I just took the idea and ran with it."

"Arwen and Her Magic Green Thumb. This is good stuff. Maybe I should write it down."

"No more interruptions, wise guy. So anyhow, I thought I had some kind of secret healing power. When a friend fell at recess and scraped her knee, I pressed my finger into her wound and it stopped bleeding. I thought it was my magic that did it. I imagined this healing traveling down through the tips of my fingers into places that hurt. I thought I could heal anything . . ." Arwen's voice trailed off.

"And?"

"That's the story. You're the guy who doesn't like spoiled endings, right?"

"Yeah, but . . ."

Arwen placed her hand over my mouth, shushing me. In the dark she traced my cheekbones, her thumb against my lips. "You have a nice face," she said. "An honest face."

I thought of all my accumulated lies. Noah's tears as he let the flyers fall away. My phony salvation and the scam I was running with Mother Sophie's people. My affair with a married woman. I wasn't a good person. I don't know what I was anymore.

"Show me where you hurt." Her cool breath washed over me.

"Uh, where? All over." Yet pain was the furthest thing from my mind. She hadn't touched me like this before and it took me by surprise. Her hands in my hair, her face close enough to kiss. I felt my body waking up under her touch, the feel of skin on skin. I had thought it would be a long, long time before I felt such things again.

"From the accident. Where are your scars?"

"My collarbone. It's held together with silicone screws."

Her fingers traced the line of bone, lingering over the puckered skin where they'd cut me open.

"I can't heal you like that old woman," Arwen said. "Though I wish I could. I'm not a little girl anymore who believes in healing or magic. I don't know anything about prayer or God or miracles, and I'm suspicious of anyone who claims to know the truth of these things. I can't heal you, Lucien, but I can know you. I'd like to know you. Where else were you hurt?"

"I broke three ribs. Punctured a lung." Her hand traveled there, sliding down my side without my directing. Instead of the old wound underneath, I felt something else. My body alive under the grace of her hands, every cell awake. It might not have been a healing, but it felt good.

"This hurt?"

"Not so much anymore."

"Where else?"

I didn't know what to say at first. How far was this going to go? Was I betraying Maura, my first love? The people at Rose of Sharon who believed in me?

But Maura wasn't here, so this was not a difficult decision to make. For one furious moment I could let all my wondering cease. Arwen repeated her question.

"Surgeon had to rebuild my hip," I said. "I'm like Lee Majors."

"If you say so," she said. Her hand rested on my hip, a danger zone, since she had to sense what jutted through the vent in my boxers. Her hand lingered there, tracing slow, concentric circles.

"Where else?"

"I already told you I'm not right in the head."

"Who is?" She laughed softly. Then, Arwen moved closer and her mouth found mine and she took me in her hand, tracing the length without speaking. "You don't happen to have any protection, do you?"

Ordinarily, I might have reflected on how that question had several levels, including metaphorical ones, but the thought and speech centers in my brain were difficult to access. I wanted to tell her I hadn't ever been with anyone else but Maura before. "No," I said. "Maybe we shouldn't?" I didn't think my newfound friends at Rose of Sharon would approve of such a midnight rendezvous. In just a couple of days I had traveled from grace into perdition and back into some kind of grace once more. I didn't deserve such mercy.

"It's okay," Arwen said. "There are other things we can do." She began to trace the same territory she'd graced with her hands with her mouth, her lips smooth against my skin.

You Will Not Replace Us

Through the iron sight, dark figures boiled up from a low ground fog, the snow exhaling as it melted in the warm morning air. Somewhere off in the trees a child was screaming. I could hear her even through the rubber plugs inserted into both eardrums, but I couldn't tell if the child was hurt or only playing. The figures were no more than silhouettes, no more than ghosts in the creeping fog, thugs with gorilla arms scraping so low they might as well have been coming at me on all fours. Like beasts. I flicked off the safety, pressing the spring-loaded stock firmly into my shoulder, my face against the cold metal as I exhaled and pressed the trigger. Hot brass casings ejected around me in a concussive burst, splinters of light, as I kept my feet planted wide and swiveled from the hip, releasing and pressing the trigger at even intervals.

"Woo-eee!" Elijah whooped beside me when I was done. I held out the smoking SIG Sauer he'd nicknamed Mjolnir after Thor's hammer, my palms cupped under the stock like a holy offering. Elijah received it reverently, his fingers brushing the runic symbols cut into the barrel. I took out my earplugs, tucked them in a front pocket, and we both pivoted to Roland who held a stopwatch.

"Eight seconds," Roland said in his gravelly voice. "All head shots. He put down four niggers in the time it takes an old lady to blow her nose into a Kleenex." The brim of his cowboy hat was so low I couldn't read his eyes, sunk deep in a cavernous face, but he sounded pleased. The peppery smell of gunpowder drifted around us in a cloud.

"Swenson, we'll make a soldier of you yet," Elijah said, addressing me by the last name he'd recently wheedled from me. He glanced over at Roland as he shouldered the AR-15 and stepped to the firing range's low fence. "Didn't I tell you? This boy here is descended from Vikings."

Roland grunted, his head dipping as he turned his attention back to his stopwatch. Off in the woods, I heard a child scream again, but it was the high-pitched holler of a kid at play and not of one afraid or in pain. They were just over the other side of the ravine, probably playing Agents of ZOG again, their favorite game. I slipped in my earplugs before Elijah could take his turn.

We were in a low valley well away from the trailers, the targets tucked against a shelf of granite to take the brunt of any errant bullets. Tacked onto straw bales, the silhouetted targets about forty feet away resembled gangbangers, their forms crudely distorted to appear more apelike, black fists clutching knives or pipes as they lumbered toward us. The ground fog that had come with the warming spell made them look even more sinister, like they had sprung up from the dark earth, demons and not men, hunting us in the rocky pine valley. I don't know where they bought such targets.

I felt a tingling that traveled from my shoulder down to the tips of my fingers. I felt it right down to the fillings in my teeth, on a level of skull and bone. It surprised me how much I liked that feeling. Holding Mjolnir, I was no longer the broken kid who had spent ten days in a hospital bed. If you knew how to hold the assault rifle carefully, in my case tucked against my uninjured shoulder, it couldn't hurt or bruise you. There is no preparing for such a feeling. Mjolnir was a marvel of engineering, a beautiful killing machine that fit naturally against my body. I stepped away from the low fence that separated us from the firing range as Elijah began to fire. I'd tried other weapons, including an M-4 and a genuine AK-47 that Roland owned, but the AR-15 was my favorite: light, accurate, and deadly.

Roland paused us for a smoke break. "You seen

the news?" he said to me. From a pocket in his vest he unfolded a clipping from the *Duluth News-Tribune* and passed it my way. I saw the headline first—"Hate Crimes Hit Duluth and Aurora Bay"—and I felt a shelf within me fall away. The article didn't just mention the racist flyers spread on the campus of NMSU, but also detailed an act of vandalism down in Duluth where a monument to three young black males, lynched at the turn of the twentieth century, had been spray-painted in red with the number "14" and the initials "ROA." The reporter didn't know yet that these were *the* fourteen words or that ROA stood for Race Over All. His article went on to describe the flyers on campus and say that police speculated the same person had done both of these acts. Authorities were also aware of a rural Christian Identity church called Rose of Sharon with possible connections to white supremacy groups. It ended with this quote from Professor Friedman at Northern, who was the child of Holocaust survivors: "This hatred must be uprooted from the dark soil and shown the withering light of day. It cannot be allowed to fester and spread underground. Only by yanking it out by the roots will we be safe."

Reading those words I felt a wash of nausea rinse through me, cold and oily. I hadn't any idea that when Roland sent me to campus with the flyers, I was part of a larger plan. What had I done?

Elijah took the article from me, his brow furrowing.

"How?" I said.

Roland exhaled smoke from his nostrils. "I sent Bjorn down there. He was itching for some action."

"You went too far," Elijah said. He crumpled it in his fist and let it fall to the ground.

"We got the attention we wanted."

Elijah shook his head. "They'll be watching us now."

"They already are." Roland smiled grimly around his cigarette, his eyes on me. He took out another paper from his pocket and handed it to me. "You ready for act two?" he said. "I'd like to see the *Star Tribune* pick up the story next."

The hand-drawn brochure he passed my way featured a comic with four frames that told a simple story. In the first frame, a young skinhead comes across a lovely young woman who is being groped by two African-American hoodlums. Was it my imagination or did the face of the woman look like Maura, her high cheekbones and aquiline nose? I tried to blink her image away, her memory, her face in a place where it should not be. Not here.

The artist had drawn one gangbanger sneering, the other with his tongue lolling as he attempts to fondle her breasts. Their features were crude and simian, huge lips and noses. In the second frame the skinhead flips into action, smashing in those faces and saving the young woman's virtue. His reward? In the third frame a Jewish judge, his long nose curling snaillike on a cruel face, sentences the skinhead to prison where he languishes behind bars. The final frame shows the skinhead out of prison and now reunited with the woman, her gingery hair flowing as they stand before wheat fields spreading endlessly, a new world bought and paid for with blood. All of this happens without a single word being spoken, the pictures doing all the talking.

I handed it to Elijah, who took it without a word. "You remember when Jones drew this for us before he went away?" Roland said to him. "I been saving this for the right moment."

Elijah looked at the woman and then back at me. Did he also notice how she resembled Maura? Had the artist used her as a model? Elijah's jaw tightened but he dropped his head as if resigned to something. "In another world, Hitler makes it into art school and finds his place in Vienna. He never goes to jail. Never writes *Mein Kampf*."

"What?" Roland said with a frown. "I swear I don't understand you sometimes." He took the pamphlet from Elijah and gave it back to me. "So you think you can make copies of this at Kinko's? Then you can spread these on campus."

I didn't answer right away. I was thinking of Noah, who now probably suspected I had vandalized the monument down in Duluth as well. Why hadn't he reported me? I let the weight of the consequences settle in my gut, where it didn't sit well. I had hurt a good person. I had made another good person afraid. Elijah kept his head down and it seemed like he wanted to look any direction but my way. Why? What had his strange comment about Hitler meant?

Ten days had passed since Thanksgiving, and in that week, I had gotten myself in so deep with these people I was having trouble telling the real from pretend. They knew my last name, knew my major, knew my skills as an artist and programmer, knew that I was from Chicago after they asked about who my people were. I didn't see any sense in lying about these things. I had been coming here every day since to play chess with Elijah and talk strategy. This was my new school. My university. The texts were the Bible that Mother Sophie had given me and the battered copy of *The Turner Diaries* that Roland tasked me with reading. This was the school where I was learning how to survive the apocalypse coming for us at the end of the year. This was where I was learning how to fight and how to hate. I told myself that I was only pretending and I tried to hide as much as possible what I was doing here from Arwen, mostly out of shame, but the real truth is that I hadn't expected how easily I would take to all of it. On some level, I came here because I liked coming here.

For a time I had to give up my moral compass. Such a compass wouldn't do me any good until I had the answers I needed. In the meantime, I was gathering information I could use against them. I knew already, for instance, that convicts aren't supposed to own and operate firearms like the ones we handled down at the range, information I could bring to the attention of authorities. I knew that in the machine shed behind Mother Sophie's cabin they were building AR-15s from custom kits bought in pieces by mail order, a way to circumvent the assault weapons ban. I knew some kind of plan was in the works, something they intended to do before Y2K, though the men clammed up in my presence. I felt sure that if I stayed with them long enough I would find out what had happened to Maura or where she had gone. For a time, I needed to get lost, but I was already so lost now I didn't know if I would ever find my way back to my old self. The old self had to die so Meshach could be born again. Meshach, who could stand in the fire.

BEFORE THIS, I WOULD have sworn to you that I was not a racist. Growing up in the predominately white conservative suburb of Mount Greenwood, I hardly gave much thought to race at all, except on trips visiting my grandparents' house in Fuller Park, which had gone from primarily Caucasian in the fifties to almost all black after white flight sent folks scrambling for the burbs.

This one visit stands out in my memory. My grandpa Logan had just been released from the hospital and was recovering from congestive heart failure. My uncle

Nolan took me with him to spend the weekend so we could help my grandma Zee around the house and finish building the prefab toolshed my grandpa wanted in the small backyard. At the age of fourteen — still reeling from my parents' divorce the year previous — I dreaded such a trip. A little man-to-man time, my uncle Nolan had pitched it to my mother. My "please don't make me go," went unheard.

We cruised the old neighborhood in his Buick, our windows down as my uncle Nolan pointed out landmarks. Rush Limbaugh squawked on the radio, his furious tirades against Clintonian sleaze at the "oval orifice" filling up the silence between my uncle and me. Rush segued into a bit about a new book called *Bell Curve* that wacko professors were censoring on campus. As "the most dangerous man in America" it was his responsibility to tell us the truth about this book and the truth wasn't pretty. The book supposedly proved that intelligence was inherited, imprinted in your DNA, and while Rush didn't say the next part out loud, it bubbled like a muddy river under the subtext of his rambling: whites were smarter than blacks from birth onward, so all the social programs in the world, from Head Start to welfare, couldn't lift black people from the squalor of their basic inferiority.

Uncle Nolan had one hand easy on the big wheel, the other casually draped on the seat rest behind me. Square-jawed and balding, he was a big man who looked nothing like my petite mother. A Vietnam veteran—he had been a clerk in the war—he was a wanderer and a vagabond, some seasons working the crab boats up in Alaska or hiring himself out as a handyman. I was just a gangly kid by comparison, beanpole thin after my first major growth spurt. I missed my father—the gap between us started growing a long time before the divorce, and I felt certain he wouldn't have left us so easily had I not been such a letdown to him as a son—but Uncle Nolan wasn't exactly father-figure material. He had once been a cheerful man, but time and liquor had not been kind to him, his voice tinged with a rough bitterness that made me miss the old Uncle Nolan.

My uncle adjusted the dial before slipping his hand back behind my seat rest. Outside our windows, liver-colored lawns sprouted crab grass after a dry summer. Everything looked yellow; even the air smelled of urine. What always struck me about this neighborhood were the iron bars on the windows of some of the houses, as if people here lived in stucco prisons. "What do you make of all that?" Uncle Nolan asked after a long silence.

"All what?" I said, though I knew he was referring to the show. I had discovered that I could kill many painful conversations with adults by directing questions back at them.

"Truth is that the law is tilted in every way to favor

these people with handouts. Affirmative action and all that shit. Take a good look around, Lucien." He sniffed. "The supposed war on poverty has been going for over two decades. This look like uplift to you?"

"It does not." I had to agree.

He gestured at the radio. Even at a low staticky murmur, Limbaugh sounded like an angry bee trapped inside the speaker. "All I'm saying is that there's some truth to the man's words."

We stopped at a corner store and Uncle Nolan sent me inside with a twenty-dollar bill while he left the Buick idling. I kept my head down as I hurried through the aisles, the only white person in a small store with too many mirrors on every wall and corner, so a thousand Luciens reflected back at me, pale-faced and skinny and trying not to look scared. I snagged a gallon of whole milk from one of the sliding cases and hustled to the cashier, an obese, Asian man wearing a stained apron as he stood behind the deli counter. We traded cash for milk without a single word passing between us, and then I hurried back outside, the plastic jug in one hand, the change for the twenty fluttering in the other like a fist of green flags.

I walked out of the store and right into the midst to a trio of young black men who happened to be wandering past at the same moment. I had been told not to make direct eye contact—no gesture that would appear challenging in any way—so I only caught a glimpse of them:

each with a single pant leg rolled up, red shoes or caps on backward, the tallest one sporting a rust-colored do-rag. They stopped at the same moment I did. "We'll be taking that," the tallest one informed me, nodding toward my fist of cash.

"I don't think so," I said. The words left my mouth before I even knew what I was saying.

He tensed, squaring his shoulders. I had no choice but to meet his eyes. They were bright as pennies, keen and alert. He was clearly the leader and not just because of his size. Maybe they were just wannabes and not real Bloods, boys playing at being gangsters, I had to hope. This could have gone either way. We each had our roles to play in this moment, but I had gone badly off script.

I looked away from him for help—any help at all from my uncle Nolan—who was watching the scene unfold, his mouth agape as he sat behind the steering wheel. He gave one toot on the horn to make sure the trio would turn his way and then he motioned like he was reaching into the glove compartment.

The teen in the do-rag showed his teeth when he looked back at me. "That your daddy?"

"Not really," I said. I glanced at his friends and back at him, saw him shove his hands in his baggy pants pockets. I was starting to realize how much trouble I might be in for, but once I committed to a course of action, I saw it through, whether it was wise or not. I don't know where such stubbornness comes from. He wasn't getting this money, not today.

"'Not really'?" His sharp laughter broke the tension. "Yeah, maybe you look more like the milkman. That's you, the milkman's son." Satisfied with insulting me instead of robbing me, he laughed again as he and his crew continued on their way. "We let you go this time," he turned to call out as he went.

Inside the car, my uncle Nolan was livid. He slammed the glove compartment shut when I climbed in and set the milk gallon jug on the seat between us. "What the hell was that? You don't walk around flashing cash like that."

I bit my lip and looked away. Here I had been given a simple task—the first thing he'd asked me to do on this trip—and I had failed him.

"And for God's sake, if some gangbanger demands you hand over your money, you hand it over. Got it? You think I want my nephew getting shot over a god-damn twenty-dollar bill? Your mother would never for-give me."

I wondered if he was right. What would I have done if they attacked me, throw milk on them? I didn't under-stand my own actions. "I guess I'm just stupid," I mut-tered.

Uncle Nolan sighed heavily and rolled up the power

windows and clamped down the power locks. "You're not stupid," he said. "You just need to use better judgment. These people. They're animals, okay? They will kill you for your shoes. For a goddamn pair of Nikes. You're not in Mount Greenwood anymore."

I stared out the window, not really seeing anything. Later I would continue musing on this. Why had my uncle Nolan sent me in alone if the neighborhood was truly dangerous? Why not warn me beforehand about not being careless with cash? And what had he been looking for in the glove compartment? Uncle Nolan had never been the type to carry a gun before. When he turned Rush Limbaugh back up on the radio, I was almost relieved.

My uncle Nolan never said the N-word. Not out loud. But it coursed under the surface of every sentence he spoke about black people.

It was a short drive from the corner store to my grandparents' house. My grandfather hadn't fled with the rest of the white people in the fifties because he had renovated his brownstone with his own two hands, adding a cupola with a round wall of windows, some of them stained glass, so the light washed through in rainbow prisms. My grandmother kept her potted lemon trees in that light. How I loved curling up on the Turkish rug next to one of her many cats, the smell of citrus filling my senses. Before this visit, before the divorce, before I realized I would never live up to the expectations of the men in my family, it had seemed a magical place.

Even bent by age, my grandfather had been a tall, imposing man who had loud opinions on everything. He would swear to you he despised racists in one breath, but in the next he would tell you that the history books had given a bum deal to Hitler since he had been a great leader, a powerful speaker who brought Germany out of the Depression. My grandmother, a tall, dark woman of Norwegian descent, didn't bother to hide her racism. She looked a little like Greta Garbo, and she kept her hair dyed black.

The day I was almost mugged she listened to my uncle's angry retelling of my mishap at the corner store and drew me aside. "I know just the thing," she said. She opened a mason jar of chocolate-covered Brazil nuts and handed me one. I downed the sweet obediently, still a child in her eyes. I knew what she was going to say before the words left her mouth because she tended to repeat herself, the same stories and jokes. My grandmother smiled and passed me another. "We call these nigger toes," she said, "but don't tell your grandpa because he doesn't like that word. I'm glad you didn't give those pickaninnies a single penny." She chucked me under the chin and walked away. For a long time afterward the sweetness of that chocolate melting in my mouth mixed with the ugliness of the slur.

I nodded and absorbed it all. My grandfather extolling the efficiency of the German war machine, which the world would never see the likes of again, my grandmother watching Aretha Franklin on the Zenith and griping that black people didn't really know how to sing, they just screamed into the microphone. My uncle talking about the persistence of their poverty despite decades of social programs. There was a war happening in the context of their stories, and in this war, white people, particularly white males who were the true descendants of our august forefathers, were losing, piece by piece, a country that was rightly theirs. What was so wrong with having pride in your heritage? How I longed for fatherly love and approval, then and now.

My grandparents had both died a few years ago. In the touch of Mother Sophie, I heard my grandmother's voice again. In Elijah's talks on history, I heard my grandfather. In Roland's sternness, my father or my uncle Nolan spoke to me again. There were times with this new family I had found when I felt I was stronger than ever before, a man with faith and purpose. I didn't just sit around complaining about the state of the world. I had become part of a group that was preparing for a real and defining action, even if they kept the details from me for now. I tried to tell myself that my upbringing had prepared me for this moment, but I knew the truth deep down. Though my grandparents had died years ago, they would have been afraid if they could see me now, afraid of who I was becoming. I didn't know what I was capable of doing anymore.

I STAYED OUT WITH Roland and Elijah for another half hour, until the targets were so riddled with bullets they no longer resembled human forms. They were shadows, monstrous and deformed. Roland eventually drew Elijah aside, out of earshot, for a discussion. This had happened frequently the last week, a plan taking shape they didn't want me to hear about. Bjorn had even gone away to scout soft targets, and he must have hit the monument in Duluth on the way. Today I had the distinct impression that Roland was talking about me this time, and from the turning down of his mouth I was sure Elijah wasn't happy about what he was hearing. What could they possibly be saying? I had done everything they had asked of me so far, but I didn't think I could spread those pamphlets on campus. I had a terrible feeling that I was being used by these men. Then Elijah signaled me to follow as he and Roland headed up the hill.

Watery sunlight broached the clouds above the treetops, gilding the tops of the pines. On the way up the hill, Elijah suggested we stop at Roland's trailer, a small but sturdy Scotty with a shell shaped like a turtle. Before this I'd only been inside Mother Sophie's cabin and Elijah's Airstream, so I wasn't sure what to expect from a recluse like Roland. He'd built a proper porch out front, complete with a slanting, shingled roof, wind chimes tinkling in the eaves. We stomped mud from our boots, which Roland requested we leave outside the door along with Mjolnir.

The trailer within was surprisingly tidy, a room both cozy and warm. Elijah and I sat at a Formica table across from a low queen-sized waterbed. I knew by now that most of the beds within these trailers were waterbeds — a practical measure in the event their wells dried up after Y2K or were poisoned by the star Wormwood falling to earth and causing nuclear meltdowns — in which case they could tap open the beds for drinking water. Elijah had given me a tour one day, including of the underground bunkers where they stored fifty-pound bags of powdered milk and five-pound bags of powdered peanut butter and enough sardines to feed an army of seals.

From a cabinet above a small fridge, Roland fetched a milk jug with some caramel-colored liquid sloshing around inside. He planted this on the table with three coffee mugs with Alaskan scenes painted on the sides — mine had Mount McKinley on it. Roland had campaigned vigorously for the Alaskan Bush as the church's final refuge in the End Times, but was overruled by Mother Sophie's fear of bears.

"You're in for a treat now, Meshach," Elijah said as

Roland uncapped the jug. The smell of liquor nipped at my nose from where I sat. "This is Roland's home brew. He's got a still back in the woods, but don't tell Mother Sophie. We're supposed to be dry on The Land. Too much hooch and the boys end up fighting each other instead of the world out there."

My ears still rang from our time at the firing range. I don't drink. The words were there on my tongue. The only liquor I'd ever touched had been the whiskey I shared with Maura the night we were robbed. The first time she held me. I thought of my mother's alcoholism. The car she'd totaled the year her marriage dissolved. The nervous nights I waited up for her, trying not to imagine who she was out with. Bailing her out of jail when I was a junior in high school. I'd seen a lifetime's worth of the damage liquor could do, but that was the old Lucien, weak and wounded. Here I could shed my weaker self as a snake sheds its skin. What was the harm in one drink?

Roland filled each of our mugs two fingers deep with his witch's brew. It smelled of molasses and turpentine. Then he motioned me up so he could sit beside the window, and I sat again, squeezing in beside him.

"To the end of the world," Elijah said, hoisting his mug. I toasted the others, clinking mugs. My first sip was nearly my last. The homebrew burned in my throat and seared my sinuses. A woody fragment of something snared in my teeth. The heat washing through my body caused me to remember Maura and the first and only time I'd ever tried whiskey. I felt my skin flushing.

"Woo-eee," Elijah whooped just like he had at the firing range. When I blinked back tears he laughed at me. I took another sip. The home brew had a smoky appley flavor that grew on you, the liquid gold of a fine autumn day distilled into this caramel concoction. Apples and gold and turpentine and some rusty nails thrown in for good measure. The heat spread all the way down to the tips of my toes. I grew conscious of the rotation of the planet, the earth spinning, my head spinning, Elijah watching me like an indulgent older brother, his eyes shining. I'd longed for a brother growing up. This odd family here that I'd found myself a part of was starting to feel more real than my own.

I downed my entire mug and Roland poured me another before I could wave him off. He cranked open the window, tapped down his pack of American Spirit cigarettes, slid one out, and lit it.

Then Elijah sighed heavily, as if he'd made up his mind about something. Whatever they'd been talking about on the way to the trailer. Elijah's eyes were hard when they settled on me again. I never saw the next part coming. "Tell us again how you found us."

The spinning room no longer felt quite so pleasant. Where had the question come from? Mush-mouthed, I repeated what I'd originally said about being out on the highway and spotting the church.

"Rose of Sharon's nowhere near the highway," Roland said, taking a long draw on his cigarette and tapping his ashes into an ashtray shaped like a glacier. So this must have been part of what they'd been talking about earlier, planning to ambush me with questions.

"I just drive some days," I said, which had been true before the accident. Once I'd driven all the way to Thunder Bay, Ontario, and back with no destination in mind, the radio turned up, windows down, my body fueled by gas station cinnamon bears and Mountain Dew. "No maps. Just go where the road leads me."

A look passed between the men. The light in Elijah's eyes darkened, like he had come to some regrettable decision. Smoke seeped from Roland's nostrils. I thought I would remember this moment for a long time afterward, the light coming through the curtains, the sharp scent of tobacco, the hooch swimming in my brain.

"I don't understand why you're here," Elijah said.

"I don't know why I'm here either," I said, trying to cut him off, since I was worried about where he was headed with this. "Or any of us."

"Don't go getting all existential on me," Elijah said. His eyes narrowed as he watched my face. "You surprised I know what that means? My certificate may have come in the mail but I studied philosophy. There are existential paradoxes even in the Bible. When God asks Abraham to kill his own son, Isaac, as a test of his faith? There is a teleological suspension of morality in that moment. God has asked him to do an act he knows is wrong, wicked, and personally harmful. But what would you do for God? Who or what would you sacrifice? Could you sacrifice a child? Who? You ever had to sacrifice anything in your life?"

I burped more hot air, the home brew turning to acid in my larynx. What kind of man has an affair with a married woman without giving a thought to the damage he might do to another? What good had I done in my meager, selfish life? By spreading the flyers on campus, I had only added more evil to the world. I couldn't stay still because of the tension in the room. I tried to meet Elijah's gaze and figure where he was heading with this. "That's a terrible thing for God to ask," I said, hoping to keep us on this subject.

Roland shifted in his seat. He looked impatient to return to the interrogation, if that's what this was. He stretched one arm across the seat behind me, ready to hold me here.

"Isn't it, though? There are a good many atheists who would agree with you, Meshach. Who cite that very passage as one reason they lost their faith. Who put themselves in the place of God. But to think that way also means reading the Bible without any sense of context or history. At the time God asks this of Abraham, the Israelites are surrounded by pagans who regularly practiced child sacrifice. The Amarites killed their own children on altars. You've heard the rule, show don't tell? Every good storyteller knows it. Well, if God exists, it stands to reason he knows how to spin a good yarn. He wanted to make an example so that every generation going forward never practices such a sacrifice. He tells the story for the sake of the children. Isaac is spared by the appearance of a lamb."

"I don't know," I said, my thinking wobbly from drink. The home brew sloshed in my brain and stomach like flaming lighter fluid and words slurred in my mouth. I thought of Maura's nightmares that these trailers would bust loose from their log foundations and slide all the way down the steep hill into the river. The small enclosed room rocked like a ship in the morning wind. "Seems like He could've just told people, don't kill your own kids and most would have gotten the point."

Roland tensed, but Elijah smiled, warming to the game. Hope rose within me that I had distracted him from his original line of questioning. "Where is your sense of drama, Meshach?" he said. "Isaac is spared by the appearance of a lamb. Generations later, God will sacrifice his own son on the altar. For all our sins. Yours. Mine. The Lamb of God is another name for Christ. Are you beginning to see how showing it as a story invites the reader into it, makes us all part of one tapestry of faith? Because the wages of sin lead to death, and death is coming, and soon. I would not want to find myself on the wrong side of the path."

Roland tapped out more ashes, his cigarette drawn down to the filter. The faintly chemical odor added to my nausea. "Meshach," he said. "Such a curious name. Never met anyone with a name like that before."

There were deep shadows under Elijah's eyes. He knocked his ring finger against the table. Why did he still wear his wedding band, if he knew Maura wasn't coming back? "I think I know who you are," he said, in a voice that sounded bruised by betrayal and hurt. "But I don't know why you're here."

"I think I'm going to puke," I told them because I felt a hot wave bubbling up from my belly, an undeniable urge.

Roland sprang into action, one hand hooking me under my left armpit, my bad side, and propelling me up out of my seat. Instant agony flared within my wounded body, but I couldn't scream because if I did I'd retch everywhere. I gritted my teeth and swallowed down burning bile. Roland shoved me from behind, urgent to get me out of his tidy trailer. I fumbled at the latch, desperate, when he reached around me, one hand looped around my belt as if he was going to carry me out of here like a child in a sling. Somehow, I made it out the door and spilled down the stairs, not bothering with my boots as I went around the side of the trailer and heaved up the liquor, a hot, noxious stream gushing from my guts. Waves of it left my body, my stomach squeezing, until I was emptied out.

I stood wavering, the cold biting my feet, my throat scorched. Both men had followed me out and now stood glaring at me, their eyes full of questions and doubts. Behind them, Mother Sophie had come out on her porch as if sensing the disturbance. Elijah fetched my boots and carried them over. He thrust them into my arms and marched me through the snow to my Continental.

"I'm sorry," I said. It looked like Mother Sophie was headed this way, so Roland must have gone over to head her off.

"You shut your mouth," he said. "I don't want her to know."

My hands were shaking as I tugged open the door of the Continental and climbed inside, setting my hiking boots on the floor. Elijah leaned in before I could close the door. I hunched into myself, expecting a fist that didn't come. "I don't think you should come around here anymore." His voice was soft instead of angry, like he didn't want Roland to overhear. "I don't think it's good for your health."

After peeling off my wet socks and tugging on my boots, I didn't start the car right away. I felt exhausted and emptied out, a man in desperate need of water, but there was nothing in the car, not even gum to take away the bitter taste in my mouth. My throat ached, but at least I had time to think as I drove home. I knew even before I looked in the rearview mirror that Roland would be following me in his truck.

I thought about driving straight to the airport in Duluth or the Cities and getting on board a flight to see my mom. Just get the hell out of here. How had things turned so suddenly? Elijah knew. He must have figured out who I was. Or had it been Roland? Maybe he had known all along or something else tipped him. But if he knew, then why had he let me go? One minute I was so deep in the inner circle I was standing at the firing range with them, and the next they were ready to nail me to one of the trees.

I decided I didn't have anything to hide. Let them follow me home. The strangest part to me was how Elijah had sounded protective even as he was dismissing me. Like he was warning me away. We aren't done yet, you and I, I thought, as I led Roland to the place I lived now with my ghostly priestess and a dying German shepherd. There was no way to save myself, no place of safety for me anywhere on earth. Yet, I still didn't have the answers I needed. I wasn't going to run. She *was* my wife, he'd said. *What did you do to her? Or did you put such a scare into her that she ran away, disappearing for good?* I hadn't forgotten that scene from *The*

Turner Diaries, a woman brutally strangled for betraying the cause. I couldn't get it out of my head. I vowed they wouldn't scare me away. Not yet. "I don't want her to know," Elijah had said of Mother Sophie, which made me wonder, what did the old woman know? I had to go back there, but first I needed a plan.

The Trouble with Angels

Roland followed me the whole way home and parked behind me in the circular driveway. I ignored his truck at first as I hobbled inside in search of Arwen. She didn't answer right away when I called for her, but the house smelled fragrantly of baking bread, so she had to be here somewhere. How was Arwen always disappearing when I needed her most? Kaiser barked once in greeting down in the den, asking to be let out. When I peeked through the blinds I saw that Roland had left his pickup idling, a window down as he sat behind the wheel and drew on a fresh cigarette. I wanted someone to tell, but there was no one. I felt exposed and alone. I let Kaiser out of his kennel and coaxed him up the circular staircase before fetching the last remaining Dr Pepper from the fridge.

This I carried out to Roland in his truck. I knew he had

followed me home to intimidate me, but I figured some-one guilty would stay hunkered down inside the house. Would he ask about my name again, or threaten me? I resolved that I would not be afraid. I was a man with a Dr Pepper, a geriatric German shepherd, and nothing to lose. Halfway to his truck, I paused as a new thought struck me. *This isn't the first time he's done this. This isn't the first time he's followed someone home. Maura, did this man know about us?* I tried to keep my hand from shak-ing as I raised the Dr Pepper, my peace offering. A geek bearing gifts. But Roland didn't wait around. He shook his head, flicked out his burning cigarette, and rolled up his window. Once he got his rig turned around, he peeled away.

Growling, Kaiser lifted his back leg and loosed a stream of urine into the snow. I cracked the Dr Pepper. "I know," I said. "That guy is going to be trouble."

I knew I'd be seeing him again and soon. I had to find out what happened to Maura, which meant I needed to go back to The Land, and when I did I would go to Mother Sophie. She owned the property and had founded the church, so everything began with her. She was a woman who held a healing fire in her hands, a woman who had told me about a living God who held me in His palms as a sparrow, a God who knew the number of hairs on my head, knew me when I was in the cradle of my mother's womb, knew the lies and deceptions I would grow up to speak and loved me still. Of all of them, she was the one I felt I could reason with. I had to find out what she knew. But not yet. I needed to think this through and wait for early morning tomorrow when Elijah was likely to be out on a call.

I found Arwen in the garage of all places. I hadn't thought of checking there. She was dressed in jeans and a black hoodie, the hood up as she sat on the bottom step with the wounded raven in her lap. She must have caught it somehow, or trained it to feed from her hand. I remembered my dream, the swaddled bird, the blood after she split the tongue to make it speak. Arwen didn't turn around at first. "You didn't hear me calling?"

When she did turn, her eyes glittered with tears. "Edgar's dead," she said, using the name I had told her about a few days before.

I walked down the steps and sat beside her. She cradled the bird as though she held a child and not some wild creature. "We should have taken him to a rescue center," I said.

Arwen stroked the glossy feathers. "How? We couldn't catch him once he got up into the loft."

The raven's eyes shone white like river pebbles, filmed over in death, the terrible tongue with its dream prophecies sealed inside the beak. "I need to tell you something," I said. I wished I had before. I spoke of the storm of ravens filling up the pines and their war in the snow, the carnage I'd seen, and how this bird had been the lone survivor. I told her about my sense of the evil driving them to slaughter one another in a time of famine and how sharing this story in the church had made me seem like some kind of prophet to the people at Rose of Sharon, one more proof the world was ending when we were living in a time of miracles and apocalyptic horrors.

Arwen listened without commenting. She lay her head against my shoulder. "You're a strange person," she said.

I had a difficult time arguing with her assessment. I had expected her to be angry that I had withheld such a story. Did that mean she believed me? Strange was a better alternative than crazy.

"So you believe in all that Y2K stuff?" Arwen said. "You think the world is going to end because you saw some birds lose their shit?"

"Maybe," I said. "All I know is that I'm living in a world right now where things are happening that I can't explain with logic and reason. I've just been trying to figure it out. There has to be some reason these things keep happening."

Arwen blew out an exasperated breath. "Maybe there isn't any reason. Sometimes nature writes a horror story about the battle for survival. Things die. Especially when you're trying to hold on to something wild. Something wild in a place where it doesn't belong." She rocked slightly on the step as she spoke. "Will you help me bury Edgar? I don't want the wolves to get him."

We dug a hole for the raven behind the ruined rose hedges while a bitter wind nipped at our cheeks. Even a grave only two feet deep proved difficult as we hacked at ground caked with ice, my steel shovel chipping away at iron soil. The effort left me short on breath. "You want to say anything?" I asked Arwen when the hole seemed sufficient.

"No. I'm just pissed he's dead." She set the corpse in the hole. In his shallow grave, the raven was so dark against the whiteness of the snow all around. "Besides, you're the prophet."

"Let's get inside," I said. "I'm cold." On the way back after tamping down the ground, the shovel loose in my left hand, I pointed out the frozen-over koi pond and we stopped there. You could see their bodies encased in their icy tomb, a blur of orange inside a coffin made of glass. It was shaping up to be a melancholy afternoon.

"Your parents didn't say anything about tending them. They're down there, a couple of fish popsicles." The thought gave me an ugly premonition. In this part of the country when the snow melts, when sheets of ice sealing shut the lakes and rivers give way to running water, the springtime can reveal ugly, buried secrets. In the spring the land gives up its winter dead.

"They're down there in the mud under the ice,"

Arwen said, bumping against me so we stood shoulder-to-shoulder. "But I don't think they're dead. Pond's deep enough to keep it from freezing all the way. A koi can slow its heartbeat to a single beat per minute when it goes into hibernation."

"They're alive?" It seemed impossible.

"You'll see," she said. "Winter can't last forever."

I was no longer so sure about that.

"And," Arwen added, "not every miracle defies explanation. There's a life force at the core of every being, stronger than any of us can realize."

Her hopefulness surprised me. I tried my best to argue against it. "We are also more fragile than we know. So easily snuffed out."

"Not the koi," she said. "They're aquatic life-ninjas, truly badass. You just wait and see."

As soon as we left the shovel in the garage and stepped inside we smelled smoke, an acrid scent. Then everything happened at once as the smoke detector in the hallway began to screech when smoke curling along the ceiling reached it.

"Damn!" Arwen said. "I forget I had bread in the oven."

I went to get a chair to silence the alarm while Arwen hurried into the kitchen. In the chaotic moments that followed neither of us recognized the sound of the doorbell ringing. I thought the sound was inside my head, a remnant of my time at the firing range, or this alarm, so loud I could imagine my eardrums bleeding into my brain. I only knew what I was hearing when I saw Arwen hurrying down the hallway after I'd yanked out the battery. She glanced up at me, still stupidly standing on a chair in the middle of the hall. "I'm not here," she said in a firm voice, and she disappeared into her room, closing the door carefully behind her.

Roland must be back, and I would have to confront him alone. Kaiser barked downstairs, stirred up by the noise and smoke. The doorbell buzzed again, insistent. When I made my way down the hall and peeked through the peephole I saw it wasn't Roland after all, but instead a police officer in Navy blues, a young man who didn't look much older than me, his face freckled, his orange hair shaved to stubble. He held his hat in one hand and pressed on the buzzer with the other.

I opened the door halfway, conscious of what the chaos inside must have sounded like to him here at the threshold. Downstairs, Kaiser continued to carry on, knowing a visitor was here.

After the officer and I exchanged greetings, he said, "You're the boy the Krolls asked to tend this place?"

I nodded, though I didn't like him calling me a boy. He had eyes like blue fire, like the twin flames of Bunsen burners. His shaved head and intense glower bothered me. He would have fit right in with the skinheads who had been coming and going on The Land.

"Who else is there in the house with you?"

"Just me and the dog," I said. The lying felt like second nature by now. "What's this about, Officer?"

He craned his neck, trying to peer past me. "Mind if I come inside?"

"Actually, I do." Corny lines about asking for a warrant flitted through my mind, straight from television. "Look, I'm really busy right now."

He frowned, his whitish lips thinning. The splash of freckles across his nose and cheeks made him look young, I decided, but those eyes were cold and calculating. "Smells like something's burning."

"I'm not much of a cook," I said, "but I can't see how that concerns the Aurora Bay Police Department."

That didn't even buy the crease of a smile. He had come here hunting for something. Or someone. "The Krolls themselves called our department and asked us to look in. Apparently, they haven't been able to reach you."

I held my arms across my chest, the chill from the open door getting to me. I hadn't been home much of the last week, spending most days on The Land.

"They're worried their daughter might try to come home."

"Daughter?" I hoped my voice sounded surprised.

From his pocket he took out a folded printout with

Arwen's mugshot. She had long black hair in the photo, ebony waves that must have fallen to her waist, a hippie princess. But her eyes were hard as she glared defiantly at the camera or the person behind it. "You seen anyone who looks like this? Goes by the name of Arwen? The Krolls think she'll try to come here."

"Huh," I said, "I didn't even know the Krolls *had* a daughter." My voice broke high with the lie.

His pale eyes scoured my face. I could tell he knew I was lying. He folded the picture again and took out a business card with his name on it, Officer Connor Sheehan. "You call me if you see anything unusual. I'll be stopping by again to check up on you."

He was halfway to his cruiser before I called out to him. I could have told him about Roland's threatening presence, his trespassing. Maybe even what I'd seen and heard on The Land: rumors of dynamite and ex-cons fresh from Stillwater. I could make trouble for Elijah, a convict who wasn't supposed to own or operate firearms. "Officer Sheehan, why do they think she's coming here?"

He turned, his hat pulled low, his eyes alight under the brim. "Seems she ran into some trouble across the country in Washington. Authorities in Bellingham want to speak with her. They tried contacting the Krolls after she vanished, and the Krolls in turn have tried contacting you."

Standing before the open door I was so cold my teeth

were nearly chattering. "What'd she do?" Not asking such a question would've raised more suspicion.

He walked toward me a few paces, snow squeaking under his boot heels. "The Bellingham PD believes she witnessed a murder. They would like to question her."

"Well," I said, "I'll let you know."

"You do that." Officer Sheehan didn't drive away at first, instead strolling the perimeter. He would see two sets of footprints in the snow instead of one. The garage door opened with a freshly used shovel lying inside. A wrong smell. A long time passed before he drove away. I had a feeling he would be back.

Before I went into the kitchen I checked the phone. Sure enough, Arwen had pulled the cord from the wall. Again. No wonder the Krolls hadn't been able to reach me. I plugged it back in and went into the kitchen, sitting in a chair to wait for her beside the burned loaf. I rubbed my hands together to try to get heat back into them.

A few more minutes passed before Arwen emerged from her back room and stood surveying the charred brown wreckage of her baking efforts. "I suppose you have questions," she said.

She carried the loaf and pan over to the sink and started scraping away burned portions. Flickers of wings beat at the edge of my vision, which made Arwen look like she floated over the floor, the aura all around her. I worried that the edges of my miraculous healing were beginning to fray and come undone like everything else in my life. She carried the loaf back to the table and fragrant steam bloomed when she cut it open. The deeper smell of pumpernickel, dark and sweet as molasses or unspoken secrets, lived on under the char. She slathered a few pieces in butter and pushed them toward me. "Eat," she commanded. "You don't look well."

"If you talk," I said. Arwen watched me eat for a while, her own plate untouched.

"You weren't supposed to be here," she said. Arwen had come home knowing her parents planned to spend the winter in the South, believing she could live here in secret. She wouldn't have come otherwise. Her childhood had been half-feral, the only happy times when she wandered the woods with Kaiser. Verbally abusive, her father made her life difficult, and her mother had been distant and distracted, a woman who only seemed to love her gardens. Arwen had run away at the age of fifteen and hadn't looked back.

She told me some stuff I already knew about finding her way out west and her life in Seattle with other kayak-activists, how much she'd loved the ocean—her first arrest came at this time, a trespassing violation during a Greenpeace protest. She told me that she eventually came to Bellingham and lived with the other flower children down in Fairhaven, where she thought she would spend the rest of her days. Until she met Gabe.

"You remind me so much of him. Before the accident." Arwen picked at the slab of pumpernickel before her but didn't eat. "That's when everything changed. Gabe was riding his bike down Alabama Hill—the steepest hill in town—when a car pulled out of a driveway and right into him. He flew over the hood and hit the asphalt head-first. The helmet saved his life when it cracked, but his momentum . . ." Arwen pushed her plate away and drew in a shaky breath. "He lost so much skin. Shattered his chin. He broke bones in his face I didn't know could be broken."

She swallowed hard before she went on. I was glad she didn't elaborate. I could imagine what someone would look like and feel like after so much damage. How well I knew.

"They reconstructed his chin," she went on, "but he wasn't ever the same. It's like the head injury opened up something mean inside of him. And all those surgeries left him in pain. All the time. He got addicted to the pills. Percs. Vicodin. Whatever he could get his hands on after his prescriptions ran out. We were living apart from the others by then. With Gabe's habits, money from the set-tlement didn't last long."

I didn't know if I should reach across the table, try to hold her hand. Arwen was dry-eyed as she told her story. "He wouldn't go into treatment. Even just talking about it made him furious. Gabe needed the pills. God, he was so pitiful. He would wake crying as he relived the accident. Half the time it was like living with a child. The other half, he raged." Arwen crossed her arms, hunching into herself. "When he got the idea to start breaking into houses, I didn't try to argue him out of it. He couldn't do it alone—Gabe wasn't a planner. He wasn't smart like that. So, I drove him, and we cruised neighborhoods. We did most of the robberies during the day, when we could be certain that no one was home. All the usual tricks. Hitting houses on the corner, houses with backyards blind to neighbors. Gabe could get in and out in minutes. He took what cash or jewelry he could find and raided medicine cabinets. I think I knew we would get caught from the beginning—thieves always do—but I didn't see it coming when it happened."

Arwen's face looked washed out in the gray light filtering through the kitchen skylight. "We had simple rules. He went in unarmed. Get in and out within five minutes. No places with dogs. No busy streets. And never, ever go back to the same house. But Gabe had made a big score at a house up on Bear Creek Road, got a whole bottle of Vikes from some old-timer's cabinets. A week later he thought we should hit the house again in case the owner had refilled his prescriptions. I couldn't talk him out of it."

Arwen returned to picking at her slice of bread, which had been fairly dismantled. "It was raining that day, one of those cold, drizzly afternoons when there would be few people out walking around. I dropped Gabe off at the corner and then pulled around the block, where I could watch from a distance. I saw him go over a low fence into the backyard. The house looked dark. I remember feeling kind of drowsy. The rain sounded pleasant, dripping down through the firs and plinking on my roof. I dozed off, for how long I don't know. We'd used the earnings from one score to buy a couple of Nokia mobile phones. We wanted to use them like walkie-talkies. I looked down at the time on mine and when I glanced back up I saw a light go on in the bedroom upstairs. My heart went into my throat. Gabe knew not to turn on any lights. There had to be someone there, someone who was waiting for him. I called Gabe on the phone to warn him. He must have picked up just as the guy was coming into the room. I screamed 'Get out!' but he didn't respond. I heard his phone hit the carpet."

Arwen's face dropped into her hands as though she needed something to steady the weight of her head, the weight of what she knew. "His phone was still on, so I heard it all happen. I heard Gabe pleading, 'Please don't kill me.' The other man's voice was muffled, but he went on for a long time, until his voice rose to a shout, and Gabe shouted back, and then there was the boom of the gun. I heard it all. I heard his body fall." One hand massaged her throat as though it hurt to speak the story aloud. "And I just drove away. I just left him there to die.

I stopped on the way home to call the police from a pay phone. I didn't want to use the Nokia. I was only thinking of how to save myself by then."

"I'm sorry," I said. I reached across the table and wrapped my hand around her cold wrist, squeezed. Arwen didn't respond. "I can't imagine going through something like that."

"When the son of a bitch turned himself in, he claimed self-defense," she said flatly.

"No wonder they want to talk to you, right? I mean, should you tell them what you heard?"

Arwen yanked her wrist from my grip, pushed herself away from the table, and stood suddenly. "No," she said, though she couldn't bear to look at me. "It wasn't just him and Gabe in that room. His wife was there, too. She told the police all about it. Gabe down on his knees. Gabe begging. The speech her husband gives about 'protecting his property' before he pulls the trigger. When the news stations came to interview her she almost sounds proud of the son of a bitch. But every night I go to bed, I hear the phone fall, I hear Gabe begging, I hear that terrible boom." Arwen sniffed and glanced my way. The aura still haloed her faintly, but there were no tears in her eyes. Why had she cried over a dead raven, but not her boyfriend? It wasn't flintiness, I thought, but the story of someone hollowed out by grief. She had been all cried out long before she came here.

"So, if I go back there," she said, "all they will do is arrest me as an accomplice. I can't help Gabe. I packed my stuff in a duffel bag and left the same night before the cops showed up at our apartment. They already have enough to convict this man. He made a speech of his own for the cameras. Like he was some kind of avenging angel. They were waiting for Gabe. Somehow they knew he would come back. They were waiting and they executed him. Whatever happens will be up to a jury. If they convict him of premeditated murder, he will go away for life. From what I could bear to read, the wife was sick and the pills were hers, so maybe they'll go easy on her. But that's the deal. Gabe's dead, and nothing I do will make any difference."

I wasn't so sure about that. I could imagine Arwen saying what she had just told me to a jury. Explaining how Gabe went in unarmed. Helping them see the humanity of a dead addict and thief. But Arwen turned and walked away before I could say anything else, shutting herself in her room.

After she left I fired up the percolator on the stove. I would drink the entire pot myself if I had to. I had work to do. While the coffee perked, I went into my own room and downed an Effexor—technically one of the antidepressants I'd been prescribed—a preventive measure to hold off the migraine. I felt guilty taking the medicine, like I had given up on the miracle, but I left my pain meds alone. I needed to think clearly.

I sat on the edge of the bed and felt a faint pressure in my back pocket. The pamphlet Roland had given me to be photocopied and distributed. I'd forgotten all about it. I couldn't even remember putting it into my back pocket. I touched the drawing of the woman who so resembled Maura, a likeness that had provoked Elijah as well. Or maybe I was just imagining the resemblance. Already her face was fading inside me.

Maura, maybe I never saw you clearly at all.

I carried the pamphlet into the kitchen. What bothered me worst about it were the distorted faces of the gangbangers and the Jewish judge. The distortions were cartoonish, meant to be comical. They invited the viewer to be on the inside of one big, cosmic joke. And if you were on the inside you gained the power to laugh, the power to mock and demonize those who were different, the power to harm those demons you had invented.

And I kept thinking of Noah, his angry, disappointed tears. Of Professor Friedman's quote in the article, about uprooting hate from the shadows. Arwen's story had reminded me that evil is a real and active force in this world. The comic book violence in *The Turner Diaries* had inspired Timothy McVeigh to bomb the Federal Building, killing over a hundred, including a dozen children in a daycare on the lowest level. What evil might I unleash by distributing this? I tried to summon the outrage I remembered from my own near-mugging. I tried to summon the fondness I felt for Elijah and Mother Sophie, that sense of unity, us against the world. No. I recognized this for what it was. Not only vicious propaganda, but a lie that robbed people of their humanity. The percolator had bubbled over by then. I fed my pamphlet into the stove's blue flame and then carried this burning page to the sink, where I dropped it in and watched it turn to ash.

I carried the entire pot down with me into the den. I felt worse than ever about the world I lived in, but I was also certain my own time was limited. If I were to die like Gabe, I didn't want to leave this world without anything to remember me by. For all these reasons I spent the entire afternoon working on coding and design for my game.

In the last section I had written, a shadowy figure hovered at the edge of the scene, summoned by my sub-conscious mind. It was time to welcome Death into my game. I knew what to do now. My fool would have to play a chess game against Death, like in *The Seventh Seal*. If he won, Death would spare him, but if he lost he would have to journey into the Land of the Dead.

This became another cutscene, the fool playing the part that Spassky had played in Reykjavík, the impos-sible task of defending white against an all-consuming darkness. There would be no safe place for him to go but into the Land of the Dead.

Here again, I could twist the story to my purposes,

because what looked like death once more would instead open up into another unexpected adventure. Bringing all this together fueled my excitement and my fingertips flew over the keys. I worked long past when my coffee had gone cold and the cursor blurred before me, dreaming in my fugue state, only taking brief bathroom breaks and a couple of short walks with Kaiser to stretch my legs. The migraine held off for now, the aura before me a blue light that past experience taught me would narrow to a dark and painful eventuality. Unless the miracle had been real. On those walks with Kaiser, I didn't bargain with God over this. I prayed, instead, that I would be able to bear whatever pain was coming my way.

Even with the new cutscenes, my game wasn't finished. The backdrop for isometric action changed from a forest to a charred landscape, a place of molten rivers and strange beings from the Book of Revelation. In the game engine I was using, the pixelated creatures had limited outcomes once they were defeated, turning to a smudge of dark smoke that vanished, but I realized I could make another modification in the coding. Instead of dying they would follow the fool, a shadow army trailing behind him, until he could challenge Death himself—the ultimate boss—bringing with him the souls he'd saved. Newly empowered after escaping from the Land of the Dead, his final task would be to defeat the evil king who had chased him into hiding. Would he be able to save the pregnant queen in time? I wasn't ready to write that part yet.

I was grateful at least the people of Rose of Sharon hadn't asked me to create a website for them. The Internet was a vast, uncharted territory. Just imagine how many people they could reach, people who could connect anonymously and act out their hate online. Or, my God, if they asked me to make a game based on *The Turner Diaries*? It wouldn't be hard to make a simple MOD of *Doom* and change the demons to people of other races instead and then distribute it. I rubbed my face in my hands, disturbed by the thought. And yet, this could be my way back in. I would never actually make such a game or website for them, but by offering it, I could get them to listen. Mother Sophie, at least, who maybe didn't know what had happened in Roland's trailer. I could get her to listen long enough to find out what I had come for all along.

I worked on my own game all day, not knowing if it would even be playable. I didn't know if I would ever get a chance to test out the beta and work out any bugs in the programming. This project allowed me for a short time to escape the problems pressing in all around me. If I was going to die or if the world was going to end, I hoped I would have something to say my life mattered.

Arwen left me to my project, and I didn't see much of her the rest of the day. I made myself a dinner of Top

Ramen with an egg cracked into the boiling water. When I went to bed later that night, I again avoided the pain meds, Arwen's dead boyfriend looming in the back of my mind. I would need to hold on to my pain for what happened next.

I WAS DRIFTING OFF to sleep when Arwen stole in and slipped under my covers. She set a tentative hand on my chest, tracing the scar along my collarbone. "You're not really going back there, are you?"

"Roland followed me here. He knows where I live now."

"They'll hurt you."

I took hold of her hand, squeezed. "I need to see this through."

"Whether she's escaped or she's dead, she's gone, Lucien. She's not coming back. But I'm here. I'm here now and I'm asking you to stay."

I didn't say anything, but I let go of her hand. Arwen was quiet for a long minute. She propped herself on her elbow, studying my profile in the dark. Then she took my hand and brushed away hot tears from her face and held my palm against her mouth. Was she crying for me, or Gabe, or the shitty place this world had become? She kissed my hand, the inside of my wrist, seemed to shake off whatever grief gripped her as she kissed her way up my arm to my neck, where she bit down, hard enough to leave a mark. I hissed in pain, surprised but unable to complain because her lips pressed against mine. Our kissing was fierce, animal-like, our teeth clacking together. She climbed on top of me and shrugged away her nightgown. I took her breasts in my mouth, one at a time, while she pushed against me with her hips. She lowered herself once more to kiss me on the mouth, her eyes open, dark with desire. Then she disentangled me from my boxers and reached over to the other nightstand. "I found some protection," she said. "If you want to?"

I nodded, unable to speak, watching as she bit it open with her teeth. When she had it unrolled she kissed me long and deep, our tongues entwining, before she climbed on top once more and took me inside her, her chin tilted up toward the ceiling, her hips rocking gently, until it seemed like she rose to another place, like wings had sprouted from her shoulder blades. I rose with her, carried into the ether by the sweetness of her mercy. What kind of idiot was I to let her go to chase after a ghost? I held on for as long as I could, but eventually we had to come back down to earth.

IN THE MORNING, I rubbed my eyes and tried to figure out the time, well past dawn judging by the splash of light coming in through the curtains. The furnace rumbled downstairs. Arwen's side of the bed was empty, yet I felt a presence in the room. A hovering. I wasn't scared, not with the morning sun washing over me like poured amber.

In this light I saw the angel for the first time. For the only time in my life. When I remember this I try to rationalize that I was still dreaming, still half-asleep, and what I saw was part of the aura haunting my vision since the accident. A crack in my skull that was also a crack in my soul. Or maybe none of those things. All I know is that all these years later I believe the angel was real.

The angel took the shape of a glowing, golden man with black wings, as if the raven had shifted form. He was there in the waking seconds after my eyes opened, for just a breath. I know what I saw and what I felt. The angel did not speak aloud. His dark wings fanned the motes of gold dancing in the light, but otherwise he did not move. His face was too bright to behold.

When I blinked he vanished, but I lay there for a long, long time afterward, basking in the glow he left behind. A peace that surpassed all understanding. For the first time I began to hope things were going to turn out okay. The angel had come to encourage me. I had work to do. I had a person I needed to see. I had this work and I had a purpose. Find out what happened to Maura. Then I would be free.

In the years that have passed since, I have never again had dreams or visions like those that came to me in the winter of 1999. I don't dream of the devil anymore. I don't see angels or demons. I don't see them anymore, but I know they are there. We are attended by angels and demons all around us. We just no longer see. It was no trick of light, no psychosis of a damaged brain. I have never told another soul before now, but here I set this down: Angels are as real as you and me.

I knew Arwen had left for good even before I got up. The door to her room lay open, her things gone. She'd left a short note:

I've been running away all my life. Coming home was just another kind of running. See you after the world ends.

Whether she was heading back to Bellingham to face her past, or just couldn't bear to see what was going to happen to me, she was gone and it was time for me to face my own troubles. And yet if I could have foreseen what I was about to set in motion, I would have stayed the hell away from Elijah and the rest of them. Was I the light or the shadow in this story? Maybe I was both. All these years later I am still trying to understand.

Wise as Serpents

Mother Sophie drew her hands back in surprise. "What'd you do?"

"I felt like I needed a change," I said. Before I left that morning I'd shaved my entire head. I liked the way the close-crop felt, how dark my hair looked in the mirror, like a winter field shaved to bone. Like a darker, harder self I'd revealed.

I hadn't come over right away, knowing I needed to time my visit for when Elijah wouldn't be around. Mother Sophie's hands found my head again, lingering on the scars. "Like Ezekiel?" she said, and there was a quaver in her voice. Some new uncertainty. She hadn't greeted me by name. Her hands felt cold and leathery against my skin.

I knew who she meant. I'd read Ezekiel along with all the other prophets, knew the passage where he shaves his head, burning a third of the leavings within the city, striking another third with a sword, letting the wind take the final portion. He does this before he curses the wayward Israelites to a time of famine and cannibalism, of parents eating children and children eating their parents. Prophets, from what I'd gathered, went around telling people what they didn't want to hear, which I was preparing to do here. "You don't like it?"

"I do. It's just unexpected." To become a true "fresh cut" among the skinheads who frequented here someone else was supposed to shave your head for you. Maybe that was the reason for her concern. Mother Sophie muttered something I couldn't discern, took her hands away, and sat beside me on the couch. "Is there anything you would like to pray for?"

"Clarity," I said. "I have some questions that need answering." I had run into Bjorn on the way to Mother Sophie's cabin and he'd said, "I guess this means you're not just a 'hang-around' anymore," and cackled hyena-like as he loped away. I didn't know what it meant that Bjorn had returned to The Land, but they must be getting close to whatever plans they were making.

"In the Greek," she said, "the word 'apocalypse' comes from 'apokalypsis.' It translates as having something made *known*. The apocalypse is the *revelation*. So we will pray for revelation and for God's will to be made known."

She went on for some time like this, her voice dark with warning, before she led me in a short prayer. Afterward, I sipped at the lemon ginger tea she'd made for me and listened to her as she carried over mementos from her trip to the Holy Lands a decade before this. She told me about the time she'd been dis-fellowshipped, how it happened when she belonged to the Worldwide Church of God. She showed me a Polaroid of herself standing before a building that had been carved from the side of a mountain, towers of basalt rising behind her. "Petra is an ancient place," she said. "Sacred. Standing there, you breathe in the dust from which man was formed and to which he shall return." The woman in the photograph looked much younger and thinner, her face unlined as she stared boldly back at the camera. Mother Sophie told me she was grateful she got to see the place before glaucoma stole her eyesight.

I nearly jumped when she put her hand on my leg. "Is there something wrong?"

"No," I said. My leg had been tapping up and down, setting the couch vibrating. "I just had too much coffee this morning. Four cups of it."

"That sounds unwise," she said. "Jesus says, 'Behold, I am sending you out like sheep in the midst of wolves; be wary and wise as serpents, and be innocent as doves.' Poisoning yourself with too much caffeine is unwise. I'm gathering this is not the only thing you've been unwise about."

I had kept my jacket on in case I needed to leave in a hurry and the heat in the cabin pressed upon me. Before I left earlier that morning I pocketed the agate Maura had given me for a gift the first night we were together. I took it and the note she had written me, which I had folded and unfolded so many times the paper had become tissue thin. I felt the stone's solidity in my jacket pocket, close to my ribs. The last thing I had done was call Officer Connor Sheehan and leave a message on his voicemail. I slipped my hand into my jacket pocket now, closed my fist around the agate, squeezing the stone to remind myself of my purpose.

Mother Sophie took the Polaroid from my hand and cradled it carefully in her palm before slipping it into a Bible written in Braille, where she kept envelopes with various oddments and old handwritten notes she could no longer read. I had the feeling she had looked at the Polaroid many times before she went blind, memorizing the scene. I wondered if she'd been in love with whoever snapped the shot. "We never know what life has in store for us," she said. "That photo is from a happy time, but it didn't last. A week later, I was accused . . . of being in an inappropriate relationship." Mother Sophie's eyes were glassy, and for the first time since I'd met her, she fumbled for the right words. "To be dis-fellowshipped is a little like excommunication for papists. I thought it was the end for me, but it was only the beginning. I did what any disgraced person would do. I came home, and once I quit feeling sorry for myself, I got busy. I founded my own Christian Identity church, free from the false prophecies of the Worldwide Church of God. I bought this land with family money. I had been banished from the Place of Safety, so I intended to make my own. Roland was one of my first followers. When I found him, he was living out of his truck. A homeless Purple Heart veteran down on his luck. This country under ZOG eats its own heroes. I suppose you could say we found each other. He's been with me ever since."

"Were you ever married?" This felt like a natural lead-in for the question I needed to ask her. The question I had come here for. I felt certain she knew something about Maura.

Mother Sophie sighed. "You could say God's timing and my timing didn't always align. Sometimes you find the right person, but it's too late or the time is wrong."

"I know what you mean," I said, thinking of Maura. *More than you know, really.* I decided to abandon any false mention of creating a website or a game that advanced their cause. It was time for me to say it. "That's the whole reason I'm here this morning."

"I know why you're here," she said, cutting me off. "Roland's been with me from the beginning. If some of us are to remain innocent as doves, then I have to let the serpents loose to do their work. You could say he's one of my serpents. Roland told me who you are and what you've done."

"What'd he say?" She didn't sound angry so much as disappointed. How much had he told her?

"I'm also telling you goodbye, Meshach. You don't belong here. Even after Roland told me what he knows about you, I didn't want to see you get hurt. You are not wise as a serpent or innocent as any dove. You are not even one of God's sheep. You . . . you're one of the wolves, and Roland has a way of dealing with wolves that you won't like."

I didn't stand up or move. "Meshach isn't my name," I said.

"I don't want to know you by any other," she said, her voice sharpening. "You go on now. The apocalypse is coming and you'll be on your own when it does. That's punishment enough."

"I can't. Not yet. I need to know what I came here to ask."

She was quiet for a long time. The police scanner squawked and went silent on the shelf. I studied my surroundings, the gleam of aluminum sheeting, the logs and white mortar, the homey woodstove and the Confederate flag and muskets on the mantel. Despite the strangeness of their belief system I was going to miss coming here. Outside a car door slammed, the metal ringing. Elijah? I hoped he wasn't back yet. I needed more time.

"Elijah's wife, Maura," I said. "I knew her. I worked with her at the bank."

Mother Sophie's jaw tightened.

"Meshach is who I wanted to be. It's what Maura would've named her child. If she had a boy. She was pregnant when I saw her last."

Mother Sophie's grayish tongue licked out to touch her cracked lips. "Pregnant?" I saw the surprise register, the short, shivery breath that ran through her and set her wrinkles trembling.

"But I don't think she ran away," I continued. "Even if she hated this place. She wouldn't leave her daughter behind. Maura wouldn't abandon Sarah."

Her blue eyes bore into mine. "Sarah is well cared for. She has a better life now. She has a future in the world that's coming."

Footsteps in the snow outside, the burr of rough male voices coming this way.

"She was pregnant with my child, I believe."

Mother Sophie settled back against the couch. "Oh, child. I was wrong about you. How could I be so wrong about you? I thought God sent you, but it must have been the devil. You stupid, stupid boy. You don't even know what you've done."

The footsteps thudded on the creaking porch and the front door swung open. Elijah stepped into the room, still dressed in his quilted coveralls with his company's insignia on it. Snow sluiced from his cap. Roland came in behind him, his jacket open to his holster.

"I thought I told you not to come back here," Elijah said.

I stood, facing him. "I came back for answers. Where's Maura, Elijah? What happened to her?"

Elijah's face blanched. The question caught him off guard.

"You shut your mouth," Roland said, stepping around Elijah. "Or I'll shut it for you."

"Not here," Mother Sophie said in a firm voice. "The children will be released for their playtime soon. Take him somewhere else."

"You hear that?" Elijah stepped closer. "You and me, we're going for a walk."

A walk. It had the ring of finality. I might get what answers I needed from him, and then I would tell him I had alerted the police in case anything happened to me. And yet I saw my fate in his eyes. That smell of gasoline burning that had come over me in church when I heard him speak of the dead, a searing memory from my car accident, my body pinned to the seat in a crush of metal as flames lapped at the fuel line. All I knew of hell.

"I'll come, too," Roland said. "He was lying to all of us."

"No." Elijah spat the words out. "It's my wife he's asking about. My wife he was involved with. He answers to me." He spoke in a low, angry whisper. Outside the voices of children shouted as they poured out of the trailer where they went to school. "You really didn't know her. You thought you did, but you didn't know her at all. Let's go."

"Elijah," Mother Sophie called from the couch, where she had not otherwise stirred. "We can't have any undue attention placed upon us at this crucial hour. Whatever you do, be discreet about it."

Elijah pulled me in front of him. As we headed toward the door I heard Mother Sophie say, "Revelation also means an ending. Goodbye, Meshach."

Apokalypsis

Outside the cabin Elijah paused to pick up Mjolnir, his holy hammer, and strapped the AR-15 behind him. His eyes were bloodshot, his breath hanging around him in a cloud. He didn't look angry to me, more like a man burdened. I wondered if the role he played in Maura's disappearance ate at him, or regret about what he'd learned about me. Snow drifted past, a few fat lazy flakes that caught in my eyelashes.

"Are you planning to shoot me?" I said.

"I didn't think you would come back. I wish you hadn't."

"There are people who know where I went," I said, in a quiet voice that I didn't want Roland to hear. "Who know everything, I suspect. You kill me, it will be the Weaver raid all over again. Or worse, Waco."

It was a weak threat, but I had to get it out there. I didn't mention Officer Sheehan. Not yet.

"Just shut up and start walking," Elijah said, gesturing to the ridge above us. Behind us, I heard a trailer door slam open followed by the jubilant shouts of children celebrating the day's freedom. "And be quick about it," he added, shoving me ahead of him.

I took my time, numb inside as he marched me past the shooting range and away from the cabins and trailers. I was both frightened and relieved at the same time. This was coming to an end. All would be made known. Whatever happened here I would not be the same person when it was done, if I lived through it. I once read an article that explored what happened to guillotine victims during the Terror, the worst part of the French Revolution, when the streets of Paris ran with so much blood that the very water supply was poisoned by rotting corpses. The revolutionaries eating their own, a wheel of paranoia and death. Most of the victims went to their deaths silently, resignation weighing on them as they shuffled up the stairs of the *poteau*. I understood that now, the kind of torpor a sleepwalker must feel. And yet, I was more scared than I had ever been.

I slipped once coming up the steep slope and fell hard, only getting my hands out at the last moment. Ice scraped my palms and the fall took my breath. I scrabbled up before Elijah could prod me with the barrel of his rifle.

"Keep going," Elijah said. "We're not there yet."

I pushed on slowly as we climbed the ridge in silence,

snow from my fall seeping into my clothing. Chilled, I held myself as we trudged ahead in silence until we reached the top of the ridge.

At the summit we stood before the foundation of an old-fashioned log cabin, boulders and stones mortared in, the bare bones of timber set on top of it, the logs above my head, thick daub calked between them. The entire place had been torched, timbers charred and blackened, but the walls held fast. Even snow-covered it reeked of smoke and failure. A space had been left for a door and a couple of windows cut into the frame. Only the logs and foundation remained, the flooring dirt, the sky the only ceiling. Elijah motioned for me to step inside ahead of him.

Within the cabin a hardwood pew from a church was pushed up against one wall. A table and chairs made from hewn logs sat amid the burned remains. Gray ashes and grime coated everything. I coughed from the chalky dust our footsteps stirred up. Even if there were no floors or ceiling, the charred timber frame largely shut us off from the outer world.

I gazed out of one empty window frame. Far below us the trees thinned and I could see down into another valley awash with gold as the sun set beyond the trees. There a meadow spread out, leading to a barn and small white-clapboard farmhouse, chimney puffing in the cold. A pastoral scene. Cattle milled behind fences, steam rising from their flanks, and a person, no more than a tiny speck from here, hauled up the driveway on a snowmobile. They were faraway, but I could hear the whine of the engine.

Elijah paced behind me. "It's a lovely view, isn't it?"

I nodded.

"Maura chose this spot," he went on in a subdued voice. "And Mother Sophie agreed to let us build here after I got out of prison. Our own place away from the others. I've been working on this cabin for the last year. I wanted it to be a home out of a storybook." I didn't know what to make of this. Maura had mentioned her worry that Elijah was obsessed with bringing them back to The Land, but why hadn't she talked about this place if it was true that she had planned to live here? Elijah gestured with his rifle at stones tumbled against one blackened wall. "The fireplace was going to be made from river rock I hauled up myself. The loft where the children slept would be right above us. A cabin just like *Little House on the Prairie*. Maura loved that show. I thought this was her dream anyhow."

"She hated this place," I said. "She didn't want to come back here."

"Speak again without my asking and you won't like what happens," Elijah growled.

He hadn't raised the rifle, not yet. Instead, he pulled off the shoulder strap and leaned the rifle against one charred wall. He squared his shoulders and cracked his knuckles, a sharp sound in the cold. "My plan was to have this finished before the end of the year. Before Y2K. If the world was ending, I wanted us to be on top of it all. A home where no flood could touch us. Solid ground for Maura and Sarah. One day we would build a church alongside it, a new Rose of Sharon. I imagined her singing there, her hymn rising to the rafters." His voice broke and he trailed off. "It wrecked me when she went away. Not a few days later this place burned. If I didn't know better I might start to think God hates me."

Wet and shivering, I wanted to get this over with. "Why have you brought me here?"

Elijah stared at his clenched fists. "Why do you think? This right here. This cabin was our dream. It would have been ours, but someone came between us."

I opened my mouth to say something when he swept in and punched me square in the solar plexus, a blow that dropped me to my knees. I could sense him circling above, a dark wolfish shape. When I got my breath back I climbed to my feet.

"Hurts, don't it?" he said. "It doesn't compare to what I've been feeling these last few months. I need to remind you of the ground rules. You don't speak unless I ask you a direct question. You will not offer your opinions otherwise."

I took in a trembling breath and watched him, wary.

"You did this. You shat all over my dream." He sniffed, as if drawing strength from my pain. "How long were you sleeping with her?"

I started to say, "It wasn't supposed to . . ." when he hit me again, a blow that caught me in the ribs. I felt sinew tearing freshly inside me. I scrabbled again in the snow and ashes of the dirt floor. I didn't think he'd broken them, not yet, but another strike like that and my fragile ribs would snap like spongy twigs. Yet I would not stay down. I inched closer to the wall and hauled myself up.

"You will not make excuses," he said. "I don't want to hear it. She was a married woman. She had a child."

What he said was true. Had I ever really given her marriage much thought? Elijah had been a villain in her stories, a dangerous and controlling person she needed to break away from. But the man before me was a man speaking from a place of deep pain. For a short while, I had even come to think of him as an older brother. "How long was it going on? How many times?"

"The last six months," I said in a thin, nasal voice. "Almost half a year."

I saw the surprise register in his eyes. He cocked his fist. I didn't flinch before it. "I need you to tell me everything. No shitty rationalizations. How it happened. All of it."

So I did. I told him about closing late at night, about the stories she had told me and how those stories drew us closer. The songs she sang and how I idealized her as a musician and a mother. How our relationship started as a friendship that deepened into something else, all emotion at first. How I romanticized her with every fiber of my being. How she had turned me away, gently at first. I didn't go into intimate details. That story belonged to Maura and I alone. I wouldn't give it up or change a damn thing about what happened. Or so I thought then, hurting and defiant.

Elijah continued to pace as I talked, circling. We were so far from anything in this wrecked cabin. No one would hear me scream. And yet I felt for him. I could imagine that loft taking shape, Sarah's delighted squeal as she climbed the ladder into her own space. Maura hanging wash on the line, the wind whipping her hand-sewn dresses, billowy as sails, her belly swelling with another happy pregnancy as Elijah came up behind her and wrapped his arms around her and they looked out on a view that stretched into forever. That was *his* dream for her. I had ruined all that. I didn't see his next punch coming. He clocked me in the side of the head, his ring finger ripping my earlobe as his fist lashed past.

This time I went down and didn't get up right away. My ears rang. Blood poured down my neck into my collar. "So you thought to replace me," he said, his breathing ragged. "Because I wasn't worthy."

When I touched my ear my hand came away drenched

with blood. I stood, wavering, and held it out before me, remembering the last time I'd seen Maura alive. *Lucien, you are going to have to take me to the hospital.* Her voice, shaking. "She was afraid," I said. Blood seeped from my fingers to the ashes below. "That's why she ran. That's why I'm better than you."

"That what she told you, huh?" He stepped closer. "I knew her from the time she was sixteen years old. You didn't know her. She had already had experiences then I couldn't imagine. She was my first and only love, but already there was something hard in her. She liked it rough. Liked to get me worked up. Oh, she could be mean."

Elijah didn't punch me, instead jabbing his finger into my chest, forcing me to step back. Until I was up against the rear wall. "Like that, but with words. Her complaints. Her refusal to be happy with anything I did. A couple of times she even slapped me. What man would take that without responding?"

I thought of Maura, holding herself. *Married people fight*, she'd said. "Not you," I said.

"Not any real man. So I would grab her hand, bend her wrist back." He did the same to me as he spoke. He shoved me against the wall, his hands on my chest, his face right in mine, his breath hot against my cheek. Like he might kiss or bite me. I was too dizzied by pain to fight him, but a new panic entered me. I had steeled myself for pain, had expected the punches, but not this strange, brutal intimacy. "Hard," he said in a low voice. "She would get this gleam in her eye. She liked it. Sometimes she fought back, slapping and clawing. Then we would be tearing at each other's clothing and I would take her standing up. That how it was for you?"

I didn't dare try to defend myself or even speak. His voice was filled with such animal desperation that when his hands gripped my shirt, I thought he might tear it away. His face so close to mine I smelled his stale breath. "No, of course it wasn't. Maura knew how to read people, how to become what she thought they wanted. In the early days of the movement, both of us in it together, she was a warrior like me. My feathercut skinbyrd. But she changed. Motherhood changed her and time. And prison changed me. Both of us changing so much that a gap grew between us until we were like strangers to one another."

"Is that why you killed her?"

Elijah whipped his forehead forward so it cracked against the crown of my skull. I slumped against the wall, but he held me up, his hands closing around my throat. "That what you think? That I murdered my own wife? The mother of my daughter? I've done a lot of bad things. I've hurt people. Far worse than I've hurt you so far. I've done things I will answer for in the afterlife. But I didn't kill her," he said, gritting his teeth. "I have as many questions as you. Tell me again about the last night you saw her."

Dizzied by blood loss and pain, I did my best. I told him about how she had been feeling sick. Her gums bleeding. How she knew something was wrong inside of her. How she came out of the staff bathroom with blood on her hands and asked me to take her to the hospital. How I didn't know she'd stolen the money. How I didn't know it would be the last time I ever saw her.

This whole time he stayed pressed up against me, as if leaning on me. "You don't understand what's happening here, do you?"

I shook my head.

"Here," he said, and he unbuttoned the side of his quilted coverall, untucking the flannel shirt beneath it. He took hold of my right hand, squeezing tighter when I tried to pull away, squeezing so hard I thought I heard bones pop. He forced my hand up under his shirt. I felt cold, clammy skin. The tautness of his abdomen and just above it something hard and metallic. Taped against his belly. A few wires trailing away. He shoved my hand away and tucked his shirt back in. "You know what it is?"

I nodded. I only wanted to lie down, press my aching head and face into the snow. I had come here for answers about Maura, not this. Elijah's voice faded in and out. "I started wearing it about a month before Maura left. You're right about her being scared. But not of me. Roland and others have something big in the works. They want to make sure we have enough of a stockpile so they plan on hitting a few banks over in Wisconsin—Superior, most likely—maybe farther south all the way down to Eau Claire. They think they'll get away with it because of the chaos Y2K will bring. No one will care about a few bank robbers when there are riots in the streets and cities burning. So they started asking Maura questions about bank procedures. Operational stuff. Maura freaked."

He stepped away from me as he said this.

"Any bank robbery involves the Feds," I told him. "They'll catch all of you, eventually."

"No shit. That's why I went to the Feds first. Maura pulled away from me. At the time I thought she was afraid of what was going to happen. I suspected something was wrong. She'd been cold to me for so long. But I didn't think she would try to leave me. I didn't want to add to her fears. I didn't know about you."

My world was suffused with light, pouring in through the cracks in my brain. Yet the migraines had not returned despite the beating I'd taken. Slumped against the wall, bleeding and cold, I only wanted to lie down and sleep. The falling dark cast his face in shifting shadows.

"Why couldn't she just wait?" he went on. "Hold on for a few months until I could gather what the Feds wanted. I need you to believe me. In the beginning I thought your coming here was a good thing. A distraction. All that nonsense about prophecy. They stopped worrying about the ways I had become different. They stopped trying to change me back into the man I was before prison. But I just don't understand how she could leave me and Sarah. How could she and not send some kind of word?"

"Maybe she didn't," I said.

Elijah stiffened suddenly, twisting his head around.

"What?" I said, my voice rasping.

He held a finger over his mouth as he reached behind for Mjolnir. "Who's out there?" he called a second later.

"Eli," Roland's voice sounded just beyond the door. "Why don't you come on out of there? Bring that boy with you. We need to talk."

Elijah didn't move. "How long you been out there, Roland?"

"Long enough," he said, his voice coming from a different spot outside. He was moving around, perhaps trying to throw Elijah off, his steps whispery in the snow.

Elijah leaned in close to me. "These people are worse than you know. Can you run?"

"I think so," I whispered. My head pulsed with pain, but I could see and move. I wanted to ask him why he was helping me, but the words caught inside me. Elijah gestured to the window, toward the farm I'd seen in the valley below. *Run*, he mouthed.

"Come on out of there, Eli," Roland called again.

"Caroline has Sarah down at the trailers. They're waiting for us. Sarah wants to see her daddy again. You'd like that, too."

Elijah took hold of me and shoved me over to the window.

Then his arms were under me and I scrambled for the windowsill, feeling charcoaled timbers crumble under my grip, and Elijah gave a heave from under me, propelling me up and out. I landed awkwardly on the other side, my boots crunching into a snowbank. I didn't run though. I couldn't.

Blood and Soil

I couldn't because in the trees below me I saw the beam of a Maglite go on and I heard footsteps in the snow and knew I could not go that way.

I stood huffing in the cold, sure that I couldn't stay right out here in the open where I would be easy pickings. Elijah had the cover of the cabin, but his defensive position meant he wouldn't be able to tell which side Roland was coming from.

I made for the woods on the other side, only stopping when I reached the edge of a ravine and slipped down behind a jack pine with a massive trunk. I didn't have gloves on, so my hands and fingers stung rawly in the cold. My ribs ached, and the blood had slowed from my torn earlobe, congealing and hardening into a red mask I could feel covering my lower face and neck. I blew on my hands and squeezed them in my pockets. I was dizzy from the beating Elijah had given me, but not concussed. Cold and pain were the least of my problems. In the jacket pocket I found Maura's agate and squeezed it for courage.

The crack of Mjolnir split the air.

"Don't come any closer," Elijah shouted from within his ruined cabin. "I don't want to see anyone get hurt."

"Eli," Roland called, coming out from behind one of the trees. "Eli's coming . . ." he said, singing the name out. "You need to come out of there. Easy like. Caroline has Sarah. You want your daughter back, you will cooperate."

I couldn't see what was happening from my vantage on the side of the cabin, so I pulled myself up by the rough bark of the trunk and crept along the border of the woods. Snow muffled my footsteps as I moved in a slow lope, my heart drumming in my ears.

"Well, then," Elijah said. "It appears we have ourselves a classic standoff. Meshach is gone. He's halfway to the farmhouse by now."

"You mean Lucien Swenson? That's his rightful name. His legal name. You come on out of there and I'll tell you all about that little idiot. He's not making it to any farmhouse. I sent Bjorn to cut off the back way."

I could see Roland now, leaning against the trunk of a bare oak tree, his .45 held casually in his right hand, resting against his leg. I crouched behind another scruffy jack pine, snow sifting down when I leaned on the trunk. I thought I could hear someone moving through the woods behind me, snapping branches as he came. This was my chance to get away. Shivers coursed through my body, though I tried to remain still.

Elijah appeared in the doorway, looking down the barrel of Mjolnir. Roland straightened and brought his pistol up. "Drop the gun, Eli. Now. Or Sarah pays the price. Neither of us wants that."

Elijah's finger slipped inside the trigger guard as he exhaled heavily, the ghost of his breath rising around him, before his finger fell away. "Caroline wouldn't do that, Roland. Mother wouldn't allow it." Yet he lowered his rifle and stepped from the cabin.

Roland kept his own pistol raised. "You'd be surprised what Mother will allow."

"I want to talk to Mother," Elijah said. "Promise me you'll take me to her and I'll do what you ask."

Roland dipped his head. "First, you're gonna have to show me some faith. You gotta drop your gun. You don't get to hold on to it if you're going to see Mother. The wire, too."

Elijah took a step closer. He didn't try to deny the wire. He lifted up his shirt and revealed what he'd shown me. The tape made a tearing sound as he peeled it away from his skin and tossed it into the snow between them. "What'd you do, Roland?"

"Just do what I say. Take off your shoulder strap and set it on the ground. Do it slow." Roland stepped from the oak and approached, his .45 still raised. "Don't you worry, now. This all might turn out right. You're one of Mother's favorites. The star preacher she picked to lead us into a new millennium."

Elijah lifted the strap from his shoulder and carefully lowered Mjolnir to the ground. "What'd you do, Roland?" he said again.

"That last day she left here. I seen Maura pack a bag in the trunk of the car. I knew she was running. Mother Sophie can't abide runners. Now, how long have you been wearing the wire?"

"Does it matter?" Elijah asked.

"You owe us that much. You owe us the truth. Mother Sophie will want to know."

"And I will tell her myself. You said you'd take me to her. So you saw Maura put a bag in the trunk? What happened next?"

Roland cocked back the hammer of his pistol and gestured at the recorder Elijah had ditched. "First, I need you to crush that goddamn thing into dust."

"It's not even on," Elijah said. "I knew I was going to have to deliver some punishment and didn't think anyone needed to listen in on it."

"Oh, I can understand not wanting ZOG to know what kind of man you are. A cuckold and an abuser. Now, do it!"

Elijah grimaced, but he still lifted his boot and stamped down, grinding the machine until it was fairly dismembered. I used the sound as cover so I could keep creeping forward, moving from tree to tree. They were only about twenty feet away now. When he was done, Elijah looked up at Roland, his fists clenched at his sides. I thought for a moment he might rush him. Roland didn't waver with his .45. "How long have you been wearing it? And why?"

"I'll tell you, but I have questions of my own. I started before Maura left. I didn't want any part of your robbery plans. I wasn't going back to jail. Never again." He massaged his right fist, bruised by battering me, as he spoke. "I promised Maura. Soon as you started asking her about bank procedures and she got nervous."

"So that means they have us on conspiracy to commit a crime. But no crime itself."

"They were going to wait until your plans were definite and you made your move. They can put you away for much longer if they caught you in the act."

I heard a twig break behind me in the woods. I figured it had to be Bjorn circling back. I twisted around looking for him, but I couldn't see him or the bob of his flashlight.

"Goddamnit, Eli. You were like a son to me. And to Mother. Here we are almost to the end of the story. Almost to our Promised Land. And you have to go and fuck everything up. All because you're afraid of a little jail time? The Eli I knew was a blood-and-soil man. He wasn't afraid of anything."

"Yeah. I'm not him anymore. I changed."

"Changed how? You don't believe?"

Barely perceptible, Elijah inched closer to Roland, both fists tucked at his side. "You know that little Jew who I beat so badly I thought I'd killed him? He came to see me. Visited me in jail to tell me I was forgiven. I've never been so ashamed. So, I believe in the Bible, just not the way you all have it twisted. There were months in prison when the Bible was all I read. The Word of God. And there's not a single passage in there telling me to hate other people because of the color of their skin. I read it and I saw Jews not as enemies who killed Christ, but as brothers who share a common father in Abraham. I read it and I saw for the first time that I didn't want any part of it anymore. I wanted to be done with Nazis and skinheads and all the other violent garbage we've surrounded ourselves with." He dipped his head. "There. That enough of a confession for you?"

"Why didn't you just go, then? Would've been better for all of us." When Elijah took another small step, Roland waved the pistol at him. "Don't come any closer."

"Because you are my people. Because I thought I could share with you what I learned. Because, deep down, I was still afraid the world might end at Y2K and I wanted to be here with the only family I have left." He swallowed. "What did you mean about Maura?"

I wondered about what he wasn't saying. If he had cut a deal with the Feds for early release from prison. Roland was likely thinking the same.

"You always did like this patch of dirt, didn't you? Setting yourself above us, high and mighty like. You can still have it. Caroline's in love with you. She's sick with it. She will be true to you in a way Maura never was. She will be a good mother to Sarah."

Elijah spoke in a guttural growl. "She's not Sarah's mother."

"Sarah's mother is dead."

Everything seemed to go still. I'd been creeping forward and was maybe only about ten feet away now. I didn't dare come any closer. My vision blurred by drying blood over one eye, the men before me were specters in the twilight.

"Bullshit. She took the money and ran. Used your own plans against you."

Roland shook his head slowly from side to side. "When I seen her pack that bag, I just knew."

"You could've come to me. You should've. She was my wife." Elijah's voice broke.

"Figured you might be in on it. Like I said, you'd been acting different. So, I was waiting for the end of her shift out in the parking lot. Seen her get in the car with the college kid. It was dark, though, and the best glimpse I had of them was under the streetlamps. I couldn't be sure who the young man was when he started showing up at Rose of Sharon. But I had suspicions."

"What happened?" In the gap between words, Elijah took another small step. I mirrored his movements.

"It was an accident, Eli. Accidents happen."

"Sure," Elijah said, taking another step, weaving slightly to the side. "I know they do."

"Stop right there. I got an itchy trigger finger. Mother Sophie still has uses for you. I'd like to bring you back without your head blown off. We can use you to feed false information to the Feds."

Elijah lowered his head. "What happened?" he repeated.

"I followed them to the hospital, where he dropped her off. She waited until he drove away without going inside. Then she started walking up the street, likely heading for the bus stop. She didn't see me coming, didn't even flinch when my truck pulled up behind her and I came out the door. Only when she seen my face did she try to run."

Roland's hand shook as he kept the .45 trained on Elijah's head.

"Go on," Elijah said.

I knew I couldn't get any closer without getting spotted. Hunched over, my hands in my pockets, I closed my fist around the agate, felt its solidity in my palm.

"I grabbed her and forced her into the back of the truck. But you know Maura. She didn't go easy, lashing out with her legs and fists. She got me good a few times. She was hollering to wake the neighborhood. I tossed her in the back of the truck and gagged her with duct tape, her mouth first to stop her screaming. Then her legs and feet. I only meant to drive her back to you. Bring her home to The Land. Thought you could reason with her. But I had been hasty with that tape. Had to stop her screaming and when I put it on I must have blocked her nasal passages, too. I could hear her threshing in the back and just figured she was fighting, like a fish on the line. I didn't realize . . . I didn't know."

When I saw Elijah tense, moving into a crouch, I rose from my hiding place and shouted "Hey!" as I hurled the stone. I didn't have my full strength behind the throw, not with my hurt ribs, but it was enough of a distraction. Roland pivoted and fired in my direction before I could duck away. The bullet missed me, blasting into the pine trunk beside me, the bark exploding. Splinters of it pierced my face as I fell to the ground, blinded. What happened next I can't say for sure. I heard Elijah roar as he bulled into Roland, heard the bone-crunch of his tackle, the hard grunt of fists punching into soft places, stealing breath. The incredibly loud boom of the pistol that ended the struggle.

I crouched, picking splinters from my forehead and

face. They'd missed my eyes, fortunately, but I couldn't see for the blood at first. Footsteps came toward me in the snow. Either my savior or killer approached.

"Come on," urged Elijah's breathless voice, "we can't stay here." When I wiped away a sheave of blood, I saw him before me, looming, Mjolnir looped around his shoulder, an angel of death. He reached a hand to help me up. "You see which way Bjorn went?"

I clasped his hand, the same hand that had beaten me savagely moments before and let him help me up. "He's somewhere back there," I said. "I thought I heard him behind me in the trees."

"Okay," he said. "We need to get you out of here before the rest come. They'll have heard the shot down at the trailers. They'll be coming."

"What about you?"

His face was a shadow in the twilight, his eyes unreadable. "I can't leave Sarah," he said. "Neither could Maura. I think I knew all along that she hadn't gotten away. I knew she wouldn't leave us. She's been here the whole time. I have to find out where. Mother will know where."

I wiped away more blood and was about to say something, when a red laser swept out from behind the cabin wall. Bjorn had circled back the other direction. Since Elijah was facing me, he didn't see it right away. The red light sliced through the trees before finding me in the space between. In the split second that I made to shout out a warning, I looked down and saw a red spot bloom in the center of my chest.

Elijah barked, "Get down!" and then I felt his body crash into mine. I heard the rapid crack-crack-crack of the assault rifle, bullets ripping past and tearing into flesh as we fell and fell through the air and his weight crushed me into the snow. He crashed down on top of me, punching the breath from my lungs. When I could breathe again beneath him, I called out softly.

"Eli?" He didn't respond. "Get up!" I said. "He's coming this way." The salt of his blood, warm as tears, dropped from his face to mine. My hand cupped the back of his head, but where his skull should have been my fingers dipped into soft tissue, wet and unspeakable.

My gorge rose in my throat and I shoved him away from me, sliding out from under his corpse.

Mercifully, when I'd pushed him away he landed faceup in the snow, his wide-set eyes open and staring, glassy in death, that spark of intelligence snuffed out. As the red laser swept the area just above us, searching for me, I knelt by his body, my fingers brittle in the chill, and unclipped Mjolnir from the shoulder straps. From the trailers below I could see a host of Maglites coming up through the pines, at least a half dozen, likely led by the watcher in the tower. The men coming this way would be as heavily armed as Bjorn.

When Elijah had tackled me, he dropped us into a small depression out of sight. I shouldered Mjolnir and worked my way on my back to peer over the edge. From behind the other side of the cabin, the red eye of the laser swept out once more.

I looked at Bjorn through the sighting, my finger on the trigger. I took in two steadying breaths—in through my nose and out through my mouth. I could have taken his head off or shot him right through the throat, where that ugly iron cross crawled from his collar. I thought of those targets at the range, their silhouettes, and how easily I had pulled the trigger then. I drew a bead and fired four shots in quick succession, aiming not for Bjorn, but the cabin wall beside him, knowing the explosion of splinters might take him out. He screamed and fell away.

On a ridge below me, the Maglites fanned out, crazed beams dancing up in the pines as they dove for cover. I kept my sighting high and fired at regular intervals, aiming for the trees around them. The crack and thump of Mjolnir the only sound until I had emptied the high-capacity clip of all thirty bullets. Then I dropped the rifle and ran in a low crouch, slipping through the snow as I slid down another ridge and lay there, panting, the smell of gunpowder and blood thick in my nostrils.

I thought about which way to go. I had no way to make it past the men in the trees to my car in the lot below. If I tried directly for the farmhouse, they would suspect that, too.

Not faraway, I heard a call and echo. Someone cursed, a garbled cry as they must have found Roland's body.

I waited, getting my breath back, not knowing which way to go.

"Here," someone shouted nearby. "I see his tracks!"

I ran again as a beam of yellow light lit up the pines nearby. I ran hard and low and didn't even see the drop-off. I was running one moment and then I was walking in midair before gravity took hold of me and I tumbled down a steep slope. I managed to get my hands out before I plunged right into an icy creek. I didn't stop. Once I got my balance, I slipped into the rushing current, soaking my pant legs, and headed upstream, the way I figured they wouldn't expect.

I heard them behind me as I made it around a bend. Maglites blazed in the pines as they closed in. Ahead of me part of the slope must have collapsed in a flood, toppling an immense oak tree that had fallen across the gulley, leaving gnarled roots exposed. Wolf tree, I thought, delirious with fear and pain, old growth. The mass of twisting roots made a doorway. Without looking behind me, I scrambled up and heaved myself inside, ignoring the scraping fingers of the roots that shredded my clothes and skin. I squeezed my way into a hollow space within the heart of the tree.

Here, I curled up, drawing my knees to my chest. Melting water rushed underneath, the icy flow of the current washing past, I clasped my wet jeans, and curled in like a fetus.

Voices called outside. I held my breath as one of the Maglites peered into the root cave, blinding me. The light found me and pierced me. I was a dead man. "Must have gone the other way," the voice said. A young voice, no older than a teenager.

The light pulled away. I stayed huddled in the dark. I couldn't run anymore, even if I had wanted. My adrenaline spent, I felt so bone-weary and cold that I could have slept for days.

They splashed off in search of me downstream.

The lights didn't come back. They were gone. Yet, I remained within the tree. Even the pain of my torn earlobe and bruised ribs felt far from me, a pain that belonged to someone else. While my boots were waterproof, my pants had been soaked up to the knees. I shivered but didn't even feel the cold. Instead a strange warmth surrounded me, embryonic, and I listened to the ebb and flow of the creek, wondering dimly if I was in shock, while the tree held me as a mother holds a child. As Yggdrasil must have held the children at the end of the world. Don't sleep, a part of my brain warned. If you sleep you will never leave this place. I wondered if hypothermia was already settling in.

THE LAND

Maura, oh Maura, you almost got away, didn't you?

The agate had been the only gift she had given me, polished and dark at first glance, but lit with many colors when you studied it. Now all I had left was the handwritten note she gave me along with it. I knew the words by heart. Huddled in the wolf tree, I pictured her elegant handwriting and the words she had set down.

Lucien,

I know we have spoken about how I wanted to study geology if I'd been allowed to finish my degree, but still you must think this agate an odd gift. It's the bad children who end up with coal in their stockings at Christmas, right? But if you study the stone you will see a rainbow of colors. It's a darkness lit with many colors.

I need to explain. In the Book of Genesis it says that the earth was without form and void and darkness was upon the face of the deep. And the spirit of God brooded over the face of the waters. That's the only creation story I will be allowed to tell my daughter, Sarah, according to the official homeschooling curriculum from Christian Liberty Press. You want to know a heresy that would get me banned from my church? I believe your professor is in the right of it. How long did God brood? A single heartbeat? A billion years? Time is a human construct and doesn't really exist. It allows us to measure day and night and try to make sense of it. But if God exists, then God must be beyond time.

Hmm . . . see how I can be philosophical, too? I promise you, one day I will go back to school.

You must wonder where I'm going with all of this. The stone you hold. Maybe thousands and thousands of years ago the lava compressed quartz to make it. Long, long ago. Down in the darkness, the earth created this light, these colors. It's a stone that holds fire. Just as each of us are made from carbon, the dust of stars. The passage of millions of years to make this stone are a greater miracle than if God magicked it from the thin air.

When you hold this agate, you hold my heart in your hands. I give it to you freely. When you hold the stone, remember me. Like this stone in each of us there is also a darkness that sometimes presses upon us. My prayer for you is that in that place deep down inside, you learn how to make light.

— Maura

As love letters went, hers was dissatisfying, but each time I read it I also felt a deepening of mystery. She was saying goodbye in the note. She knew our relationship couldn't last. She knew the darkness was going to press down on us both.

I might have fallen asleep because the next I knew Maura was there in the hollow with me. The sandalwood scent of her, the brush of her long hair as she bent over me, her voice whisper-singing a hymn in a tongue that time had forgotten. How I loved you, Maura.

I reached for her in turn.

But her hands were not soft when they found me. Her fingernails, coils of horned bone, scraping, her hair white, sallow skin rotting and peeling away from her cheekbones. She smelled of ashes and rot as she reached for me, grabbing hold of my torn earlobe. "Wake up!" she hissed. "You have to get out of here!"

I lurched, lashing out with my feet, hands threshing and tangling in the roots. There was no one here, just the tendrils of roots and the warm dark of a dead tree and the teeth-chattering cold that returned with my waking. I had to move.

I pushed past the twisted-root doorway and dropped down into the stream. I didn't even pause to look for the lights. How long had I been out? I didn't know. I couldn't go back to the trailers. I didn't know the way. Numbly, I followed the creek to its source where it spilled out from a crevice in the hill. I kept going, up a slope of granite scree, until I could see the dark valley spreading below the trees. I cut down the slope, keeping well away from the cabin where Elijah and Roland had been killed. I could no longer feel my feet, my tread heavy, every step an agony. I only wanted to curl up in the snow and sleep. I willed myself to keep going.

I don't know how long I walked, but eventually I made it down to the main road leading to The Land. I kept to the treeline, trudging, my thoughts empty. If I tried to think, the terrible memory of Elijah's death came back to me. At one point I heard tires crunching over the gravel behind me and instinctively I threw myself down in the brush. A pickup rolled past, its headlights off, and in the bed of the truck I saw the cherry flare of a cigarette and heard a low murmur of voices before they were gone. They were still out here, hunting me.

I forced my stiff limbs to get up and kept limping along the road, stopping now and then to listen. I passed the first farm I came upon in case they were watching it and kept going. To walk up any of these quarter-mile-long driveways would leave me exposed. The first gray fingers of dawn spread along the horizon. A crow cawed from a pine and flitted off into the woods. I followed it, cutting through a grove of bare apple trees, which gave way to a fenced meadow and then an L-shaped farmhouse. I hobbled across the meadow. The kitchen light was on, a gray-haired woman in a blue nightgown rinsing something in the sink.

I knocked at the back door, which had a small glass window. A dog snarled from within the house and the kitchen light went dark. I was too numb with shock and desperation to wonder what it must have felt like to have someone knocking at your back door in the early morning light, or if she glimpsed the horror of my face through the window, the mask of dry blood around my eyes and mouth, and what she must have thought when she saw me. I knocked again, my fists numb against the wood.

The pale oval of the woman's face appeared. She blinded me when she turned on the porch light. "I have a gun," she said in a shaking voice, "and I will not hesitate to use it if you try to get in this house."

"Please," I said. "You have to help me."

At World's End

When the ball dropped on Times Square there was a single moment when I caught myself not breathing. Just one split second when I found myself praying that it might really be true. I knew that I was thinking with the part of my brain still under the strange spell of Rose of Sharon's apocalyptic teachings. I wanted all the sickness of this world wiped away—the world that had killed Maura and Elijah and Roland and left a little girl orphaned—and for a better one to take its place. Maybe in some ways that's what happened. Inside of me.

I watched the ball drop from my mother's living room in Mount Greenwood. She rose and cinched the belt of her bathrobe tighter. "Let's go make some noise," she said, which is something we've done ever since I was a boy old enough to stay up until midnight. My mom rummaged in the kitchen and got out some pots and pans for each of us and lugged them to the back deck overlooking the cemetery. A cloudy night with ever-present drizzle dripping from the bare trees.

"You ready?"

"Ready," I said, and drew in a deep breath. "Ready to sound my barbaric yawp over the rooftops of the world."

I hoped she wouldn't hear the false joviality in my words and was grateful she laughed. "You and your poetry," she said, and we commenced with such a clatter to wake every sorry soul that had already gone to bed, bored by the passage of yet another year, a clatter to wake the dead on Judgment Day. We banged those pots and pans and hooted like two fools, my voice more like a wolf pup yipping than a barbarian yapping. A neighborhood dog yowled in response and was joined by several others in chorus. Down the street someone laid on his horn. I hollered with all the breath in my body, the names of the dead rising up inside me, all my pain and frustration contained in the sound. My pots clanged together, a tinny ringing. When we finally ran out of breath, the world seemed too silent, the darkness too vast.

"Fucking Y2K," I muttered, for it was clear the world would go as it had before.

"Well," my mother said, ignoring my profanity. She clinked one of her pots against mine. "We gave them heck."

We trudged back inside and put away our sundry noisemakers. My mother yawned and apologized for it. In her bathrobe and slippers, her hair prematurely silver, she looked older than she was. I know I looked the same. I felt like I'd lived ten years in the space of one.

"You go on to bed," I told her. "I'm going to stay up a little longer."

My mom nodded, her eyes watering. There were a thousand unasked questions behind those eyes, but she let me be. I loved her for that. I had told the story too many times already to the police and Feds. Every time I told it I felt like some piece of me peeled away and died. My mom didn't try to hug me, but she lingered for a minute, perhaps considering how to bridge the space between us. I hoped not to wake her up again, screaming with another nightmare, my fingers dipping into the back of Elijah's skull, the weight of his dead body crushing me into the snow. "Good night," she said at last and went off down the hall.

I traipsed to my room down in the walkout basement. Maps of Middle Earth mixed with posters of Sarah Michelle Gellar from *Buffy the Vampire Slayer*. A boy's room. The room of a stranger. Why was I still alive when others had died?

I had brought my two computers back from the Kroll house and hooked them up again with the LAN line on a single Sauder wood desk, which sagged under the weight of those clunky monitors. The only refuge I had found after coming home was in this game.

I sat in my desk chair and booted up *The Land*. In the final scene, when the fool returns from the Land of the Dead, he learns of the queen's public execution and how her body was left out as food for the crows. The fool has no choice but to lead his shadow army and make war on the king. In this version, you return as revenant and destroyer. You must burn down the old, sick world that killed your queen to make it new again. I played the game out and the screen lit up with the final triumphant image, a painting I had digitized, The Land bathed in gold.

"In another world," Elijah had once said, "Hitler gains admission to art school and never goes to prison or writes *Mein Kampf*." I was only able to sleep again at night when I dreamed up other worlds, a different ending for each of them.

IN THE STORY I told myself, Elijah takes Sarah with him and moves to a new town. Maura gets away and stays on the move, never settling in any one place too long. Maybe you have seen her at a bus station or a park bench, a new guitar and case beside her, and have been struck by the shifting light in her eyes. The light holds her face in such a way that she reminds you of someone you knew, so you sit and listen to her sing a hymn so sad and sweet that you can dream of a world where there is no death any longer. Perhaps you tell her that her name is written down in the book of life and are surprised when she weeps. In this moment you have touched something vulnerable inside her. For if the dead are all around us, wearing the faces of strangers, perhaps only in this way can they be held.

The morning I appeared at the door of the woman's farmhouse she hadn't called the police right away. She hadn't wanted any trouble between her and the "crazies" on The Land, so she drove me to hospital herself, carefully spreading newspapers so I could lay down on the backseat of her station wagon. I would end up spending the next two days in the Aurora Bay hospital I already knew so well, recovering from hypothermia and telling the feds what I knew.

The ATF did end up raiding The Land, going in at night, and managed to take Bjorn and others into custody without further loss of life. Mother Sophie was sentenced as an accessory to commit a crime, the money from Maura's robbery recovered from her cabin, and Sarah went into foster care. The Feds found Maura's body exactly where I told them they would. I had remembered how her spirit had come to me in the tree, smelling of ashes. They found her buried under the cabin Roland must have set on fire to cover up his crime.

I never saw Arwen again, though I searched for news online. The articles I read in the *Bellingham Herald* detailed the testimony of Gabe's partner and girlfriend, which ultimately helped put his killer away for life in prison. Arwen was not charged as an accessory to any crime, so far as I could see, so they must have cut a plea bargain deal with her.

A couple of days after I arrived home in Mount Greenwood, Albert Kroll called and screeched at me through the phone. He was furious that a book had gone missing, a very important book. He didn't say the title, but I knew he was talking about the *Gemäldegalerie Linz*. When he threatened to sue me over my failures as a caretaker, I simply said, "Maybe you should talk to your daughter." He was still screeching threats when I hung up the phone. I was not surprised a week later when the online version of the *Bellingham Herald* reported an anonymous donation to the Whatcom Museum of an album featuring artwork stolen by the Nazis.

The game didn't get me the job I coveted at BioWare, but it became a small legend on the shareware scene. It would be a long time before I created another; in the early 2000s I followed the path of most computer science majors into the burgeoning telecom industry. I went where the money said to go, but programming and game design were in my blood already. I went on to found my own company, Golem Dreams, and to make games with overtly religious themes: as Noah you plot how to conserve resources and keep the animals on your ark alive (including creatures that never existed or were lost to time) as you search for land; as Moses you battle the Pharaoh's sorcerers, turning the Nile to blood, before you lead the Jews out of slavery in Egypt; as young David, you slay giants and hide out in a cave as King Solomon hunts for you. These games were published under the Jewish idea of Midrash, a way of honoring ancient stories through imaginative retelling. I like to think that had Elijah lived — the Elijah I came to know and not the one I had been expecting — he would have approved.

The migraines never returned, but sometimes I still see an aura around people, and at the furthest corners of my eyes, a swirling of dark wings. The aura that surrounds people is a kind of liminal glow. It's how I met my wife a few years later. She was in the campus library, books and notes scattered before her. The aura made her strawberry blond hair glow like burnished metal. It transfixed me and she must have felt my staring because she looked up from her studies, pale brow furrowing. "Can I help you?"

I liked the sound of her voice, quiet and assuring. My ribs and hip had mostly healed, but I walked with a limp and would the rest of my life. I would never run again. I limped over and sat down across from her. She appeared to be a few years younger than me, her eyes a clear, cornflower blue. "My name's Lucien," I said. It wasn't much of a line, but it was a start. "What are you studying?"

"Angels," she said. "Their hierarchy. It's for a paper on *Paradise Lost.*"

I nodded. This was a subject I knew well. "The poet Blake said that Milton did the devil's work when he wrote *Paradise Lost,*" I said. "He made Lucifer too sympathetic."

She shook her head. "Maybe Lucifer is in the beginning, but by the end he's a wretch. 'Better to reign in hell than serve in heaven' is not the speech of a hero. Even his best monologues are packed with self-serving lies. He's an egoist who only causes harm unto others."

"In the beginning, he dreamed of a better world," I tried to argue.

"With himself on top. Typical dude stuff." She laughed. "I'm Rachel, by the way." She held out her hand. I took it and held on.

NOT A DAY PASSES when I don't think of that winter. A season of omens and miracles. The winter when birds fell from the sky and an old woman laid her hands on the crown of my head and healed my pain with a touch. For a time, I walked with angels. For a time, I was haunted by demons. I no longer see them, the hole closing up in my skull, the cracked places healing over. I no longer see angels or demons, but I know they are there.

There is a house in my mind where it is always winter and the snow falls without ceasing, a house perched on a cliff of anthracite above a boiling blue river. An ageless hound bounds ahead of me, leading me to the edge of the world. At night the stars are so close I can touch them like leaves, and ravens with forked tongues cry out from the pines in human voices.

Years later I visited a koi pond at the Japanese Garden in Jackson Park after a bad cold snap. I remember thinking of the agate Maura had given me and that I had thrown away. I wanted to tell her about the smothering weight that pressed upon me for years after that winter. I wanted to assure her that down in the darkness, I had learned how to make light. The koi were there, muffled tongues of fire obscured by ice. It was true, what Arwen had told me. A koi can suspend its heartbeat to one beat per minute, burrow into the mud and wait for warmth again, a season of light. Dreaming in the mud, they survive the cold that presses upon them, stealing breath. And in that natal darkness, as the ice melts away, oh how they rise again into the shining.

Author's Note

No church like Rose of Sharon existed in the Arrowhead region in the late 1990s. The monument to the Duluth lynchings was not defaced during this time. So, why is the novel set in Minnesota, a progressive state with a reputation for tolerance?

This story started with a dog, or rather a husband and wife who asked me to care for their house in the country while they were gone for the winter. They gave me one strict instruction: make sure the dog survives. Over winter, the loneliest winter of my life, I did just that, and when the owners returned in spring they put the old dog to sleep. It's not much as anecdotes go. I have never liked irony. Yet that winter haunted my imagination. Here I was out in the country, surrounded by wilderness, visited at night by coyotes. I hadn't ever experienced such cold, or waded through such deep snow. I worried over their koi, frozen in the pond.

THOMAS MALTMAN

A curious thing happens when memory mingles with
the imagination. When I started this novel I meant to set
it in the Inland Northwest, which was where I was living
at the time I cared for that house. I wanted to set it there
for family reasons as well. You see, the title for The Land
comes from family history. My family knows the pull of
the wilderness. In the 1980s my grandparents purchased
heavily forested land in Northern California. The entire
family, all six of their children, invested in the purchase of
this land. Legend has it they were inspired by the publication of Hal Lindsey's *The Late Great Planet Earth*, a book
that predicted the End Times were upon us. I grew up
hearing about the Great Tribulation from my grandparents, listened while great uncles debated gravely about
the Mark of the Beast and the coming of the Antichrist.
My grandparents named the property they bought The
Land. It was meant to be partly a vacation spot, but also
as a refuge against the Apocalypse. Later in 1999, as fears
about Y2K spread, some members of my family looked
again to the property as a place of safety. One relative
talked openly about a man he knew who could dynamite the only bridges heading into Scotts Valley. While
The Land as described in the novel bears a resemblance
to the place we knew and have long since sold, I want to
be clear that my family never belonged to any Christian
Identity church. This novel is not about my family or
anyone in it, but instead explores what happens when

the fearful eschatology of dispensationalism intermingles with racist belief systems. As a Christian, I have long been concerned with how American Christianity has been co-opted by nationalism and other toxic ideologies. And while I have sometimes been accused of having an overly gothic mindset, if your grandmother reads to you from the Book of Revelation when you are a child, it does things to your imagination. I have kept the faith in my own way. Writing the novel allowed me to return to The Land.

So, how and why did the novel's setting move from the Inland Northwest to the Upper Midwest? In the mid-1990s the botched Federal raid of the Weaver cabin and the violent deaths of three people during an eleven-day siege had left enduring scars on the region where I lived. Yet as I did research, all signs kept pointing me back to the Midwest. Randy and Vicki Weaver were from small towns in Iowa and were married in Fort Dodge. The 1990s spawned the Posse Comitatus in North Dakota while the Aryan Republican Army was busy robbing banks across Ohio. Timothy McVeigh, who lived for a time in Michigan, committed the worst act of domestic terrorism the nation had yet experienced in Oklahoma City.

Local research offered no reprieve. I discovered a Christian Identity church like the one described in the novel right over in Fridley, Minnesota, no more than ten miles from my home. (The church is no longer active.) I found out that Charles Weisman, a prolific publisher of racist propaganda for the Christian Identity movement, operated his press out of a home in Apple Valley, Minnesota. The white supremacists whom I had been ready to consign to the mountains of Idaho or to the Deep South? They were right here living among us, in our very backyard. As I wrote, I thought about how white supremacy and the violence such groups engender are a little like natural disasters. They only happen in other places, not where we live, and certainly not in the private spaces of our hearts. The more I read and researched, the more I knew I had to bring this novel home.

For all these reasons, the setting moved to the wildest and most beautiful place I knew in Minnesota, the Arrowhead region. Meanwhile, as I wrote, residents of Grand Marais were unable to stop the leader of a fundamentalist Mormon cult from settling on a property west of town. It was another reminder of how this can happen anywhere.

Dreamers and visionaries have long known the inexorable allure of the wilderness, a part of our American psyche. It's The Land that calls to so many of us.

Acknowledgments

I owe a debt of gratitude to the writers of the Upper Mississippi Young Writer's Association who saw early drafts and provided crucial feedback. Nick Healy, Roger Hart, Hans Hetrick, and musician Nate Boots are lifelong friends and writers whose judgment I know I can trust. They helped me see early on that this was a story I needed to honor. I am likewise indebted to my campus writing group at Normandale, including Dan Darling, Loli Dillon, and Eric Mein, who inspired me to make some important revisions. Amit Bhati provided crucial advice about game development and programming in the 1990s. My wonderful agent, Laura Langlie, saw the novel when it was halfway done, and spurred me on to finish.

I knew when I was halfway through the novel that I had to send this to my editor, Mark Doten at Soho Press.

This needs to go to Mark, I thought. We worked together on my last novel, *Little Wolves*, and I felt strongly that sending this to Mark and Soho would also complete a Minnesota trilogy that started all the way back with my novel *The Night Birds*, set in 1862. There are few things writers appreciate better than the natural completion of a story arc. Mark Doten helped shape this novel into what it is. I'm grateful to him and to the entire team at Soho, including Rachel Kowal and many others.

To my mom and dad and my siblings, who have been champions and great supporters of my work, and to many others in my family, I thank you.

Last, but certainly not least, I need to make sure I thank the one who makes all of this possible, my wife, Melissa Jean Dahlke Maltman. A long time ago, she was my first reader, the one who nudged me to go back to graduate school, the one who helps me find the time to write and to create as we raise three daughters together. It's a good life.

—Tom Maltman